The Other Lover

Also by Sarah Jackman

Laughing as they Chased Us

The Other Lover

Sarah Jackman

POCKET BOOKS

LONDON • SYDNEY • NEW YORK • TORONTO

First published by Pocket Books, 2007
An imprint of Simon & Schuster UK Ltd
A CBS COMPANY

Copyright © Sarah Jackman, 2007

1 3 5 7 9 10 8 6 4 2

Simon & Schuster UK Ltd
Africa House
64–78 Kingsway
London WC2B 6AH

www.simonsays.co.uk

Simon & Schuster Australia
Sydney

A CIP catalogue record for this book is available from the British Library

ISBN-13: 9-780-7434-8935-5
ISBN-10: 0-7434-8935-7

Typeset in Garamond by Palimpsest Book Production Limited,
Grangemouth, Stirlingshire
Printed and bound in Great Britain by
Cox & Wyman Ltd, Reading, Berkshire

For Dean

acknowledgements

Thank you to friends and family for their encouragement and support, especially to my parents Michael and Gwynneth. Thanks also to Teresa Chris, and Rochelle and everyone at Simon & Schuster.

Autumn

1

Adam doesn't hear me come into the hall, he doesn't sense my presence but something about the tone of his voice – some half-heard sentence – has alerted me. His hand rests on the phone which he's just slowly put down. And I'm standing barefoot on the cold tiles behind him, waiting for the bad news that I know is coming.

His jeans are saggy at the bum, his T-shirt half tucked-in; his hair sticks up like brown feathers on a cockatiel's head. The tattooed dog on his arm comes jerkily alive as he rubs the side of his face, his hand rasping across the bristles on his jaw.

Names travel across my mind – a ticker bar of the people I love – but I blink them away. I'm certain that the bad news won't be about anyone close. It's more likely to be a great-aunt, known to me only by name, the real sadness being that we never had the chance to become involved in each other's lives. Or perhaps it will be a distant relative from Ad's numerous clan up in Yorkshire, who gather in numbers in celebration – and now sorrow – and who all look the same to me.

Outside the wind blows rain against the glass front of our porch. As I watch Adam, I realize that in over two years of being together, we've never before had to share the experience of imparting or receiving bad news. Now, as he turns to face me, I have time to feel curious about how this moment will unfold.

'That was William,' he says, his voice sounding hollow. 'I'm sorry, babe, but Rose is, um . . .' He clears his throat, shakes his head. 'She died last night.'

He steps forward. Our eyes are locked. His pupils look immense.

An image of Rose flashes into my mind. Lying in bed, weakened by the flu bug but still on form: one hand flapping, the other pressed to her chest, wheezing, 'Oh my God, Laura, that's so funny.' Her eyes wet with tears of laughter, which I wipe away. My own, too.

'She can't have,' I tell him. 'I was there in the afternoon, with her.'

Adam's closer now. I'm trembling all over. My teeth go chatter, chatter, chatter like a clockwork set of dentures let loose on a table.

'We laughed,' I tell him, and I hear my voice squeak in its urgency. 'All afternoon. We *cried* with laughter.'

It had been a beautiful day – sunny but with a strong sea breeze that blew most of the heat away. I'd walked to the house along the seafront. Brighton beach had been full of hopeful people huddled behind flapping, stripy windbreaks; the fringes on all the abandoned parasols rippled like jellyfish tentacles.

When I turned into Kings Crescent, the sun was soaking

into the honey-yellow brick of the Georgian houses, and in the sheltered square, the temperature was several degrees hotter. By the time I'd ascended the three flights of stairs of the Claymores' house I was beginning to sweat. The urban thermals, as Rose called them – the odours from the nearby hotel and restaurant kitchens – had pervaded her room at the top as usual.

I stood for a moment by the open windows to cool off. A slice of cobalt blue stood out between the white shoulders of the Grand and the Plaza Hotels that commandeered the seafront. The slice – which William had been amused to discover meant that he and Rose could legally claim to have a sea-view – was unusually clear. That day, there was no film of mist or cloud; no blurring by rain. Instead, picked out like tropical fish in a narrow tank of blue, were the colourful triangles of the windsurfers, and the dinghies of Brighton Sailing School. I described what I was looking at to Rose.

A gust whipped at the curtains, giving me goosebumps. I hurried over and tried to cover Rose's bare arms with the sheet, worrying that she'd get cold in the draught.

'You've made me want to feel summer on my skin,' she told me, pulling free. She needed her hands out anyway. Her gestures were as exuberant as her mind was sharp; her wit was a silver thread in the golden afternoon.

When I'd left we'd both been on a high.

'No,' I say to Adam now. 'It's not possible.'

Adam envelops me; he rocks me to and fro but I rush out of his embrace to hide my dry eyes.

In the bathroom, I stare at my reflection for a minute before filling the sink with warm water. I bend low, scooping handful after handful over my face.

When I come out, Adam calls from the living room. 'OK, babe?'

I stand in the doorway. 'What did William say?' I ask.

Adam is slow to turn his attention from the TV. 'William,' he says, as if orientating himself. 'He just said to tell you Rosie had passed away.'

'They're the words he used? "Passed away"?'

Adam nods.

I can imagine William choosing that phrase – it's dignified while containing a weight of meaning. I see him pushing his hair back off his face as it falls forward, pausing a moment before he makes the next call. Rose has been tricking death for months. I'd thought – we'd all believed – that there was still plenty of time to be won.

'How did he sound?'

Adam thinks for a moment. 'Sad. You know, quiet and – well, sad.'

'And?'

Adam rises from the sofa. 'Look, Laura,' he starts to say, head bobbing, shoulders slack.

I take a deep breath. 'I'd like to know exactly what he said, that's all.'

'OK.' Adam shoves his hands through his hair, frowning in concentration. 'OK. He said: "It's William here, William Claymore. I'm afraid I've some bad news. Rosie passed away last night." I asked him if he wanted to talk to you and he said no – only please could I let you know, and to say that he'll speak to you soon.'

'Is that it? Didn't you say anything else?' A burr of irritation sits in my chest. I think how differently the conversation would have gone if I'd answered the phone.

'Just that I was sorry,' Adam tells me. 'What else could I have said? What would you have said?'

He looks crestfallen: he thinks he's let me down. He shrugs, the way Adam does – with his whole body. 'Sorry. I'm no good at this kind of thing.'

'It's fine,' I say. 'Really.' And I mean it. I'm being unfair. After all, what more *is* there to say? What words could I have come up with that would have helped William or made a difference?

'Come and sit with me.' Adam gestures to the sofa. 'We'll see if there's some no-brainer film on to watch.'

But Adam's offer of comfort seems too easy; I choose to lie on the bed on my own instead. From the flat upstairs I hear the abrupt clip-clop of heels, a brief screech as something is pulled across the parquet floor, then everything goes quiet again.

'Hello, Laura, dear.'

Rose was sitting at her desk, emailing one of her friends back in Barcelona – 'back home', as she always referred to it. 'I won't be a moment; I'll just finish this.'

I stood outside on the balcony ledge. At the end of the road, between the hotel blocks, I could see the mayhem of traffic. Madeira Drive had been closed for the Car Rally and half the streets nearby had been cordoned off, too. I'd parked in the NCP earlier and walked down.

The Lanes had been busier than usual and slippery from dropped food and the drizzle earlier in the day. I became caught up in a large group of spectators, all sporting baseball hats with the Rally logo, and had trouble escaping, finally breaking through to a near-empty back street where I'd felt suddenly weightless and rapid.

'Did you see William?' Rose called to me. I heard the tiny click of her laptop as she closed the lid.

'Just to say hello. He said he's going to get some shopping in a while.'

Rose joined me. 'I have to tell you something.'

I noticed she was wearing lipstick but no eye make-up. Up close in the daylight, her skin was so clear and smooth it reminded me of the fawn, speckled pebbles you find on the beach, the ones that are like birds' eggs. 'I have to talk to you about the reason William and I came back here to live.'

Rose was one of the most vibrant people I'd ever known, so when she stood there and told me that she had terminal cancer, I laughed because the idea seemed too ridiculous. But in the next instant, I also knew it was true and I couldn't look at her. I hung my head while she stroked my hair, played gently with the curls that had fallen in front of my face.

'Laura,' she said. 'You've got to think whether you want us to keep on being friends.'

This made me look up. 'Why wouldn't I?'

'We've not known each other long and it's never going to be a normal kind of friendship. It's not . . .' She struggled to speak. 'I – don't think – it's going to be easy.'

I took her hand. She was shaking and this made me feel stronger.

'No,' I told her. 'You're not going to get rid of me that easily.'
She gripped my hand tightly. 'Thank you.'

'Rose is dead – she's dead,' I say out loud into the silence but
I still can't believe it and the tears still refuse to come.

2

The weather this week has been schizophrenic. One day it's as hot as summer, the next there are thunderstorms which cause the temperature to nose-dive and leave the pavements awash with a gluey mixture of water and fallen leaves. When I come straight out after work for a run, it's so muggy I feel the heat in my throat when I swallow. Huge clouds hang motionless; their grey underbellies paunchy with rain.

My body is sluggish, as if all the energy's been punched out of me, and a headache is looming; the vein on the left side of my head pulses each time my trainers hit the ground, and when the low sun briefly emerges, I have to squint against the reflections which are glancing off the damp pavement and piercing my retina. My mind keeps returning to the same thought: that usually at this time of day, I'd have stopped off to visit Rose.

Fifteen minutes on and I'm already battling against the desire to give up and walk home, but unless I keep going for at least half an hour, this run won't count. I can't bear the thought of missing a day so I grit my teeth and urge my legs into action.

I'm heading down the main road which I plan to cross at the Seven Dials roundabout when my body is suddenly released from the struggle. Everything feels perfect and easy; I am relaxed and loose, muscled and powerful. The rush-hour traffic is backed up all the way from the parade of shops. I run alongside the queuing cars with their bored drivers and catch myself grinning with each stride.

Bounce, grin, bounce, grin, bounce.

I don't care if I look crazy. I just don't care because these moments make you understand what running is all about. I love it, I love it, I love it.

I cross the road at the zebra crossing and run into a subdued street which looks pretty much the same as the one we live in. In fact, all the residential streets round here are more or less identical with their rows of bay-fronted Victorian houses, the majority of which have been split into flats and maisonettes and become the preserve of young professionals with the same taste in Habitat curtains and Ikea lightshades. When I first moved in with Adam, I kept getting lost, and even now if I get too wrapped up in the running, I can become briefly disorientated – although I'm really only ever seconds away from a landmark and quickly find my bearings: BlockBuster's video store, the parade of shops with the deli which sells amazing olives, 'Bert's Best' organic grocery shop, Theo's wine-bar, the odd house which has been painted a colour other than cream or which, like ours, has had the outer doorway closed in with glass at some point.

Today though, my mind is locked into my exact location and as my energy surges, I change my route to include a shorter, more challenging uphill climb at the end. I duck my head against the wind – sudden and forceful as it always is at this spot – because today I'm determined not to be defeated by its bluster. My lungs are scraping and my calf muscles popping but I push through. The wind exacts its revenge by tugging and playing with my hair, creating a bird's nest of curls and tangles in the time it takes to reach the corner of our street.

I ease back to walking pace. Puff pant, puff pant; my heart is walloping against my chest, my face is burning and my legs are like jelly.

I walk the last few metres in the dusky light with every inch of my body fizzing.

Nibbling on a piece of kiwi fruit, I heap chunks of banana and mango into the food processor. Under the *rrr-rrr* of the machine I think I hear a noise. I turn it off to listen; it's the guttural sound of our doorbell. I turn the blender on again.

'I'm ignoring you,' I sing above the noise because I know it won't be anyone important. It'll only be a salesman, or canvasser, or, most probably, an estate agent. Hardly a day goes by without one of them calling or pushing a glossy leaflet through the letterbox saying they have clients desperate for properties in this area. The other week, one had added a handwritten, poorly spelled note on the back. *Waiting list of purchesers for you're flat – you name the price!*

'Dream on,' I sing out loud, but as soon as I pause the machine, I hear the prolonged raspberry *phtuup* of the bell again, and something about its persistence makes me change my mind.

'OK, I'm coming!' I yell as I hurry down the hall.

As I'm passing the living room I catch the name Claymore

on the TV and, stopping in the doorway, I see William's face filling the screen: a younger, sandy-haired William with a thinner face. The picture vanishes so rapidly that for a second I wonder if I've imagined it.

Scraps of dialogue begin to take shape in my mind. 'Taken in for questioning.' Is that really what they said? The ringing's been replaced by urgent knocking.

It's the police.

'Laura Eagen?'

I nod.

'Sorry to disturb you, miss. We're from the Sussex Police, Brighton Central District. May we come in?' the WPC asks, stepping forward as if I've already agreed.

I'm aware of my backside horribly outlined in my Lycra running pants as the two officers follow me into the living room. I look down: there's a smudged handprint of the peach-coloured smoothie on my thigh, and more blobs which smear across my top when I try to rub them off.

I feel strangely nervous. I try to compose myself but my cheeks are burning, making me look guilty even though I've done nothing wrong. I'm too flustered to catch their names.

'Shall we sit down?' the male police officer suggests.

They squash into the two-seater opposite me and remove their hats, which they both balance awkwardly on their knees.

'We won't take up much of your time,' Mr Policeman says. 'It's just a routine enquiry about a friend of yours, William Claymore.'

'I thought it must be.'

'Really?' he says quickly. 'Why?'

They both lean forward.

'There was something on the TV,' I say. 'Just now. On the news.'

'Christ,' I think Mr Policeman says under his breath, his forehead creasing.

'What's going on?'

They act as if I hadn't spoken.

'The Sergeant and I would like to ask a few questions, if that's all right?' the WPC says after a short pause.

Her skirt has ridden up and my eyes are drawn to the cellulite on the back of her thigh. Every time she shifts her weight, the dimples on the flesh become less or more defined. Smooth, puckered, smooth, puckered. I'd hate to wear a uniform, I catch myself thinking. She looks frumpish though she's probably a few years younger than me, and the sergeant, despite his thick beard, has a youth's scrawny body and a cluster of spots around his nose which makes me suspect he's barely past his teens either.

'OK.'

'What do you do, Laura?' the WPC asks suddenly. She gives me a friendly smile but as I begin to reply their hands reach to their pockets as if they've practised synchronized notebook removal and I realize that everything I say from this moment on will be recorded. It's a scary thought which has the unwelcome effect of making my mouth go into overdrive.

'I'm a business consultant – all my clients are down in the North Laine. You know? All the funky, unusual shops?' I cringe as I hear myself sounding so full of it, but I can't seem to stop. 'I love dealing with them. There's a great atmosphere, and—'

'The New Age crowd?' the Sergeant interrupts.

'That's what some people call them.' I flash him a look. I can sense the 'whacky baccy' attitude a mile away and it really winds me up. I could quote a few figures at him: the substantial revenue raised here in Brighton by these businesses, for example, but there's no point wasting my breath. The cogs in his brain have already ground into work in the light of this information, and as his gaze sweeps over our décor, taking in the mismatched furniture and the untidiness and the shelves crammed with books and magazines and CDs and all manner of other things, and alighting first on Adam's collection of garden finds – the clay pipes, glass bottles, pieces of ceramics and Roman coins – then moving on to the plastic lime-green polka-dotted chair and finally coming to rest on the giant bowl of pink pebbles on the hearth, I can almost see the light-bulb illuminate above his head and sense his relief at being able to slot us into the same New Age pigeonhole.

'I meet a lot of interesting people,' I nevertheless add, though half-heartedly.

'We've met quite a few of them ourselves,' Mr Policeman replies and laughs, his mouth wet and red in the wire of his beard.

I decide that I really, really hate beards.

'I still don't understand why you're here,' I say.

The WPC glances at her colleague and I wonder, briefly if she's hating every minute of being pressed up so close to him.

'We have to ask these things, love.' The WPC looks encouragingly at me, her face showing concern, and even though it's probably false, it still makes me feel a little better.

'Do you know William Claymore well?' she asks.

'Pretty well,' I tell her. 'I knew Rose – his wife – better.'

'Did you see a lot of Mrs Claymore?'

'Yes. Especially the last couple of months when she got worse. You know Rose was terminally ill?'

The WPC nods.

'When did you last see Mr Claymore?' the Sergeant asks this time.

'A couple of days ago when I took a condolences card round.'

'How did he seem?'

He had looked awful, had seemed stunned. He repeated: 'Thank you, Laura,' several times as if he was on auto-response. I left feeling stupid and useless and my stupid, useless words had kept returning to me for the rest of the evening: *I'm so sorry about Rose. If there's anything I can do* . . . I still wish I had said something much more meaningful, or been able to express how I was really feeling.

'How someone who's just lost their wife would be, I suppose.' I'm beginning to resent their questions and I shoot a defiant look at them but their faces remain impassive. There's a short pause during which they both watch me in silence. I feel sure they're expecting me to pipe up with a whole heap of information but the truth is I've nothing to tell them. I'm not even sure what they want to hear.

'When did you last see Mrs Claymore?' the Sergeant asks in the end. He stretches out his leg and knocks against the coffee-table. I feel a brief moment of satisfaction as he bends forward to rub his shin.

'The afternoon of the day she died.'

'And how did she seem?'

I don't tell them that Rose had been better than I'd seen her in weeks. I suddenly feel protective of her last day and want to hide it from these two with their clumsy manner. It's none of their business; that afternoon was about Rose and me and not anyone else.

So I say, 'The same as usual.'

'Nothing memorable?' the WPC probes, perhaps sensing my hesitation.

'Memorable? In what way?'

As she opens her mouth to reply, the phone starts ringing.

We avoid each other's eyes as we wait for it to stop. The Sergeant fidgets, the WPC crosses her legs, swiftly uncrosses them, tugs her skirt down.

I think of that afternoon.

The door was unlocked as always when I arrived, I called out, 'Hello!' as I walked in, and William came down the stairs to greet me. To begin with, there was nothing different about our brief conversation, but whereas usually William would head off to the kitchen and I'd go on up he didn't move. I waited, expecting him to say something more, but he didn't and his eyes kept jumping around, never settling on my face.

'Is everything OK?' I asked in the end, and William suddenly brushed past me without speaking. I felt dismissed; blood flooded my cheeks as I watched him walk down the hall.

'I'm not going out today,' he called over his shoulder. Then he stopped and turned round, fixing his gaze on me. 'I'll be here, Laura, if you need me.'

It's getting dark outside and the backs of my visitors' heads are reflected in the bay window behind them. In between is my face – a pale oval surrounded by a huge blonde frizz. I instinctively start pulling my fingers through my hair to tease it back into shape. Then I notice something which freaks me out. My eyes are absent. I blink and there's no corresponding movement. There are only dark holes. I squeeze my eyes shut but there's no change when I re-open them.

The WPC is studying me.

I have to look elsewhere. The phone has stopped ringing but I can't remember what was said last, whether she's waiting for my reply. The TV's been turned off, but I don't remember doing it. I shiver. The sweat from my run has dried on my skin, leaving me cold, but I'm reluctant to get up in front of these two to fetch a fleece so I hug a cushion instead.

'Did Mrs Claymore ever express any ideas or intentions of finding a way to deliberately end her life?'

'No, never.' I begin to laugh at the absurdity of the thought but I'm pulled up short by their serious faces.

'If you knew Rose, you'd understand,' I explain. 'She hated the idea that everything and everyone would go on without her.'

'I can't imagine myself not being here,' Rose had said once. 'Even though I'm wasting away in front of my own eyes.' She'd plucked at the flaccid skin covering the withered muscle on her arm.

'I'm being cheated out of my chance to grow old disgracefully, to be an interfering, eccentric, flamboyant old bat. It's not fair,' she said, making a joke of it, although her voice was off-key and harsh as if she was upset and angry all at once. 'That role was made for me – I was only just getting warmed up.'

*   *   *

'Did Mr Claymore ever mention assisting his wife to die, if ever she should need help?' the Sergeant asks, stumbling a little over his words.

'Of course he didn't. Neither of them talked about anything like that.' My headache is threatening to return. I need some food; I sense an energy crash round the corner. 'I don't know what else I can tell you,' I say. 'It's Rose's funeral on Friday,' I add for no reason other than it seems important that they should know that.

They exchange sideways glances, as if they've got a secret between them, then the WPC sits forward and smiles – a genuine smile for the first time – and the atmosphere suddenly lightens.

A moment later, they're standing, doing all the hand-shaking, and saying things like: 'Thank you for your time,' and 'If you think of anything, here's our number,' and I'm left alone holding the little white business card that I didn't know the police used, and still wondering what's going on.

I press my face to the window. Threads of rain glisten in the streetlights and render the humps of the car roofs a neutral shiny grey. Parking is less of a nightmare since the Council introduced Residents' Permits last year and stopped commuters using the road for the station ten minutes away. We're still packed in bumper to bumper though, and the only spot still free even this early in the evening is Adam's.

I try his mobile but it transfers straight to his voicemail which means he's on his way home.

In the upstairs flat of the house opposite, I watch a woman in her kitchen. She's talking to someone I can't see. She keeps stopping what she's doing to listen; she leans against the work surface, nods furiously, keeps nodding.

I pull the curtains, switch on the TV and the radio too and start searching all the channels for the news. The local radio has William as their lead story.

I hold my breath.

They call him 'an award-winning photographer in his own right', though they say he was best known for his work as part of the renowned husband and wife photographic team. They imply an unexpectedly sudden death for Rose, who had been 'fighting a long battle with terminal cancer' since their return to the UK from Barcelona just over a year ago.

After the headlines, euthanasia is the evening's 'Discussion Point'. There's a quick sweep through the issues before a heated exchange between representatives of the opposing sides. The 'for' camp go on about the rights of the individual; the 'against' utter dark thoughts about terrible motives. Someone mentions mercy killing and a croaky-voiced female caller uses the word 'Murderer' before she's abruptly cut off.

I can't believe what I'm hearing. I shout at the radio. No matter which side of the argument, there seems to be an assumption that William has performed this act and done it as nonchalantly as administering Rose with her everyday painkillers. If they had seen Rose's passion to live, if they knew how devastated William is, they would be ashamed to be coming out with such rubbish.

I turn everything off and the silence is overwhelming.

I hope that the police are treating William well. I know they must be trained for dealing with this kind of situation, but I can't help thinking that no matter how sympathetic you are with someone who has recently lost the person they love most in the world, you must still have to treat them as a criminal.

I hope William won't be misunderstood. I hope they don't mistake his self-containment for aloofness, or worse, the demeanour of a man coldly in control. I could kick myself for failing to impress on the pair who came round how Rose's death was a shock to everyone, William included.

My mobile goes off. It's Debbie.

My finger hovers over the green button. I've bitten the nail right down without noticing, like I used to do as a child whenever I was nervous. I hesitate between the consolation of a chat with Debs to fill the time before Adam gets back and the feeling I have that she's been listening to the news and is greedy for gossip.

'Come on, *Loz,*' I imagine her saying. '*Dish the dirt. What's been going on?*'

I ignore the call in the end because it doesn't seem right to talk about Rose like that and because a memory of that afternoon has just washed through me which I need to think about for a moment, to work out what it means.

William wasn't in the kitchen where I expected him to be. I found him, sitting in the lounge, without any music or TV on, staring into space. The room seemed closed-in and gloomy in contrast with the bright and airy feel upstairs.

'I'm off now.' William hadn't heard me come down and he jumped a little when I spoke. 'Are you OK?' I asked him.

'I'm tired,' he'd replied, after a moment's hesitation. 'Just tired.' Then he'd leaped to his feet. He was halfway up the stairs before I'd reached the front door.

'She said she was going to have a sleep,' I called up, but he carried on anyway.

I peer behind the curtains and after a few minutes I'm relieved at the sight of car headlights coming down the street. I hang on until the white form of Adam's van is clearly visible before rushing to the door.

'The news? What news?' Adam asks in response to my questions. He shakes his hair like a dog and a few drops hit my face. Water forms a puddle around him on the stone floor.

Adam is a giant in the lilliputian front porch. As he shrugs his coat off, his arms skim the walls, and as he's straightening up from removing his boots, it wouldn't have surprised me if his head had touched the ceiling.

We both look out as rain begins to hammer down and I have to raise my voice above the noise from the guttering. 'About William.'

He looks blankly at me.

I throw my arms around his neck as he steps forward, and smell the fresh air on him mixed with the sweet scent of soil and cut grass. He clutches my bum, a cheek in each hand, and squeezes gently, then lifts me by my buttocks and takes a couple more steps along the hall before letting me drop.

I know why he hasn't heard anything. After working outside all day he always listens to CDs on the drive home – never the radio, as if he's reluctant to tear himself away from the solitude and peace of his gardens.

Sometimes he arrives home looking bewildered, as if he's

been plonked down in the middle of a metropolis and doesn't quite know what to make of it. 'You only need a piece of straw hanging from the corner of your mouth,' I tell him when he's in his country bumpkin mode; he just smiles, his eyes dark and unfocused until he comes round.

'The police came, they've arrested William. It's been on the radio and the TV. They think he helped Rose to die. They wanted to know if I knew anything.'

'Whoa,' Adam says, pushing me towards the living room. 'Slow down a minute.'

I leave him to settle on the sofa while I fetch him a beer and myself the smoothie I'd forgotten until now.

Adam's tired. I can see it in the way he holds himself. His limbs look heavy, as if his muscles are saturated with physical effort. He props his feet on the coffee-table and stretches. He lolls his head back on the settee, clasping the beer bottle on his stomach.

'It's probably some routine enquiry which has been blown out of all proportion,' Adam declares with certainty once I've told him everything I know. He's always doing this: bringing 'a bit of reality to the situation' as he likes to call it. He'll say something like: 'Hang on, aren't you going over the top here?' or 'Let's get a bit of perspective going.' But today, the magic of his level-headedness fails to work.

'I've been thinking about it,' I say. 'For one thing, there's no smoke without fire, is there? I mean, who on earth would have dreamed up something like this out of the blue? And that afternoon I was round there, something definitely felt odd. Rose suddenly seemed better than she'd been for weeks, and yet William was completely on edge. He never, ever stays in when

I get there, but that day he obviously had no intention of leaving the house.'

I've got Adam's attention now. He frowns. 'I'm not sure what you're getting at.'

'So maybe Rose did know she was going to die.' I sit forward. 'Maybe they did plan it.'

Adam slurps his beer, and some trickles down his chin. He wipes it away with the back of his hand.

'This all sounds a bit far-fetched to me, babe,' he says. 'From what you said before, I had the impression Rose wasn't going to give in lightly.'

I slump back, deflated. 'Oh, God. I just don't know what to think. I mean, if she'd been planning to die, she wouldn't have let me walk out of that room without saying some kind of goodbye, would she?' I glance at Adam. 'I can't even remember what we talked about, and I should, shouldn't I?'

I feel tears gathering in my eyes at the thought that I might have missed something important that Rose had said. I'd been so caught up in the mood of that afternoon; I'd indulged myself in her company without savouring her words and committing them to memory.

Adam takes hold of my hand. 'Laura,' he says, rather sternly, 'I think the fact that nothing momentous was spoken about, probably goes to prove that Rose wasn't planning anything. OK?'

He strokes my fingers. I want to believe him.

'OK?' he asks again and I nod. I'm too tired to think any more.

'Now,' Adam says, 'I've got to eat. I'm starving.'

I jump up, feeling guilty. 'I'll make some noodles.'

Adam goes to shower while I prepare the food. I clear away my earlier mess, fry up some peppers and courgettes and put the noodles on to boil.

I open the back door to clear the steam and cool air floods in; I breathe in its freshness. The rain's stopped and the garden is illuminated by the kitchen light. The tall tree fern drips with water; the huge plate leaves of the banana tree that will soon have to be blanketed to survive the winter, look so polished, you could believe they were fake.

This summer – a rare hot one – we've made love several times out there in our tiny, secluded tropical paradise. One night we both fell asleep afterwards and I woke up, hours later, chilled by the early-morning air. Adam was lying on his back, his face twisted towards me. There was a furrow between his eyebrows as if a dream was puzzling him. The new air smelled secretive. The leaves and ground were slick with dew; the towel underneath me was soggy with it. It was turning light but the shadows were deep, making holograms of the plants. The longer I looked at them, the stranger they became.

I shivered. We were both naked and my skin was numb with cold. When I moved against Ad, expecting to find his usual warmth, it was shocking to encounter a body as icy as mine. I scratched at my arm, and examined the lumps I discovered there – mosquito bites. I was covered in them. A culprit attempted to execute a landing on my stomach and when I wafted it away, I disturbed Adam. He stirred, then twitched – and in one rapid move, he was on his feet. I giggled as he began slapping and jumping around like a lunatic.

'Jesus, I'm fucking being eaten fucking alive!'

He held out his hand to pull me upright, then set straight

off indoors. I followed him, and as I reached the doorway a blackbird hit the first note of the dawn chorus.

In our bedroom, Adam was holding the duvet open for me; I slid in and he pulled me close. Clamped together, wrapped tight in the duvet, we shivered and rocked ourselves warm. Ad muttered and cursed and swore that we'd never do that again, but I thought it was worth it. I knew I wouldn't hesitate about doing it again.

Now, in the exact spot where we lay on our makeshift bed of roll-mats and towels, there's a pile of flagstones. Adam has lifted them and started to dig a trench for the cabling which will transform the musty, cobwebbed shed into my new heated and illuminated office.

It had seemed an inspired solution when Mum made the decision to put her house on the market, leaving me office-less in the near future, as the flat is way too small to fit in my stuff and I can't afford to rent business premises yet.

Talking it over with Adam a few months ago, I could picture myself out there – my desk by the window so that in the summer I'd be able to smell the honeysuckle which climbs all over the shed. I loved the idea of taking a few steps across the patio for work instead of the nightmare of crossing town in Brighton's rush-hour. Now all I can think is how lonely it will be.

I shiver and close the door.

'You're very welcome, any time,' David's told me several times, and once he even said, 'I hope you'll think this house is as much your home as mine and Trudy's.'

He's a sweet man and I'm so happy that Mum's finally met someone special after twenty years alone.

'I'm not going far,' she keeps saying. David's house is on a new estate on the outskirts of the city, only twenty minutes' drive away – 'Wrinkly Ville' as they call it round here – where everything's neat and ordered, and the bungalows have exactly the same allocation of curving drives and flat, mown lawns.

This past week, since they've been on honeymoon, has made me realize how much I shall miss my daily chats with Mum.

I hear the TV go on and when I take the food in, Adam's lying stretched out on the settee. He's wearing tracksuit bottoms and no top, and the lamplight on his tanned skin accentuates his muscles. I love his wide chest, his big arms – and if my hands weren't full, I wouldn't be able to resist touching him, sliding my hand across the curve of his bicep, squeezing his shoulders until he sighs, 'Mmmm.'

He yawns over the bowl before eating quickly. Noodles hang like string from his mouth.

'This is good,' he says, jabbing his fork in the air although it's nothing special and is more to do with the fact that he's so hungry.

'I might drop by tomorrow and see you,' I say.

'Cool.' Adam grins at me.

I've done this a few times when Ad's been working locally. We never make a firm arrangement; I turn up if I've got some time free. Sometimes when I arrive, he's midway through some task – pouring concrete, nailing fencing or laying paving stones. I have to wait until he reaches a stage which can be left, but I don't mind. I like watching him work. I like the way he focuses entirely on the job he's carrying out. I like his confident handling of the tools, his firm gentleness with the plants.

We usually head for the nearest pub, and even if we can only spare half an hour, that time together changes the whole mood of my day, turning it from ordinary into something special.

One time when Adam was working very close to home we returned here, to the flat. The moment we closed the door, we began to kiss. Adam undressed me in the hall and carried me into the living room where we made love with the curtains open without even stopping to think that we might be seen. It had felt as if we were the only ones around; that somehow we'd slipped through the net of weekday drudgery.

Adam's looking at me as if he's reading my horny thoughts. We both watch as I slide my foot across the carpet and rub it up against his.

There's a clap of thunder which makes us jump. The room immediately blinks white with lightning.

'This weather doesn't look good,' Adam says, mid-munch. 'It'll be hard going with the ground so wet.'

And then I remember that last week when I'd been with Rose on one of the stormy days, she'd told me how, the previous autumn, she'd followed the progress of a violent storm from the top of the house. She'd opened the French windows wide and nudged her chair forward so the front was outside on the narrow balcony ledge. She'd watched the dark clouds massing and had felt the energy in the air intensify.

'I felt like God, sitting so high up in the middle of it,' Rose had said. 'It was thrilling – sexy!' She laughed. 'I thought how exciting, how *dramatic*, to end it all with a bolt of lightning. So I stretched out my bare toes . . .' as she spoke she pointed her foot out in front of her '. . . and placed them on the balustrade. I was going to shout up to the sky, "Take me now!" but all I could think was: William will be so mad that I'm not wearing my slippers. Those wretched things!' She rolled her eyes. Rose's slippers were a constant source of contention; they made her feel frumpy and inelegant whereas William saw only the practical benefits of keeping her warm and less likely to catch a cold.

'So I rushed indoors and I couldn't find them. I was dashing round the room, thinking that after all the waiting, I'm going to miss the best part – like having to go to the loo right before the end of a film.' Suddenly her voice sounded strained; I thought she might begin to cry and so I was relieved to see her smiling.

'When I got back to the window, the storm broke. The thunder shook the glass, the lightning was breathtaking – bursting the sky open, time after time.' She held my gaze for a long moment. 'And do you know what? After all that, I stayed inside to watch. It just seemed too risky to go back out there.'

'You don't give up, Laura,' she told me a moment later. 'You can't because there's always something. There's always the next day.'

I start to speak and Adam says: 'Not this again, babe.'

But I can't stop. I'm nauseous from the words tumbling out; a kind of sick excitement fills me at the idea that I'm mixed up in something dark and dangerous.

Adam looks at me first in disbelief then he frowns deeply. 'So what are you saying?' he asks, cutting in. 'Are you seriously suggesting that William bumped Rose off? Get real, Laura.'

'It's just I can't explain it . . .'

'Exactly,' he says, sounding annoyed. 'You're guessing. No.' He stands up. 'Worse than that – you're making things up.'

He towers above me but I already feel three foot tall.

'I know you're upset about Rose,' he tells me, his voice softening, 'but there's no point getting worked up when you haven't got all the facts.'

I blush furiously. Poor William. I wish that I could take my awful words back. I can't believe I allowed those thoughts space, never mind spoke them aloud.

Adam leans down to kiss me on the top of my head, then on my nose. 'I'm off to bed. Want to join me?'

Adam's already asleep when I get in beside him after my shower. I cuddle up to his back and just as I'm thinking I'll never fall asleep, I do.

3

Mum's been away for a couple of weeks now and each morning that I come over to work here, the house feels less welcoming than the last time. It seems to have sensed her imminent abandonment of it and has taken note of the bags of clothes she's sorted out for charity, has worked out the meaning of the piles of boxes in the dining room and is sulkily protesting by emitting unfamiliar noises and producing strange odours.

This morning, I dump the few contents of the kitchen bin into the wheelie bin, hoping that this will eradicate the bizarre smell. I then turn the heating up higher and carry my takeaway cappuccino upstairs to my office, where I stand looking out of the window.

Now that a lot of the leaves have dropped from the big beech tree which overhangs the back of the garden, the red and yellow climbing frame and the blue slide in the park are visible. I can make out a couple of mums over there with pushchairs, but this park only really comes alive in the summer when it's full of students soaking up the sun.

It wasn't until Mum decided to sell the house that it occurred to me how much the area has changed from when I was a girl. The majority of the houses have now been converted into student accommodation; there's an internet café down the road, a launderette which taints the air with the smell of soap powder, and the cycle path runs down the street to the seafront one way and to the university buildings the other.

The only familiar faces I see nowadays are those of Maureen next door and Mrs Percy from across the road who's over ninety years old and looked as if she was hanging on by the skin of her teeth even when I was a girl.

'We'll get you the top price,' the estate agent told Mum when he came to give a final valuation, and I could practically hear him smacking his lips with the thought. 'Investors are falling over themselves to get hold of properties like this.'

I thought Mum would be upset over the thought of her home of thirty-five years being chopped up into student boxes, but she was pragmatic and purposeful.

'It's time to move on,' she said to me afterwards. 'I just don't feel I belong here any more.'

I sit at my desk and prepare to start work. When I open up my diary on the pc, the first thing I see is my weekly meet-up with William for coffee at Alessandro's.

I've no idea if he'll make it today. This morning when I mentioned the arrangement to Adam, he assured me that the police wouldn't be able to hold William for no reason; they can only keep him there if they charge him. Adam spoke with the authority of someone who watches a lot of detective series on TV and he refused to admit that real life might not work in quite the same way.

But even if William is able to meet me later, I'm not sure he'll bother. I've always had the feeling that it was Rose who was the keenest to continue the weekly 'assignations' as she called them, ever since she got wind of William and me meeting at Alessandro's one time by accident. She always made a point of reminding me the day before, that William would be free to escape on Wednesday as her care assistant would be with her for several hours.

Once, early on, she quizzed me about our get-togethers and I told her that William was good company. I wasn't saying it just to please Rose. Time passes quickly with William; he's interesting and funny; he talks eloquently about travelling, and his passion for the sea and for diving is infectious.

I felt rather awkward afterwards when I thought how Rose would probably repeat what I'd said to William, and although he's never given me that impression, it's hard to shake the feeling that he considers me to be a bit silly, not very sophisticated or intriguing; a pale comparison to Rose.

I busy myself with lots of phone calls all morning so that I don't have a chance to worry at the situation, but even so I'm glad when the clock grinds round to twelve. I try ringing William before I leave the house but there's no reply so I leave a message to say I'll be there at Alessandro's as usual.

I'm surprised to find that my stomach is jumping with nerves.

With disposable gloves and a plastic apron cinched tight over her red dress, Natasha's deep in chocolate as she slices up a giant cake. A tendril of hair has escaped from her hairnet and she blows it off her face before saying hello to me. The teenage lad ahead in the queue can't take his eyes off her, as if he's seeing the star of his wet dreams in the flesh.

'I'll have a piece of that,' he squawks, going crimson, and

grabs his plate insolently when Becky, the part-timer, serves him a slice already cut, from the display cabinet. She rolls her eyes at me before making my cappuccino. She, like me, is used to blokes swooning over Nat.

I search the room for William but can't spot him; as he always arrives before me, this doesn't seem a good sign.

I sit in one of the big comfy chairs; it's squashy and low and I feel tiny in it. When I sit back, my feet only touch the floor because of my three-inch heels.

I'm facing the door and no matter how hard I try to focus on the magazine I've brought with me, I can't quell the reflex of glancing up whenever anyone enters.

I absentmindedly follow the progress of a grey-haired man to the counter, and am caught red-handed when he turns round and finds me staring. I look away, my face hot. I twist round to keep my back to the door, suddenly aware how totally stood-up I look; I picture my face upturned, wide with expectation and hope, then crushed each time the person entering turns out to be a stranger.

I distract myself by watching Nat.

Her long hair is free now that she's out from behind the counter, and it seems to flow behind her as she navigates her way confidently through the tables, pausing briefly now and then to adjust a chair, a table flower arrangement or to talk animatedly to a customer. You can tell just by looking at Nat that she loves this place; she's so at home here, and her customers seem to respond to that. I've witnessed Nat charm the stroppiest complainer into a fawning puppet, grateful to be allowed to buy their coffee and cake in her establishment, just by sitting down and chatting to them.

Nat's always been able to talk to anyone. When I first knew her, as one of three Saturday girls in the boutique on Nile Street, she was the only one of us completely at ease with all the clients. Even under the critical eye of Miss Goldspenk, the uptight owner, Nat didn't flinch.

Women would walk out of that shop with clothes they'd never normally consider wearing and they always came back – not to return their purchases but to ask for Natasha again, full of their wonderful evening and the compliments they'd received. She loved talking to them and hearing their success stories, and I think it was – and is – her genuine interest in people which makes the difference.

Natasha kisses me hello and props herself on the arm of the chair.

'You heard about William?' I ask.

'That poor man,' she says softly. 'After everything he's been through.'

'We were supposed to meet today,' I tell her, 'but he's obviously not been able to make it.'

She pats my hair. I sense its springiness under her gentle touch.

'I feel I should be doing something more to help,' I say.

'I'm sure he'll be in contact soon.'

We sit in silence for a moment.

Nat sighs. 'This place badly needs a face-lift.'

'It's shabby chic,' I reply. 'It's supposed to look like this.'

She points out the flaking paint on the windowframes, the worn floor and a long crack in one of the walls.

'It's got character,' I insist, looking at the high ceiling with the elaborate rose in the centre, the mouldings and picture rails. I know people come here, like I do, because it doesn't have the sterile perfection of some places where it seems improper to linger for too long. The furnishings are Nat's choice and taste – a blend of elegant and comfortable. My favourite feature is the huge, marble fireplace. There is nothing better than sitting near it on a rainy winter's day with a cup of hot chocolate.

'And as for the loos . . .' She shudders, a little dramatically.

I protest. 'I love those loos!'

Nat looks pityingly at me. 'You're just being sentimental. They're grotty and out of place. I've put off redecorating them for far too long.'

The toilets have remained the same since I can remember; fuchsia walls and rose-pink woodwork, with the up-lights above the mirrors in the shape of ice-cream cones. When I was a girl, the bulbs behind the glass swirl of ice cream used to be changed frequently and I'd visit the toilets just to see which flavour they were – pistachio, strawberry, lemon. Nat knows about the tradition but refuses to continue it. It's been strictly vanilla ever since she's owned Alessandro's.

'Do you know?' I say, suddenly. 'This is where I first met the Claymores.'

'Are these seats free, dear?' A plumpish woman with a broad face and full mouth smiled down at me. I immediately noticed her lively brown eyes – the kind that give their owner a mischievous air. She wore linen trousers with a loose tunic top, and a large, unusual blue pendant. The sort of hippy-chic look that is quite common in Brighton, particularly among women in their fifties, as I judged her to be.

I gestured for her to join me and hurried to move my belongings which I'd spread out on the table.

'I think this place used to be an ice-cream parlour,' the woman said, glancing round.

'Yes, it was – there's a photo over there.' I pointed out Nat's 'before' shot behind her.

'I thought so. We brought our sons here a few times when they were young. I remember it was very pink and red, and there was a mural of a sundae covering one of the walls.' She rested her chin on her hand and looked at me. 'But I like this; there's a nice atmosphere here. They so often mess up these old places when they're refurbished, don't they?'

'I used to come here too when I was a little girl, and I'd imagine I was an ice-cream fairy sitting inside a giant Knickerbocker Glory.'

'That's adorable.' Rose clapped her hands lightly together. 'That's really very sweet.'

Then William arrived.

'Do tell Rosie if she's being a pain in the bum,' he said to me. 'My wife doesn't think twice about accosting perfect strangers when they're trying to have a bit of peace and quiet.'

William had the air of someone who has just walked off a yacht. He wore a loose open-neck shirt, jeans and deck shoes. His hair was grey and wavy and it kept falling in front of his face; his eyes seemed very blue because of his deep tan.

Rose was witty and amusing and did enough talking for both of them, and my lunchtime flew by. William was quiet, and whenever I caught his eye, he met my gaze openly. I felt myself wanting to impress him, even then; he was simply one of those people for whom it seems worth making an extra effort.

As I was leaving, I looked back at them. They were a very striking couple; they stood out from everyone else in the place and I thought, too, how well-suited they seemed.

'I only met William's wife a couple of times,' Nat says.

'You'd have liked her, Nat, I'm sure.'

'She didn't go out much, did she? Even before she became really ill.'

'She was happy staying at home. She said she didn't want to be anywhere else other than in her room.'

'I couldn't do that,' Nat tells me. 'I'd need to stay in the thick of things.'

'But Brighton had never really been Rose's home – it was William who had inherited the house – so she never felt she belonged here. They only came back to the UK to be near their sons.'

'I guess you have a different outlook when you're in that position,' Nat says, 'but I can't imagine spending my last days anywhere other than this place. I'd sit over in that corner ordering everyone around, boring the pants off any customers who came near.'

'I'll keep you company,' I tell her. 'I can't imagine life without Alessandro's.' I mean it. This place knits the threads of my past and my present together. When we were kids, Debs and I used to end our Saturday shopping trips here, sitting for hours over a shared sundae, poring over our day's purchases – hairclips, clothes, CDs, sweets – and on the last day of the school summer holidays, Mum would bring me here for a final treat. And now, all these years later, I still come most days to this swan of an Italian coffee shop grown out of the gaudy duckling of an ice-cream parlour to see my friend who owns it.

'Remember how Adam was convinced they were swingers when they left you that note here,' Nat reminds me.

Rose had asked Nat to pass on their telephone number and Adam had been highly suspicious of their motives. He insisted that I shouldn't meet them anywhere other than Alessandro's or somewhere 'public'. His concern was very touching but I always knew the Claymores were OK. Rose and I had clicked immediately; it was friendship at first sight.

Nat places her hand lightly on my shoulder. 'It doesn't look as if William's going to come, sweetie.'

'And I can't wait any longer; I'll get clamped if I don't leave now.'

'Are you going to be OK?'

I nod.

'Well, you know where to find me,' she says. 'If you need me.'

4

William's been released. I hear the one-liner on the radio in the car as I'm waiting to drive into the shopping-centre car park.

The newsreader says: *'Released without charge.'*

My heart bumps. I shout, 'Hooray!' out loud several times before realizing I probably look mad to the other drivers in the queue.

As soon as I find a free space, I try Adam's phone. 'Guess what?' is the opening line that I'm holding in my mind for when he answers. 'Guess what? You were right.' But when his voice-mail clicks in, it doesn't seem the kind of news you can leave as a message.

The main thing on my list is to buy some new sports gear because today, when I go out later, will be the hundredth consecutive day I've been running. Earlier, even though it was meant as a reward, my heart hadn't really been into the idea, but now, serious shopping vibes kick in.

Some cherry-red running pants attract my attention, and as I head for the changing rooms, I spot a matching hooded top and grab a couple of electric-blue T-shirts with trainer motifs.

The pants and T-shirt look great. I peer at my reflection from all angles, turning to the side to examine first my backside, then my stomach. I pose self-consciously; I'm still getting used to seeing taut curves instead of lumpy bulges under the tight material, but when I catch myself grinning in the mirror, I decide to buy everything. I'm amazed how easy clothes are now that I don't have to fiddle with belts and seams and layers to disguise and deceive. I put them on and that's it.

I've tried explaining this pleasure to Adam – someone who's never been overweight in his life – but he looks at me as if I'm peculiar, and when I told him how I think of each run as a mini-adventure, I could tell he thought I was seriously obsessed.

'But you're not a runner,' I told him once. 'So you wouldn't understand.'

'Try me,' he said, crossing his arms in front of his chest. 'Come on, convince me.'

'Often you really don't feel like going, and that's where a lot of people go wrong because you have to force yourself through that. You have to avoid thinking about the cold and the rain blowing against your face and dripping into your eyes. You have to block out the idea of dark roads and dodgy corners, dog-dirt, cat-calls from drunken men, and uneven paving slabs. You have to pin your willpower down, sit on its chest and make it submit.'

Adam was pretending to listen seriously but I could see from his eyes that he was finding my explanation very amusing.

'It's worth it,' I tell him.

'I'm failing to see why,' he said, breaking into laughter. 'Sorry, but I am.'

I nudged him and he coughed and assumed a mock-solemn expression.

I persevered. 'I feel free and my mind clears, so it's like I'm emptied out but in a good way – a satisfying way – and I notice lots of little details that I would normally miss, and somehow that makes me feel connected, as if I'm part of everything.'

'What sort of details?'

I thought about how I've noticed in the summer that older couples always emerge for walks around ten in the evening. They hold hands, conversing quietly or sometimes maintaining a peaceful silence. Their love seems so much more subtle and quietly romantic than that of younger people, who tug and push and grab at each other; and when I pass by, the man will often hold his partner closer, or take her arm in a thoughtful gesture of protection.

I didn't tell Adam though; it seemed too girly to say out loud, unlikely to lend weight to my argument.

'Like how I knew autumn had arrived,' I said instead, 'even though the days were still sunny and hot: because the air smelled smoky in the mornings.'

'Don't get her on the subject of running,' he warns our friends now. 'She'll try and convert you.'

And a few weeks ago, when Adam sneaked up behind me and discovered I'd been secretly ticking off each run in my diary, he shook his head like a concerned doctor and said, 'This is serious. You may have an illness.'

'There are worse things to be fanatical about,' I told him, batting him away before finally submitting to his advances.

5

'So what did happen?' Debbie asks.

Sweat drips into my eyes and I wipe my forehead. There's a film of perspiration on Debbie's face but, as always in the sauna, her eye make-up remains perfect. It occurs to me that it's been years since I've seen her without any make-up on at all.

'I don't know.'

The whole episode seems to have dropped into a black hole. I can't get hold of William on the phone and the story has disappeared from the news. Adam is convinced that it's a good sign – it obviously means it was all a mix-up or a misunderstanding, he says, but I won't be able to shift the worry out of my mind until I have some definite answers.

Adam also said that I shouldn't be getting so involved. 'But I was there,' I told him. 'I was with Rose only hours before her death – doesn't that mean I've got more reason than most to take it personally?'

'I always thought it was Rose you were close to. Why are you worrying so much about William?' he asked me.

'This is about Rose.'

The sauna coals creak.

'I didn't know they were famous photographers,' Debs says. 'You kept that quiet.'

I'm pretty sure I had mentioned it several times but Debs had the habit of tuning out every time I'd talked about the Claymores. 'They won some awards,' I tell her. 'William got other prizes, too.'

'So what was their thing? Porno, celebrity shots, war scenes or what?'

'Holiday brochures, travel books, that kind of thing. And William also does underwater stuff.'

'Oh, boring.'

'Some of their photographs are amazing. You should see them, Debs.'

'Yeah, right. Another time, maybe.'

Rose and I had spent hours looking through the photographs on her laptop; it had been a good way to pass time and to springboard her memories. I could see why the Claymores were popular for holiday brochures as they were good at capturing the serenity of places – but my favourite shots were those where you felt you were at the start of an adventure, on the brink of discovery: a rutted pass through the low shrubs on a hillside, the mouth of a dark, dripping cave. I wanted to jump in and see where they led.

'So, what do you think? Did Mrs C ask him to help her do away with herself, or do you think he got so pissed off playing Nursie that he did it of his own accord?' Debs stretches and looks evenly at me. I know she's teasing me a little so I don't let her wind me up.

'This isn't *Inspector Morse*, you know,' I say. I search in my head for a diversionary topic – today I'd really have preferred to stick to the girly trivia we usually cover in the sauna – but I'm not quick enough.

'He might have cracked up one night, lost the plot and smothered her.'

'Remember, he's been released.' I can hear my voice rising, and try to pitch it lower. 'So the police obviously don't think he's done anything wrong.'

'Sure.' Debs shrugs. 'But you've got to ask yourself why they took him in in the first place. They don't go around arresting people for nothing, do they?'

I ladle more water on the coals. There's a satisfying sizzle and then a few seconds before the wave of intense heat hits us.

Debs gasps. 'What did you do that for?'

'To shut you up,' I tell her. 'You're like a walking, talking gutter press.'

Debs grins. 'Cynical and realistic.'

'Anyone would think you'd grown up in the Bronx, the way you go on sometimes,' I tell her.

'You'd swear *you'd* grown up in My Little Pony Land.'

I lie down on the hot wooden slats. My ring grazes the skin on my leg and I flinch at the burn.

'You could see they were really in love, even at the end,' I tell her. 'Rose talked about William all the time and there was an intensity about them; and they were always touching each other, too.'

'Stop.' Debs wrinkles her nose. 'Gruesome. Spare me the detail of two old fogies fumbling away at shrivelling flesh.'

'Come on, Debs, being in your fifties isn't old these days and they're attractive people. I mean, Rose — before she became really ill — was striking, and William — well, he still is handsome.'

'Huh?' Debs pulls a disbelieving face. 'If you say so.'

Water drip, drips.

'It's pretty passionate stuff though, don't you think?' Debbie says thoughtfully. 'What he's done — is supposed to have done,' she corrects herself quickly, as I flash her a look. 'God, I wouldn't risk prison for Josh so that he could wimp out on a bit of pain. No way. Not even if he begged me.'

Of course Debbie would say that. I don't think I've ever heard her admit to any tender feelings towards the blokes she goes out with; the most complimentary she ever gets is to say he's nice-looking, has a hot bum, or is a good shag.

I look across at her. Just imagining her being all soft and sweet, saying 'I love you,' even to Josh, makes me smile.

'What?' she asks without even turning towards me. 'I'm serious,' she says, and in an instant my opinion is flung up in the air and I don't know what to believe.

'Would you do it for Adam?'

I am assailed with a sudden image of Adam's head on top of a body like Rose's: shrunken and weak, flabby muscles, distended stomach, folds of grey, flaking skin. I sit up, try sipping in air, because deeper intakes seem to make my head spin.

'Well — would you?'

I close my eyes. My heart has begun a rapid *tappety-tap*.

'I suppose we'd talk about it,' I manage to say. I've never felt so strange in the sauna before. I cast sideways glances at the emergency pull-cord and wonder if I reached out, whether I could pull it from here.

Debs pounces. 'Talk? That would be just like you pair. You either know or you don't; it's a gut kind of thing.' Her voice filters slowly through as if it's reaching me down a tunnel. 'I was only joking, Loz.' She's leaning up on her elbows, staring at me. 'Are you OK?'

I lick my lips and nod. She sinks back into a prone position. Water drip, drips and the coals creak.

'I'm thinking about having eyebrows tattooed on,' Debs announces, and as my mind swerves to consider what she's just said, I feel a slackening in my chest and my breathing eases.

She's placed a flannel over her face; her tiny nose makes barely a bump in the cloth but where her mouth is, the material sucks in and bubbles out as she talks.

'You're kidding?'

'You get a really good shape and it's one less thing to do in the morning before work.'

'I think they look strange – OK from a distance but close up, it's weird, like a shop dummy or something.' I instinctively touch my own. I had them dyed a darker shade of brown once and felt unnatural – clown-like – for ages afterwards. 'And what if they did it wrong?' I say. 'Got them lopsided.'

'Or permanently surprised.' Debs removes the cloth and turns her face to me, her eyebrows held in an exaggerated lift.

I laugh and heat rushes into my throat. My eyes sting and begin to water.

'That's the only thing stopping me – the error factor,' she says as we both get up to leave. 'Would you come with me?'

'No way. Accompanying you for belly-button piercing was traumatic enough.'

'That wasn't my fault. The man was a sadist.'

Debs holds the door open for me and the cold air I step into is a pure relief; the icy tiles under my feet feel wonderful.

I shout, 'Hi!' from the living room and by the time I've heaved myself up from the settee and followed Adam into the bedroom, he's sitting on the bed, bent over, pulling his socks off. I am comforted by how substantial he looks as his T-shirt pulls tight across his back.

'Are you OK?' he asks, looking up.

'Yes, why?'

'Because you're staring at me and it's a bit unnerving.'

'Sorry.' I bite down on the question that I'm desperate to ask him. I walk over to the window but it's dark out and all I can see is Adam's reflection. He stands up, unzips his jeans and lets them fall to the floor. I pull the blind down before turning around.

There's a growing bulge in Adam's boxer shorts and a 'How about it?' look in his eyes. I mustn't get distracted. I shift my gaze to the door and head for it, but just as I'm passing Adam, I stumble. He catches hold of my arm, turns me to face him.

'You're pissed,' he says happily, as if he's won top prize at a guessing game. He pulls me closer and kisses my neck. 'Naughty Miss Eagen.'

I protest. 'I've only had two glasses.'

'Two *large* ones, by the looks of things.'

Irritation pours into me; I pull away and plonk down on the bed.

Adam sits next to me. 'What is it?'

My breath catches.

'Laura?'

I can't look at him. 'Would you help me die if I asked you to?'

'Of course,' he says without hesitation.

'You're just saying that. You didn't even think about it.'

He shrugs. 'I didn't have to think. I know I would.'

There it is. His reply. The gut reaction.

I hold my hands in between my knees. Any minute now, Adam's going to ask me the same question. My brain coasts over the idea – I can't reel it in. When the question comes I want to be able to say, 'Me, too.'

But Adam doesn't ask.

I let him push me back on the bed, I let him kiss me.

'You taste like wine,' he says.

6

Bumping into my ex is the last thing on earth I'd wish to happen when I've got a severe hangover. I've had nightmares about this day, dreaded it and steeled myself for it, and now, now when I'm least expecting it, Peter has materialized in the street and is heading straight towards me.

I cross my fingers, praying that he'll be as reluctant to chat as I am but he stops dead in front of me. He comes up so close that for a second I think he's going to kiss me hello. I quickly take a step back.

'Laura. Lovely to see you.'

'Oh, hi, Peter.'

'I'm shopping,' he tells me needlessly and shakes the bags he's holding. 'Wife's birthday.'

I cast an appraising eye over the names until I realize – too late – that he probably intended me to register the posh designer names on them.

'Are you in a rush? Do you want to go for a coffee?' he asks. 'I don't have to be back at work for another hour.'

'I'm on my way to Alessandro's,' I tell him, and groan

inwardly when he says he'll accompany me. I wish I'd kept on walking; my stomach is beginning to churn, my head is pounding. What I really need is half an hour's peace to get my act together. I've an important meeting planned this afternoon with a couple of clients who are considering a merger of their businesses and I need to be much sharper than I currently feel.

'I haven't been here for ages.' Peter gazes around as if he's been asked to give the place marks out of ten.

Good job too, I think. Judging by the daggers Nat is shooting his way, she'd probably have suspended him by his balls from the ceiling if he'd dared to enter on his own. When he adds, 'Always was a bit too theatrical for my tastes,' I offer to get the drinks to keep him from going anywhere near the counter.

'What on earth are you doing with *him*?' Nat hisses.

'We ran into each other,' I tell her. 'What bad luck is that?'

'Tell him to piss off, the bastard, or can I?' she says rather loudly so I have to shush her.

'Don't,' I say quickly. 'The last thing I want is for him to think it still bothers me.'

When I glance behind me, I see a conservative, boring bloke who I wouldn't look at twice these days. As Peter reaches down and searches through one of his bags with fussy and, shockingly, rather camp movements, Rose's voice suddenly fills my head: *'He sounds truly awful, Laura darling. What on earth were you thinking?'*

I carry the tray to the table.

'Well,' Peter starts before I even get a chance to ask. 'I'm still at the old place. Got promoted again this year. It means longer hours, of course, but money is always useful with a baby and a beautiful wife to upkeep.' He chews on his lips, looking infuriatingly smug – as if he can hardly contain his happiness. 'Yes,' he says. 'All in all, things are working out pretty well.'

He looks expectantly at me, for what I can only assume is some kind of congratulations. Surprise and irritation consume my power of speech. A pain jabs through my eye into the back of my head, bringing with it a wave of nausea.

'I've got to go to the uuh . . .' I stand up quickly and take a few steps before remembering that the painkillers are in my handbag, which is down at the side of my chair. I vacillate about returning for them – I don't want to look as if I have some gushing female problem but I'm desperate.

I march back to the table, fish the packet out of my bag, wave them in the air.

'Hangover,' I say as cheerfully as I can muster. 'Bit of a wild night. Don't suppose you get many of those these days, do you?' before stomping off.

My reflection is scary. My eyes are puffy and darkly shadowed. The two tiny pops of the foil as I press the pills out are music to my ears. I cup my hand under the tap and swallow them gratefully. I let my forehead rest on the cold glass of the mirror above the sink and close my eyes.

Peter never thought to draw the curtains in the sitting room.

'You can't see through the blinds,' he'd say.

'You can with the light on,' I used to tell him.

And the light had been on.

Peter's naked profile was silhouetted. How embarrassing, I was thinking. What if one of the neighbours sees him like this?

A bloke out with his dog walked up to me.

'Some people have no shame,' he said, laughing companionably as we stood there for the few seconds it took before Peter's form was joined by Debs and they both dissolved into the whiteness of the window.

'Show's over,' the man said and set off, the dog trotting happily beside him.

Nat's clopping heels announce her arrival.

'Are you OK?' She stands so close to me that I can feel her warmth; she rubs my back.

'I'm hungover,' I tell her, straightening up. 'Oh yes, and Peter's so up his own arse, it makes me want to puke. And I've just remembered how much I hate him. I hate what he did to me and I hate that I care about being made such a fool of, and I hate having to sit there and pretend how pleased I am to see him and to hear how wonderful his life is.'

I catch Nat's eyes in the mirror.

'And why do I have to look such a wreck, today of all days?' I wail.

'Go out there,' she says. 'Right now. Pick up your bag and just keep moving.'

'I can't.'

'Sweetie . . .'

I shake my head. 'I need to do this.'

'If you're sure,' she says. 'But I honestly don't think he's worth bothering with.'

'It's OK,' I tell her. 'I'll be out in a minute. I just need a minute.'

*   *   *

'She came on to me, Laura,' Peter had said, sitting perched on Mum's sofa like a nervous suitor; a skinny crow with his dark cropped hair and his best business suit on, pecking out his words. 'It was Debbie who started it.'

When I didn't respond, a shiver of irritation passed across his face. He frowned it away and cleared his throat. 'I got caught up in the moment.'

'Three moments,' I said, and he looked startled. 'Debs told me. It was three times.'

I turned my head away then because I wanted him to leave; I'd already decided it was over before he'd spoken.

'Still not married, Laura?' Peter asks when I've returned to the table.

I sit back in my chair, stunned. He can't be that insensitive, I think, but Peter gazes blankly across the table at me, seemingly oblivious to his faux-pas.

'I live with Adam,' I tell him. 'Although it's none of your business, of course.'

'Oh yes, the gardener,' he drawls. 'I heard about that.'

'What's that supposed to mean?'

Peter huffs out a laugh, like he does when he's telling a joke. 'Well, you've gone all very eco-warrior lately, haven't you? All this New Age business stuff and now your plant man. Whatever next?' He laughs again. 'What happened to the smart, up-market executive Laura I knew?'

I stare at my untouched hot chocolate. God knows when, but Peter's finished his. Not only that, but he's actually had the cheek to eat both his and my chocolate flake that accompanies the drink. Something flips inside me. I clench my jaw, my fists, and hold tight onto the edge of the table.

'You mean the idiot who nearly married you?' I say, leaning forward. 'She's long gone, thank God.'

'Calm down, Laura,' he says, casting his eyes around the room. I remember now how he hated 'scenes'.

'Don't tell me to calm down because it will only make me worse.' I glare at him, willing him to leave, leave, leave.

'You're a bloody lunatic,' he mutters and stands up abruptly, scrabbling with his bags in his rush to get away.

'Does the beautiful wife get cheated on too?' I shout at his back.

I watch his head, held stiff and averted, bob above the length of the printed *Alessandro's* on the window like a cut-out ship on a cardboard wave.

When he's finally out of view, I turn and see Nat grinning at me across the room, her thumb up in the air.

7

The next morning, I go for a run before starting work. Winter is gaining ground; the rain is the icy, wispy kind which looks light but actually drenches you in minutes, and the air drills sharply in my nose each time I breathe in, making me want to sneeze. I'm glad I'd returned to fetch my gloves; even with them on, the tips of my fingers feel bloated and sensitized.

I hear the drawn-out, metallic *clunk-clunk* of a train pulling into the station just as I pass under the dimly lit railway bridge. Ahead of me is the dark outline of a sprinting commuter. I catch up with the man in the station forecourt where he stops dead in front of me once he sees the train begin to move out. I swerve away from him and glance back as he raises his arms, his briefcase swinging in the air, lifts his face to the sky and wails: 'Fucking hell-l-l-l-l-l-l-l-l-l.'

A few steps away and the streets are empty and hushed. When my mobile rings, it reverberates shrilly in the sleepy street. I'm anxious to stop the noise and curious to see who it is, calling so early, but my mobile is slippery like a fish between my sheathed fingers. When I see *the Claymores* on the display,

I stop running, pull a hand free from my soggy glove and answer.

It's Ben, William's youngest son, though, not William, phoning to say that his mother's funeral is being postponed.

'Sorry it's such late notice,' he says. 'I've been trying to get hold of everyone who's travelling from abroad first and I'm just starting to contact those who live more locally today.'

It's too cold to stand still. I start walking.

'When will it be now?' I ask. The rustling of my waterproof and my puffing breath make it difficult to hear Ben's reply. I press the phone close to my ear.

'It's hard to say; they'll release the body once the autopsy's done,' Ben is saying. 'Dad's going to come and stay with me,' he adds, and underneath his business-like tone, I catch the strained emotion in his voice. 'Get him away from here for a few days.'

'That sounds like a good idea,' I tell him. 'Can I speak to William? Is he there?'

There's a pause in which I have the impression that Ben is mouthing my request to his father. I hurry towards the Monkey Garden, where I'll be able to sit and talk properly. I'm fully expecting to hear William's voice next but it's Ben who speaks again.

'I'm afraid he doesn't really feel up to chatting.'

'Oh.'

'Nothing personal, Laura,' he reassures me. He speaks in hushed tones presumably so that William can't overhear. 'Dad's not been in the mood to talk to anyone.'

After I've said goodbye, I go into the park anyway. The gate squeaks as I push it open and I have the feeling I always do when I come here – that I'm trespassing into a private garden. On the left side of the entrance there's an old iron plaque which shows the locking times, and it's the only thing that makes me confident this is a public place because the park is so tiny – the smallest I've ever known.

This is the earliest I've ever been here; the park's only been unlocked in the last half an hour and I feel sure I have the honour of being the first visitor of the day. As usual, I'm struck by the extraordinary quiet. It's like stepping inside a magical world – the monkey world; the instant you're in, you feel cut off from the streets and traffic, the houses and people. The raindrops pattering on the fallen leaves seem only to accentuate the silence rather than disturb it. The monkeys are waiting – their chattering and calls have been stilled by my entrance. Their eyes are watching me.

It's a good time of year to spot any new additions to the family now that winter's approaching and the trees and shrubs are losing their leaves. I look for my favourite – the little Hanuman monkey god who peeps out from the lilac bush. He's more exposed than the last time I came and I can see the detail picked out on his iridescent, golden jacket.

I start mentally noting the others that are familiar to me – the large, handsome bronze orang-utan adjacent to the trunk of the old holly tree; the two ceramic, painted masks tied to the railings behind the bench; the simple clay monkey with the spiral tail. It's like taking part in an interactive Spot the Difference puzzle, comparing what is before me now with the positions they were in before. But I soon give up, as I always do. I never seem to be able to retain an accurate picture, not only because the changes in the season continually bring a different perspective but because I am 99 per cent convinced that once again they've been moved.

I'm getting cold. My hands have that bluey-white shine of a dead person's. I recoil from the thought, but it's too late to avoid conjuring up an image of Rose lying in the morgue, waiting to be picked over and poked around.

I remember how Rose had sometimes talked about dying.

'I can't help wondering how it's going to happen,' she said once. 'Will I be fighting for every last breath? Or will I let go – just close my eyes and drift off? The thing is, no one can tell you what it feels like. There is no one alive who can tell you that. Isn't that the strangest thing?'

But I had never imagined it would be like this afterwards.

8

On Saturday, a postcard arrives from Mum. It's a view of Rio de Janeiro. I read it out to Adam over breakfast.

'Dear Laura and Adam. We're having the most wonderful time. Have seen some incredible places – my favourite so far is the one on the card, but we're rather spoiled for choice! I miss you and send my love. David too. Mum.xxx.

'That reminds me.' Adam leaves the room and reappears a couple of minutes later with a notepad and pen. 'It's time we finished converting the shed.'

'Mum isn't back until the middle of November,' I tell him. 'I can't imagine her buyer will want to move until after Christmas.'

Adam keeps quiet. He fiddles with the pen.

'What?'

'I know this is hard for you,' he says.

'It's just there's so much to sort out. I'll have to change my stationery and my brochures – there's a lot to do, Ad.'

'I meant with Trudy selling up your old house and moving in with David,' he says softly.

'I'm fine about that,' I tell him.

'I'm not sure you are.'

Adam gives me a long look which I can't hold. I gaze instead at a puddle of coffee on the table, then at my empty plate. His perceptiveness has caught me by surprise. Of course I'm not fine. I lick the tip of my finger and press it onto the crunch of crumbs on my plate; I contemplate the brown and black flecks there before dusting them away with my thumb.

There are times when it seems that Ad knows me better than I know myself.

'Can you be homesick for a person?' I ask him, my voice faltering at the end. No matter how furiously I blink, a tear escapes. I wipe it away. 'First Rose, now Mum – I seem to be losing the people I care about one by one.'

'You've not lost your mum – you'll still be able to see her as often as you want – and I'm not going anywhere,' he adds. 'For what it's worth.'

I meet his eyes. He grins a little sheepishly, scratches the top of his head with the pen. I reach for his free hand, feel the prickle of hairs as I stroke them the wrong way, touch the swirl of callus on the side of his index finger.

'It's worth loads, Ad, thanks.'

I release his hand, tap the blank piece of paper in front of him. 'You're right,' I say, sitting up straight. 'The sooner we get on with the new office, the better.'

In the afternoon, Adam heads off to the builder's merchants with his long list of materials while I head to the Downs for a run to cheer myself up.

The sky is patchily blue. I hope the strong wind will keep blowing the rainclouds away from me until I've finished my run.

The ground is soggy underfoot; mud soon coats the soles of my trainers, making it laborious work, like running in platform shoes against a head-on wind. My thigh muscles are burning after ten minutes so I take a breather, only half an hour in, once I've reached the top of the Mound. There's a bench there, thoughtfully placed for the best view around. Miles of flat heath and marshes stretch in front of you and – at eye-straining distance – you can sometimes make out the thin thread of the sea.

Today, on the scrubby grass to my left, there's a man practising with one of the large surf kites. The wind is making his life hard too; everything is flapping – his hair into his face, his jacket, even the legs of his trousers ripple. He's bent over, moving up and down, up and down, trying to lay out the lines of the kite which are continually blown out of place.

'I hate being a cliché,' Rose once said, 'but when it comes to the crunch, even a hardened atheist like me can't avoid thinking about life after death. There's this thing about the sky, isn't there? You know, heaven's there, spirits float around, angels descend. I mean, why the sky?' She paused briefly before continuing. 'Anyway, I can't help but notice how busy it is – aeroplanes, birds, kites, balloons, butterflies and bees, fireworks, smoke, helicopters, lightning.'

We were in her room as usual, Rose in her chair, me on the cushion on the floor next to her, both of us facing the window although the view that day was obscured by heavy rain and a dull light which was darkening by the minute. The window was open a little and Rose got up to fetch me a pair of socks as the draught was beginning to freeze my toes.

She switched on the lamp and the room instantly turned

cosier. I watched her dig around in the little chest of drawers which was the most recent addition to the furniture. The more time Rose spent up here, the more she accumulated, and I knew from comments that both she and William made, that she rarely ventured downstairs any more.

It was easy to understand her reluctance to leave her room; the rest of the house was still full of William's aunt's belongings from years ago when he inherited the house. In the past, when their stays in the UK were mostly limited to a few weeks a year, the Claymores had never felt it worthwhile replacing 'the monstrosities' as Rose sweepingly labelled everything, from the large, dark furniture to the dainty figurines that filled the glazed mahogany cabinets. 'But living with them is a whole other matter,' Rose had declared, eyes narrowed, her hands on her hips, when I came over one day and discovered her ankle-deep in paper and bubble wrap, unpacking the belongings they'd shipped back from Barcelona.

These items soon provided an idiosyncratic edge to the surroundings: in place of an old-fashioned hunting scene hanging over the fireplace there was a five-foot-high photograph of a cactus in bloom, and at the other end of the lounge, they'd installed two white floor-to-ceiling MDF bookcases to house their considerable collection of books and papers. A large eggshell-blue ceramic bowl and a collection of dumpy rustic pottery jars jostled the elaborate silverware on the top of the sideboard, and a lamp with a bulbous candy-pink glass shade took pride of place on the bureau.

Rose, however, remained unsatisfied with the results because the Claymores' possessions still looked – as she often complained – like squatters waiting to get kicked out.

The top room, though, was Rose's domain through and through.

The candy-pink lamp was eventually moved upstairs, along with the small oak desk and armchair which had been passed down from her mother, her grandmother's faded red satin quilt, a Japanese screen, two crooked red vases and a couple of rustic wooden Italian chairs.

The one thing that did surprise me was Rose leaving the walls bare. I thought she'd want lots of their photographs around her but she said that she could look at those any time on the laptop. What she liked to do, when she was resting in bed, was watch patterns come and go on the walls as the clouds moved across the sky and the sun shone through the rain droplets on the windowpanes.

'Is there any moment,' I wondered aloud as I pulled on the socks, 'when the sky is absolutely clear of everything – including clouds?'

'Good thought,' Rose said.

We remained silent for a few minutes. Rose was the first to pick up the conversation again. 'I was thinking what if – in the afterlife – you got to select the element you wish to exist in? Wouldn't that be great? Give me the ocean to splash around in for eternity; it would be so beautiful down there amongst all that amazing colour, all those wonderfully weird plants and animals.'

'Like in one of William's photographs.'

'Exactly.'

'You could be with him,' I said. 'Like a ghostly mermaid companion.'

Rose didn't reply and my sentence looped round my head.

Each time I felt more stupidly insensitive, but I couldn't take it back, no matter how much I wished I could.

The man still hasn't succeeded in launching the kite. I take a last look at him before jogging back to the car. I've stayed too long on the bench and my muscles feel tight enough to snap. My skin is cold and clammy. I pull a fleece on, switch the heating on full blast. The windows begin to steam up so I have to buzz one down.

As I hit the traffic coming into Brighton, I suddenly think of Adam. I picture him sprawled on the settee in a Saturday snooze. I imagine waking him up, straddling him, doing all sorts of dirty things to him, using his heat to warm me through.

But when I get home, there's no sign of him. There's evidence that he's been back in the form of a stack of wood leaning against the shed and a huge mountain of screws and brackets and coils of wire on the kitchen table.

When I emerge from the steamy warm bathroom, the rest of the flat feels dreary and cold in the gloomy early-evening light. I discover a faint, scrawled note on the reverse of a till receipt, half-hidden under the kettle.

Gone 2 Boar's Head

X

I stop just inside the door of the pub. Adam and his mates are, as expected, in the back room by the pool table.

Even from a distance, I can tell they've already had a few drinks; suddenly they all explode with laughter, their heads roll back, their bodies rock forwards. I watch Adam; he slaps Rob on the back in consolation as he takes his turn at the game.

I only have to take a few steps to join them. They'll welcome me – they always do. 'Here's Adam's missus.' They'll clear a space for me, raise their pints in greeting; their jokes will change focus briefly as I become the object of some gentle joshing. Adam will kiss me hello, play with my bum secretly whenever he gets the opportunity.

If one of them had spotted me, I'd have gone forward, but nobody does and when a couple come in, pushing past me, I turn round and go home.

The evening stretches ahead of me. I sit on the sofa and turn the TV on.

I start to cry. It comes from nowhere and seems to go on for ever. When I finally stop, I examine my face in the mirror. I look wrecked. My eyelids are swollen up like a pig's and my face is flushed. I go to bed and watch TV on the portable to keep out of sight in case Adam brings any of his mates home with him.

9

William's appearance is alarming: the skin under his eyes is so dark that at first I think someone has punched him.

On the drive over, I'd run through numerous naff phrases to say when I first saw him, so cringeworthy I'd vowed not to use them, but now I can't help thinking that any words would have been better than standing mute in the doorway, my mind completely empty.

I follow William down the hall and into the kitchen. It's always been a lovely bright room and now it's the tidiest I've ever seen it; it looks spotless. I open my mouth to comment, then shut it almost immediately.

William switches the kettle on. He adjusts the line of the toaster, the espresso-maker, perfects the angle of some of the jars on the work surface while I desperately search for something to say. This silence is awful but the subjects which consume my thoughts – Rose's autopsy and his arrest – seem totally inappropriate to raise and everything else seems insultingly trivial.

'Why don't you go into the living room?' William suggests in the end. 'I'll bring the tea in there.'

William passes me my drink and sits down opposite me in one of the chairs. The cushion sighs and sinks underneath him so that he ends up awkwardly low, sagging forwards with his chin almost in his mug.

Behind him, I'm startled to see Rose's lamp back in its original spot on the bureau, almost as if it has never been absent.

I force myself to speak. 'How are you doing, William?'

'Not so bad.' He looks vaguely at me, blinking for a long moment. 'Well, tired to be honest. I feel as if every bone in me needs to sleep for a thousand years.'

He sets his drink on the floor and pulls himself more upright. 'The police were great, though – very kind,' he tells me. 'Apparently, this kind of thing happens more often than you realize; all manner of accusations can fly around following a death.'

'But who on earth accused *you*?' I ask before I can stop myself.

He rubs his chin as if he's thinking about my question. 'Emma,' he says finally.

'Your son's wife? I don't understand. Why would she do that?'

William speaks slowly. 'The suddenness of Rosie's death took them by surprise.'

This doesn't explain anything. I wait for William to say more. He rests his arms on his knees, drops his head and his hair falls across his face. He talks into his lap. 'Emma's – um – loyalty to Alex may be a little misguided but she does have his best interests at heart.' He turns to look at me. 'It seems that when it came up that you were there in the afternoon . . .'

'*Me*? What have I got to do with it?'

'She seemed to think there had been some kind of ceremony that she and Alex had been excluded from.'

'A what?'

'She knew Rosie had a living will and she became suspicious, added two and two together and came up with five.'

I stare at William. I hadn't known there was a living will. 'Surely Alex could have talked her out of going to the police?'

'He had no idea she'd contacted them until it was too late.'

I bite my tongue. I have to watch what I say to William. Rose used to refer to her son and daughter-in-law as 'Emmalex'. 'They move as one,' she used to say, but William didn't like her talking that way.

'You met her, didn't you?' William asks. 'Emma?'

'Yes, once. At Rosie's birthday party last year.'

I hadn't known what to expect that evening.

'Please come,' Rose had said, looking at William for back-up though she didn't need to; I hadn't known the Claymores long and I was flattered to be invited. 'We throw a good do, don't we, darling?'

Rose had gone on to describe some of their 'classic pool parties', jazz evenings, a picnic in the mountains, thirty friends on a Spanish fishing boat, conjuring up such a vivid atmosphere, I could almost feel the bitter tang of icy gin fizz, the brush of soft, warm air around the nape of my neck.

As I left, William had hurried after me. 'I'm afraid you may have been misled,' he said, flushing a little. 'There will only be our two sons and daughter-in-law at Rose's party.'

It was my turn to be embarrassed; I felt as if I must have somehow engineered an invitation to a family occasion. I hastily told William that I had no intention of intruding.

'I didn't mean that at all,' he said. 'It's simply that our social life is not what it used to be over here. It's what comes of abandoning your country for years – you can't expect to pick up where you left off – and our group of friends is somewhat diminished.' He pinched the top of his nose. 'The thing is, Laura, it would mean an awful lot to Rose if you – and your young man – could come.' He hesitated. 'It would make the evening a little more special for her.'

Rose had been so excited on the run-up to the party that I had dressed for the occasion in my favourite swishy, cream jersey dress and forcibly encouraged Ad into a jacket and linen trousers, but when William showed us into the living room, Alex and his wife looked as if they'd made zero effort. They had on the 'his and her' City uniforms of black trousers/skirt, white shirt/cream blouse.

They sat side-by-side on the settee and looked oddly uncomfortable and formal, considering they were family. Alex greeted us in a very stiff manner and as Emma shook my hand she studied me with such ill-concealed curiosity that I wondered what Rose had been saying.

There was no obvious resemblance between Alex and either of his parents. He was tall and thickset, his face looked heavy for his age, and his hair was the matt black kind which goes grey early.

Adam shifted beside me and when I glanced at him, his face said it all: *You owe me. I've given up a night in the pub for this.* I felt a rush of gratitude and lust for him – he looked very horny in his smart clothes – and I fished for his hand and he squeezed mine back.

Ben appeared from the kitchen with drinks for us. He grinned as he handed them over and introduced himself. He was as broad and tall as his brother, but without the extra pounds; a rugby player's physique, I instantly thought. Dressed in jeans and a shirt, his whole demeanour was much more relaxed than Alex's. His hair was a dark brown version of William's and when he made a joke, I caught in his expression a look of his father there too.

It was then that Rose made her entrance.

She looked wonderful in a strappy apricot dress and a matching bandana; her pendant earrings sparkled whenever she moved. William hugged her close and I was surprised to see that there were tears in his eyes.

When I kissed her cheek, I whispered, 'You look beautiful.' Over Rose's shoulder I caught Alex's sullen expression, so I stepped back quickly.

'Ah, Adam,' Rose said as he stood up to shake her hand. She held on to his fingers. 'I've been wanting to meet you for some time,' she breathed at him.

I was surprised how embarrassed he was by that; he'd blushed, which he so rarely does, and afterwards he said that he thought Rose was rather too intense – a bit over the top for his taste. He wasn't happy either when Rose 'borrowed' me for a few minutes, leaving him alone with a bunch of strangers.

I hadn't been to the top floor of the house before. I followed Rose into a small square room, with a low-angled, white ceiling and white walls. It was empty save for an iron single bed. Short, bare French windows faced the front; a glowing man-in-the-moon was framed in the centre.

'What a lovely room!'

'Isn't it? Doesn't it feel peaceful?'

Rose pointed out a wooden slatted door which turned out to be an ensuite bathroom when I peeked inside. It was all white, too.

Rose rattled the key in the French doors. 'This lock needs oiling.'

She finally pushed them open and fresh air rushed in. 'It's always been my favourite place in the house,' she told me. 'We made it into a guest room but it's hardly been used. We've never really spent enough time in the UK to have many visitors, and any friends of the boys slept in their rooms.'

'Is it strong enough for two?' I asked as she stepped out onto the narrow balustraded ledge.

'Yes. It's safe.' She beckoned me to join her.

'It's wonderful up here,' I said. The breeze was warm but strong, blowing our dresses against our legs. I leaned forward; ahead were the huge phosphorescent-white blocks of the hotels. Once my eyes grew accustomed to the hazy dark I could see the clean Georgian lines of the other houses extending out on either side, and the ugly backs of the hotels with the paraphernalia of fire escapes, huge extractor vents and water tanks on the roof.

'I've been spending quite a bit of time here,' Rose said. 'I've been thinking of bringing a chair up and making myself more comfortable. There's so much going on, you wouldn't believe it.'

A bat twisted and turned in front of us. Another joined the

dance. They were so close I could hear their leathery wings fluttering.

'Sometimes I wonder whether it was right to come back,' Rose said suddenly. 'It seems completely different to how I thought it would be.'

'You sound like you're back for good,' I joked, but Rose stayed silent. 'Are you?'

'Laura,' she started, and sounded so serious and looked so wistful that I felt my pulse begin to race, somehow nervous of what she was going to say next. 'Sometimes you find yourself making choices that you'd never in a million years imagine you'd make.'

'Yes,' I agreed, although I felt that the full meaning of her words was just out of my grasp.

'Our sons didn't have a conventional upbringing. We travelled a lot when they were little – job to job, country to country. Ben thrived wherever he was, but Alex didn't.' She paused. 'Alex was never a happy boy and he's become an unhappy young man. It's sad to see that with anyone, even harder when it's your own child.' Rose faced me. 'We decided it would be best for the boys to go to boarding school rather than keep moving them around. We hadn't bought our place in Barcelona then and they needed to get a proper education.' She sighed and held her palms out. 'But Alex hated that, too.'

The shriek of a cat echoed shrilly around the buildings, making me jump, but Rose didn't appear to have heard.

'They'd come over to us in the summer holidays, and in the shorter breaks we used to travel back here as often as we could. As they got older we saw less of them once they started to do their own thing, but while Ben was at university, he joined us in Barcelona each summer vacation and he lived with us there for nearly a year after he graduated.'

'And Alex?'

Rose shook her head. 'Alex and Emma have managed one trip to see us in the last five years and that was disastrous.' She giggled. 'They were so dreadfully unsociable that in the end we had to ask our friends to keep away until they'd gone.'

I thought I was beginning to understand what Rose was trying to say. 'So you're here to try and get closer to your sons?'

'Yes, darling, that's exactly it. We hoped to get to know them better; to make amends a little, if it's not too late.'

'I'm sure it's not – too late, I mean.'

I felt Rose's warm hand cover mine; the cold metal of the railing dug briefly into my palm as she gently squeezed my fingers.

'You've never talked about your father, Laura, have you?'

'There's nothing much to say.'

'You don't see him at all?'

'No, not now. Not for years. He and Mum divorced when I was two and she worked hard to bring me up on her own; she didn't want any help from him. He used to come and see me when he was in the area sometimes, but he never stayed long; and he stopped coming altogether when I was still young.'

Rose studied me for a moment. 'Does it bother you?'

Out across the Crescent, the liquid blue of TV screens shimmered in several of the hotel-room windows.

'Only sometimes,' I told her, which I had never admitted to anyone before.

* * *

William, picking up his mug of tea, brings me back to the present. His face is sunken with tiredness.

'And,' I say slowly, 'what about now? Are Alex and Emma all right with everything?'

'They say so, but in all honesty, I think everybody's waiting for the results of the autopsy.' He pauses briefly and then the words spill from him as if he's been holding them back until now. 'I wasn't there, Laura. I wasn't with her when she died and I should have been.'

He looks at me, shaken.

'But you weren't to know. It was completely unexpected,' I tell him, realizing as I speak that this means Rose would have been alone. The one thing she told me she feared. I shut that thought out.

'But I did know,' he says. For a brief second, as the sunlight falls across William's face, all the contours of his bones are visible, as if his skin is transparent. His mouth is thin and rigid as he speaks. He hardly looks like William at all. 'That's why I didn't go out when you came round. Rosie woke up that morning with a sudden, strange energy – and I was sure something was going to happen. But when you left and I went upstairs, she was sleeping so peacefully that I told myself I'd been mistaken.' He frowns. 'I made a cup of tea, sat and watched the telly – the news – for twenty minutes or so. I felt relaxed, the house felt calm, and I didn't question why. I pottered around with some domestic stuff before I went back up with her pills. I took her an ice-lolly that she liked to have afterwards to take the taste away. But when I went in, she was dead.'

The appeal in William's eyes squeezes my heart.

'There wouldn't have been anything you could have done,' I

tell him. I sound calm but I don't feel it. 'She died in her sleep, the best way to go.'

William continues to look at me.

'You did all that you could for Rose, and more.'

'God,' he says quietly. 'I miss her so much.'

That night of the party I had gone downstairs to rejoin the others, leaving Rose on the balcony.

Emma immediately cornered me in the kitchen where I was topping up on wine. Adam, Ben and Alex were outside smoking; William was with them. Smoke swirled above their heads in the patio light. The back door was ajar and a faint smell of cigarettes drifted in.

I offered Emma some of the open bottle of wine. She propped her bum against the kitchen table and held out her glass.

'So then, what was the big secret?'

'Sorry?'

'I assume Rose whisked you away to speak to you about something.'

'Oh, not really. We just chatted.'

Everything about Emma's face was sharp. Her chiselled nose, her narrow eyes, her thin slash of a mouth; even her eyebrows had been plucked to dagger-ended lines. She raised one of these and looked sceptically at me. 'Mmm.'

She wandered over to the back door, nudged it shut with her foot, then returned to lean against the table.

'So there's nothing going on, then?'

'Not that I'm aware of, but I'm sure you and Alex would know before me, anyway.'

'You're joking. Those two would rather tell a complete stranger their business before they spoke to me and Alex.'

I felt my face going pink while Emma looked at me as she sipped her wine. 'So how did you meet them?'

I told her about Alessandro's and the note they had left me. I explained how I'd hit it off with Rose straight away.

She nodded. 'They're always doing this, you know. Well, Rose is.'

'Doing what?'

'Finding young friends. You're really only the latest protégée in a long line.' Emma tapped her fingers against the wine glass, cocked her head to one side. 'I hope I haven't upset you. I thought I should warn you, that's all. There's more to our "Rosie" than meets the eye.'

'I think you're wrong,' I said, struggling to remain polite. 'Rose is a wonderful woman.'

Emma laughed and winked as the men came in, huffing and puffing, making a show of being back in the warmth, bringing the smoker's stink inside.

'Don't say I didn't warn you,' she whispered as we herded back to the lounge just as Rose walked in, too.

Rose's high heels were unstable on the carpet: 'What happened to the music?' she asked brightly as she wobbled her way over to the CD-player, and my heart went out to her as it does now. She should have been in a different setting, at a different birthday party – the fun one, where she was Queen Bee – with terracotta-tiled floors and cocktails, on a soft summer evening surrounded by her ex-pat crowd.

I wish, looking back, that I'd at least tried to persuade her to go back to the life where she was happy, to the friends who loved her, now that I know what Alex and Emma have done.

10

It's two in the morning, and the phone shocks me awake.

'Who the fuck is that?' Adam grumbles. 'Leave it,' he commands, reaching across, his hand sliding off my back as I launch myself out of bed, grabbing my bathrobe, struggling to tie it round me as I slide-run into the hall.

There's no way I couldn't answer it. The only reason people ring in the middle of the night is to report bad news. My mental ticker bar is already in motion, but this time only one name appears; a thread repeated over and over. *Mum Mum Mum.*

'The bastard's left me,' Debs wails into my ear.

I shiver from the cold and from the adrenalin coursing through me. It takes a moment before Debbie's words really make sense.

'What happened?'

'Were you asleep?' Debs asks accusingly.

'Uh – yes. It's gone two, Debs.'

I take the phone into the lounge and shut the door. I pull a throw off the back of the sofa and wrap it round me, then prop my head comfortably against a stack of cushions. Relieved there is no emergency, I forget to be pissed off that Debs has rung me this late for a drama which will blow over tomorrow. I snuggle down for a long phone session, feeling like a teenager doing a post-date dissection. *And then what did he do? What did he say? What did you say?*

'We were arguing all the time.'

'You've always argued,' I remind her.

'But it was different lately. We never made up properly. He kept telling me that I was selfish and childish and all sorts of other fucking ishes . . . Oh yes, brattish. That was the latest.'

I can tell from the way Debs is picking her way through her words that this is an alcohol-fuelled melodrama.

'When you've both had time to cool off, you'll talk and sort it out,' I tell her. 'Josh never stays mad at you for long.'

'You're not listening,' she says. 'I told you, it's different this time. Why won't you believe me? What can I say to prove it to you?'

Suddenly I remember the last time that I saw them together – how withdrawn Josh was – and it dawns on me that she might be right.

'He took his computer,' she tells me. '*See?* You know that means he's not coming back.'

I hear a gasp and then Debs starts crying. She cries as if she's never going to stop, and the hairs on the back of my neck stand up. I haven't heard her cry properly like this for years.

'Shush,' I breathe into the phone. 'Shush, it'll be OK. Debs, it'll be OK.'

I keep repeating this over and over, over and over. I don't know what else to do.

*   *   *

In the morning, Adam stands with a slice of toast heaped with marmalade poised in one hand, a mug of tea in the other.

'Did I dream it?' he asks. 'Or did some idiot ring at some stupid o'clock this morning?'

'Debbie. She's split up with Josh.'

'He's seen the light, has he?' Adam says, and then he sees my face. 'For real? Oh bollocks. That means trouble.'

Later that same day, William phones. He tells me that the autopsy results are through and that Rose died of natural causes: massive heart failure.

'There's no doubt about it – they're not going to pursue anything,' he says.

'What a relief. Thank God.'

'Yes. Now we can put Rosie to rest,' he says in a rushed voice. 'Ben's sorting it all out. He's here with me. Now we can have Rosie's funeral.'

'Oh, William. At last.'

He clears his throat. There's a brief silence on the other end of the phone before his voice starts up, quietly at first then gathering strength.

'I wanted to say thanks – for listening the other day, Laura.'

'You're very welcome,' I hurry to tell him, embarrassed. 'There's no need to thank me.'

'I wanted to say it anyway.' His tone lowers, deepens. 'Because I really appreciated it.'

At seven, I get to the bar where I've arranged to meet Debs. It's an earlier start than I'd have liked but Debs is on a mission.

'I want to get slaughtered,' she told me over the phone.

I was pleased that Debs chose to come here tonight – she's brought her sales team here a couple of times since it opened ten months ago – but I've been wanting to check it out now for a while. Millie, one of my clients, owns the business next door – a sex shop for women called *Girls' Toys*, which up until recently had been struggling to make money because of the location. We'd had a series of meetings to explore restructuring or diversifying, but the future hadn't looked promising. The last time we'd met, though, it was a different story altogether.

'Loads of girls have started coming in on a Saturday afternoon when they're pissed and buying tons of stuff,' Millie said, grinning broadly as she showed me figures for the dramatic upswing in the last two months' takings. 'I've started opening on Sundays as well and that's pretty successful too.'

The girls are absent in numbers tonight though, despite it being Happy Hour with cocktails at two for the price of one – the main reason, I suspect, for Debbie's choice. There are a couple of people sitting at the bar who look like the barman's mates and a group of three glum young women who have the air of being stood up en masse.

Debs hasn't arrived either and so I take the opportunity to order a latte – much to the barman's irritation – which I'll need to line my stomach for the night ahead if her mood earlier is anything to go by.

All the available furniture is inflatable, and once I get over the unnerving idea that it will go pop under my weight, the armchair is surprisingly comfortable. A comical underwater scene is set in see-through Perspex flooring over the whole of the centre of the room. There's seaweed and shoals of gaudy fish, a trail of air bubbles leading to a diver who's swimming on the opposite side, and the character near me who I like best is a saucy-looking mermaid with huge pointed breasts sitting on a rock; crabs are pinching her nipples and one is hovering near her bum with a goofy smile on its face.

It reminds me of Rose and her aquatic heaven, and even though I don't really believe in anything like that, I can't help hoping that she's having fun somewhere else; that she's making her jokes and telling her stories just as she did with me.

Debbie's sandalled feet, with her trademark *Hot Cherry* varnish on her toenails, walk across the mermaid's tail.

'I'll get the drinks in, shall I?' she says, taking off her jacket and throwing it onto one of the chairs.

'I'll have whatever you're having.'

Before Debs has even reached the bar the barman, who spent the whole time I was up there chatting to his mates, is leaning across, smiling at her.

She's wearing silver jeans and a very tight black camisole top. I really, really hope that these are flirting not pulling clothes; that she's not about to start getting off with loads of guys to prove a point to Josh, and herself. We've been down that road so many times before, and all it means is I suffer weeks of having a knot in my stomach every time she phones, fearful that this could be the time she's pushed it too far and got herself mixed up in something nasty.

'Cheers,' Debs says, clinking her glass against mine and looking in the direction of the barman. 'These ones are free.'

'Do you two want to get a room?' I ask her.

'Jeez, Loz. Stop being such a Miss Prim.'

I ignore her and ask the question I need to ask before we both get too drunk to make any sense. 'What happened?'

'Don't know, don't care.'

'Have you heard from Josh?'

'He left a couple of messages.' She pouts a little, as if to say it's beneath her to be having a conversation about him. 'I haven't called back. I've been too busy.'

'But is it over, for definite?'

'I wouldn't take him back even if he begged me,' she says, narrowing her eyes at me over the rim of her cocktail glass. 'No one does that to me. If you walk out – you stay out.'

'But if you only talked to him . . .'

Debs interrupts me. 'I don't want to. The idea makes me want to throw up. Let him find someone else and me too. I'm back on the market. Where you should be too, if you ask me.'

'Hey, hang on a minute, I'm perfectly happy,' I tell her. 'What are you going on about?'

Debs shakes her head pityingly at me. 'You two are like Mr and Mrs Married For Twenty Years. You're sooo boring.'

I let this remark go.

Three hours and a lot of cocktails later, we hit on the same subject.

'Don't you miss that?' Debs asks. 'The thrill of the chase, the excitement of meeting someone new? You can't tell me you don't miss that kick.'

'Ad and I are contented,' I tell her. 'There's nothing wrong with that.'

'Nothing except that you're *twenty-eight*, for fuck's sake,' she says.

'So?'

'I'm only saying that you shouldn't settle until you've tried a few different things.'

'We do try different things,' I joke.

Debs rolls her eyes. 'Give me a break.'

'We're fine,' I say. And because I'm drunk and Debs is beginning to wind me up, I rush off to the loo and text a frantic message to Adam.

debs crazy. wish I was home in bed wiv u sooo much. Xxxxxxx

I sit on the loo, clutching my mobile, hoping for a quick reply but none appears. My world spins gently.

There's no loo paper. I rifle through my handbag for tissues or anything else I can use instead; I am studying my cash-point receipts as a real possibility when someone comes in and bangs shut the door of the adjacent cubicle.

'Chuck me some loo roll, please?' I call out.

A hand shoots under the partition, waving a handful of paper. It's Debs, her nail polish a giveaway.

She shouts over the noise of her loud, copious peeing, 'What you should do is get him jealous. Wake him up a bit, Loz. He'll just start taking you for granted otherwise.'

I make *yadda-yadda* gestures with my hand at the partition. My spinning world has gathered momentum and I stagger when I stand up and nearly end up with my face pressed against the door.

I'm too drunk to shower and can barely undress myself; I'm trying to be quiet but keep teetering and landing against the bed. I think I hear a grunt of laughter from Adam, but when I stand still to listen there's silence.

He's awake though, and as soon as I get into bed, he pulls me against him. His tummy is lovely and warm against mine.

'You stink of cigarettes,' he tells me, sniffing my hair. 'And booze,' when he kisses me. 'How was it?'

'You didn't reply to my message.'

His eyes are close to mine and in the dim light they look glossy as if they've been polished; I'd like to touch them, I think. There are more than two, I notice with interest.

'I didn't have my mobile on,' Adam says. 'Was it a rude one?' He starts to caress my breasts, bends his head to suck on my nipples. 'Tell me what you said.'

Drink churns in my stomach, rising in stale, bitter burps. I twist away from Adam and turn over, so that he won't discover how disgusting I am.

'I'm very drunk,' I tell him.

'Never.'

He pushes up behind me, slips his finger between my legs and inside me. It feels nice. I wriggle to make myself more comfortable. He nibbles on my ear, pushes his finger in higher. In and out.

After we've made love, the nausea returns, stronger and more alarming.

Adam is sleep-heavy against me.

I try and concentrate on not throwing up, hoping that I will fall asleep instead so that I don't have to make the long, long, long journey to the bathroom.

11

'Emma's here,' I hiss into Adam's ear.

'Why wouldn't she be?'

'Because of what she did, perhaps?' I reply sharply.

'Sssh,' Adam says, glancing from side to side. His hushed voice comes out as a low rumble. 'You said it was all a misunderstanding.'

'I know, but it seems a bit hypocritical . . .'

Adam shoots me a look. 'William's obviously got over it.'

Meaning I should have, too. I seethe quietly at his side and look round.

I had imagined that the crematorium would be a sad, rather soulless place, but in fact there's quite a party atmosphere – an occasion that Rose would probably have enjoyed herself. There are loads of people here, and most of them seem to be from abroad – they're the tanned ones who looked frozen when we were waiting outside. It's a blustery day and even colder up here on the hill.

The room is crammed with flowers – the sweet stink of lilies and freesias catches in my breath every now and then. And of course there are roses everywhere.

It's much more relaxed than a church. Most people are wearing informal clothes, as they were requested to, and there's a lot of chat and the occasional burst of surprised pleasure as new arrivals are greeted by other guests. Only William and his little family group sit like black blocks of wood at the front opposite Rose's coffin.

When I first came in, I had this swift and hideous image of me doing something daft like running to the coffin and holding on to it once the conveyor belt started. A crazy, slapstick thought which threatens to return. I swallow hard.

Adam finds my hand, squeezes it. 'You OK?'

I nod.

Suddenly William swivels in his seat. Some of the chatter is stilled as his eyes travel across the room. He looks ill, putty-coloured; his face remains blank. His gaze passes in my direction and hesitates when I smile at him. He lifts his hand, just slightly, in acknowledgement.

Emma whirls around and glares at me before turning to the front again. Blood boils up to my face.

'Did you see that?' I pull at Adam's arm.

'What?'

The other three are all listening to Emma. Her head jabs forwards; her mouth works away in a pinched rush of words.

William reaches out behind Alex and pats her shoulder.

'Doesn't matter.'

The service begins. Several people go to the front. They tell anecdotes, read passages and poetry.

Adam next to me is solid and warm. I lean against him, grateful to be close, and he puts his arm round me and pulls me tight to share the service leaflet, but the wording dances in front of my eyes and I struggle to follow it.

I laugh with the rest of them and snivel a little too. I think, That's beautiful; that's so Rose; that's such a nice thing to say. But I sense their words slipping away almost immediately.

My eyes keep being drawn to Emma. I am aware of her every movement, every twitch of her head as she constantly glances at Alex, every shift she makes in her seat. Everything else around me is hazy; only the spot where Emma is sitting is burned clear.

Neither William nor his sons get up to speak.

Outside, the wind has dropped and it feels eerily silent and still as if we're being sheltered inside a glass dome. Memorial stones stretch as far as the eye can see down the slope to the trees at the bottom; their bright autumn colours look incredible.

Ben shakes my hand first then Adam's. Adam says we'll be happy to give anyone a lift back to the house, but there's no need in the end. Everyone's sorted, Ben says. The two of them chat briefly about the pros and cons of certain cars, in that intense but impersonal way men do, before Ben heads off to talk to other guests. Alex and Emma have gone ahead to open the house for the guests.

William hasn't managed to move far from the door; people keep approaching him to offer their condolences. I watch how the expression on his face changes from open pleasure at seeing a friend, to a creased sorrow. I catch his eye and he manages a wavering, sad smile before his attention switches to someone else.

Adam and I drive to the house. When he unclips his seat belt, I don't move. 'I don't really want to go in,' I admit.

'Me neither; I hate this kind of thing.' Adam gets out and stretches. He finds my car cramped because he's used to the rattling space of his van. He bends down and looks at me. 'We don't have to stay long,' he suggests hopefully.

Inside, chatting groups have already formed. Adam and I stand like spare parts on the edge of the lounge while other people who arrive after us seem to be immediately welcomed in. I can't help wondering where they all were when Rose was dying.

'We'll make our getaway once William arrives,' Ad says quietly.

Emma's outside the downstairs loo when I open the door.

'Oh,' she says. 'Hello, Laura.'

She sounds friendly so it briefly crosses my mind that I'd imagined the horrid look she'd shot me earlier, but my heart starts beating quickly as if my body knows better.

'I hear you and William have been having a few tête-à-têtes recently,' she says, still pleasantly but her eyes have a hardness about them.

'I've been around when he's needed to talk,' I tell her, carefully. 'And I'm happy to listen.'

Emma seems to consider this. 'That's great, thanks,' she says. 'We're grateful, but – well, that's what his family's for now, so there's no need to feel you have to keep in touch.'

I must have looked confused because she puts her hand on my shoulder and gives me a sickly-sweet smile. 'Look. I'm just saying whatever Rose put you up to, you can forget about now. She's not here any more to know, is she?'

'Rose didn't put me up to anything.' I side-step to move past her. 'I'm sorry, but I can't just abandon him.'

'There's nothing in it for you, you know, whatever she might have told you,' she calls after me.

I ignore her and continue walking.

I find Adam, touch his arm. 'We're leaving,' I say. 'Now.'

By the car, I hand Adam the keys. I'm trembling. 'You drive.'

'Where to?' he asks when we're inside.

'Just drive,' I say.

'OK, lady.' He doffs a pretend cap and winks. 'At your service.'

He takes the road out of Brighton and stops after twenty minutes in a car park overlooking the Downs.

The scenery is bleak; the trees bare, the grass scrubby and churned up with mud. We are on the cusp of winter. The thought hangs over me, like the clouds which are filling up the sky – slate-grey and ominous.

'Do you want to walk?' Adam asks.

'Not really.'

We sit in silence. Emma's words repeat over and over in my head.

'What's wrong? Babe?'

Tears are running down my face. I wipe them away furiously. 'That fucking Emma; she's such a cow,' I tell him, yanking tissues out of the box that Adam drops into my lap. They smell of my perfume.

'Whoa,' he says. 'What the hell happened?'

I blow my nose hard. 'Why does she have to make everything sound so sordid and calculating? Rose and I were friends – that's why I went to see her. And that's why I want to help William. Not for any other reason.'

'I know, babe.' Adam takes my hand, rubs his thumb across mine. 'Don't take any notice of anything Emma says; she's upset and she's jealous and she's bitchy. Some people just have to be bitchy.'

Big splats of rain drop onto the windscreen, then suddenly it's drumming down, bouncing off the car. The view is obliterated.

I shiver.

Adam starts the engine. The wipers squeak into action and fight to keep the window clear.

'We'll wait for this to ease,' he says. 'Then we'll go home.'

I leave it for a few evenings before I go round to visit William. There are lights on and when I knock on the front door, the dark blur of someone's head appears behind the thick glass, but nobody answers and the shape seems to fade away.

I put my ear close to the pane and think I catch the muffled sound of voices. Perhaps Ben is still staying with him.

I knock again – louder this time, but nobody comes. I must have been mistaken; William must be out.

On the street when I glance back, I see William standing at the lounge window with the curtain pushed to one side. I wave and immediately head towards the house. William disappears.

On the doorstep, the bottle of wine I've brought is slippery in its tissue-paper wrapping. I adjust it, wondering again whether the present is appropriate or not. Adam had said absolutely yes. 'What? He's got to be miserable *and* sober for the rest of his life, has he?'

William still hasn't come to the door and I'm beginning to doubt that he saw me after all. He was hard to miss, illuminated in the window, but that doesn't mean he'd spotted me out in the darkness. I feel stupid though, standing there waiting, unsure what to do next.

From the corner of my eye, I sense movement. William's face appears from behind the curtain, and then a second later is gone. But that glimpse tells me enough: he doesn't want to see me. I'm not wanted there.

William's strange behaviour has really upset me. I'm worried that Emma's said something to turn him against me, but Adam disagrees. He thinks I've been watching too many soaps.

'I expect the poor bastard needs a bit of peace, that's all.'

Normally I'd be happy to agree and say, 'Yeah, Ad, you're right. *Again.*'

But Adam hadn't been there.

'You don't think he's pissed off that we left the wake before he got there, do you?'

'Ring him up,' Adam replies. 'You don't have to tell him the truth, just give him a reason. Say it was an emergency – I got the shits or something.'

I wrinkle my nose at this suggestion.

'He's not answering his phone,' I say.

Adam's getting ready to go over to Matt's to work on some garden designs for a chain of small funky hotels; it's their latest commission. He passes from bedroom to lounge, to hall in great, clomping strides, accumulating all he needs: price lists, his battered old briefcase, a portfolio which contains some of the prototype designs Matt's produced and which Adam's been considering for their viability.

He kisses me goodbye. 'We might go for a few beers at the Lion afterwards.'

I don't think might's got anything to do with it. Ad and Matt's business meetings always seem to finish in the pub.

'Do you think you could pick me up, babe, if I call?'

'Why not?' I say. 'I might even join you for last orders.'

When Adam's gone, I put a CD on loud and gather all my stuff for a pampering session: manicure set, nail varnish, face mask, magazines. I place a towel on the bed and sit in my underwear in the middle of it. I put my mobile next to me in case anyone rings when I can't move. I run my hands up my shins; my legs badly need waxing. I make a mental note to book an appointment this week.

While my mask is drying I phone Debs. There's no reply from her either.

Adam gives me a big kiss and points to the bottle of beer he's bought for me. I sit down next to Matt, who squeezes my knee.

'How's the lovely Laura?' he asks.

'Fine, thanks. You?'

'As ever,' Matt says, which means chilled. I don't think I've ever seen Matt anything but happy and relaxed. He swigs down the last of his pint.

'Better get back to the missus,' he says casually. 'The little one's playing up, and if I don't go and relieve the pressure, the mother of all arguments will erupt.'

Matt weaves through the tables, shaking hands with people along the way. He always knows someone wherever you go. I watch Adam watching Matt. They make a good business team. Matt loves all the networking and is great at the spiel, and Ad is happy to step out of the limelight and just get on with the work he loves.

We turn to each other, and judging by Adam's grin, I'd say we've both realized at exactly the same time that we are alone.

He reaches under the table and touches the top of my thigh. I've put on my black trousers – the ones that Adam says 'fit your arse just perfect'.

'Hello you,' he says, and when his hand adventures up further, I squeeze my thighs together and trap his fingers there.

'Mmmm,' he says, leering at me.

But then I remember my hairy legs. It's like a cold shower on me. I push Adam's hand away.

'What's up?' he asks.

I shake my head.

'Come on,' he says. 'You can tell me.'

'My legs need waxing,' I say, and look defiantly at him. He grins.

'I don't care,' he says. 'I'll take you any way you are.'

Debs winds her hair slowly on top of her head and secures it there with a clip.

'Guess what?' she shouts above the motor and broiling froth of the Jacuzzi. 'I'm seeing someone.'

'Already?' I say before I can stop myself.

'God!' She rolls her eyes like a stroppy teenager would to her mum. I keep quiet, slide along the seat until I find a jet to pulse directly on the small of my back.

'Well? Don't you want to know the gory details?'

'OK, but what about Josh?'

'What *about* Josh? I told you, it's over with him.'

'Why does he keep ringing then?'

'God, Loz,' she says, shaking her head. 'You're such a useless romantic. He's ringing because he wants to know whether I've trashed his precious belongings which he didn't have time to take with him on his midnight flit; and if I haven't, when he can pick them up.' She raises a foot out of the water, points her toes. Her skin is a deep brown against the blue-tinged foam, her toes the usual explicit red. 'There's no delicious making-up scene on the horizon; it's strictly the practical tying up of the end of a not-so-beautiful thing.' She lowers her foot. 'Call me a bitch but I thought I'd let him sweat for a while.'

She looks at me.

'What?' I ask. 'I didn't say anything.'

'You don't have to; I can read your disapproval a mile off. The trouble with you, Loz, is you fall for that love crap too easily and you think everyone should be the same.'

'I liked Josh, that's all.'

'Well, get over it. I've had to.'

The sauna's empty when we go in.

'So who's the guy?' I ask. 'Do I know him?'

'He's new around here. I met him at a party,' Debs says. 'His name's Andrew and he's a journalist for the local rag.'

'And?'

'Good company, nice meals, v-e-r-y good sex. *And* no lovey-dovey stuff, which suits me fine.'

'You've slept with him then.'

Debs goes to the stove and ladles on water. The water hisses and spits off the coal; steam gathers then quickly dissipates.

'Yeah, well, last time I looked it was the twenty-first century and apparently there's a shortage of chaperones these days.' She stands with her hands on her hips and grins. 'We shagged on the first date, if you really want to know, Miss Prissy. He's sexy as hell – I'd defy anyone to resist him.'

She removes her bikini top and flings it onto the top bench. 'He loves my tits,' she says, contemplating them, and I can't help but look, too. Her breasts are small and high. Mine are fuller – the kind that will collapse as soon as I've given birth to my first child.

As Debs steps onto the bench I spot small saddlebags of fat on her thighs, some cellulite on her bum. For the first time ever, my body is tauter and leaner than hers. I find this idea disturbing somehow, as if the balance between us has gone awry. I lie down quickly on the hard bench and fold my arms across my stomach. My back protests at the harshness of the wood, and I have to wriggle around until my spine is fitting comfortably between the slats.

'Ugh,' Debs squawks, picking at the hairs on my leg. 'Do you have a hair-growth problem you'd like to discuss?'

'I keep meaning to get them done.'

There's a tiny pause before she asks, 'Doesn't Adam mind?'

Debbie's feigned innocence doesn't fool me. I know what she's implying with that question.

'Of course I like to look good for him,' I tell her. 'But it isn't the most important thing in the world if it doesn't always happen.'

'Each to his own. I just know I couldn't.'

Of course she couldn't. Debs follows the fake-tanned, mani-cured and plucked to perfection way like I used to. I spent years dressing myself up, hiding myself, constantly on edge waiting for the crushing comment from Peter, the needle of self-doubt he liked to poke into my skin time after time. Peter – whose head would swivel at any woman, who even with his skinny chest and receding hairline made me feel I never came near his required standards.

But Adam isn't like that. Adam still wants me when I'm less than perfect, and that's the biggest turn-on going.

Adam is the only man I can imagine giving birth in front of, who has a share in my pussy, to whom I can say the word 'pussy' or sometimes even 'cunt', instead of 'down there', or 'my you know what'; Adam is the only man I can picture myself with, standing side by side in front of a mirror joggling our old, slack bellies together and laughing, who would help me shower and dress and put nail varnish on my toenails when I couldn't manage any more, like William did for Rose. I could have described to Debs how such intimacy feels, but I pull back from exposing these thoughts to her. They might be brought up later, distorted by a joke; made to seem ridiculous. 'How is the man who would change your incontinence pad doing?' I can imagine her saying.

Instead I tell her about Mum's house sale going through.

'I can't believe she's actually doing it,' Debs says. 'I've got so many memories from there. I feel kind of let down, don't you?'

This is what I like about Debs. One minute she's the wicked Ice Queen and the next she shows this sweet, vulnerable side.

I'd forgotten how Debs always suggested playing at my house, never over at hers, because her three brothers would constantly barge in or her mum would nag her all the time to run errands. I remember how she used to hang around the kitchen, eating biscuits and chatting with Mum about school and boys and anything, while I'd be fidgeting, desperate to get upstairs and for us to be on our own.

'I don't think I really believe it will happen yet,' I say.

'I had my first orgasm at your house,' Debs tells me now, restoring the wicked balance a little. 'Self-performed, naturally,' she adds.

'Where was I?'

'In your bed, on the other side of the room, of course. Sleeping the sleep of a little angel, as always.'

'You were corrupt from an early age,' I tell her.

Grinning, Debs pretends to play with herself. A woman opens the sauna door, sees Debbie's writhing, moaning body and slams it shut again.

'Time for a cold shower,' I say.

I try phoning William again and finally someone – Ben – answers.

'Hi,' I say brightly, to cover my nerves. 'It's Laura. How are you?'

'Laura, um, hi.'

'Is William there?'

'Not really,' he says, and I catch an odd tone to his voice.

I lick my lips. 'Is everything OK?' I ask. 'It's only, I came round the other day and I'm sure William was in, but he didn't open the door.'

There's a pause, some background noise. I think I hear William's voice. I press the receiver to my ear. I'm trembling.

'I wondered if he was upset with me for leaving so soon after Rose's funeral.' I talk on into the silence. 'I was hoping I could explain to him about it.' I pause. 'Ben?'

'It's not about that.'

'What's not about that?'

'Not wanting to speak to you. It's about what you told the newspaper. And to be honest, Laura, I'm not surprised he's pissed off. I am, too, really, if you want to know.'

'Which newspaper? I don't know what you mean. I haven't told any newspaper anything.'

'Well, they've got it from somewhere,' Ben says sharply. 'And let's face it, there's only you who knew that stuff.'

'What stuff?' I ask but Ben says: 'I've got to go, sorry.'

The phone goes down.

12

The article that Ben was referring to is on page five of this week's edition of the local paper. I stand reading it in the newsagent's. It seems to be a kind of unofficial obituary on Rose and I scan the first paragraph quickly, anxious to discover the reason why William and Ben are so angry. Instead, I find a rather flattering and well-written account, successfully evoking Rose's glamorous, adventurous nature and the exciting, flamboyant aspect to the Claymores' life abroad.

I force myself to concentrate, and discover in the third paragraph an explanation of Rose's return to the UK as an *attempt to improve her relationship with her sons, who spent most of their childhood separated from their parents, in UK boarding schools* . . .

This is followed in the next sentence by: *Family complications continued when a misunderstanding led to the brief questioning by the police of her husband, William, following Rose's death.*

Although it doesn't directly mention that it was Emma who had contacted the police, it doesn't take many brains to read between the lines and to guess it was either the Claymores' sons or someone else closely related; and to picture an unhappy family embroiled in rifts and bitterness.

I stare at the paper. Somebody mutters, 'Buy the bloody thing,' as they push in front of me to reach the shelves.

I re-read the whole article through. Certain phrases jump out at me: *magnetic charm, incisive wit, flamboyant lifestyle*. I can almost hear my voice saying those words, and yet I didn't – not to a journalist.

And then it clicks. I look for the author's by-line. The initials ARW are printed at the end of the piece – and I'm convinced.

This is down to Debs. This is her, opening her big mouth to her journo boyfriend, Andrew.

It's nearly Bonfire Night and premature fireworks bang and crack and squeal, lighting up the sky as I power-walk home. I picture my anger exploding into a million stars inside my brain. This time I'll let her know she's pushed it too far. This time I'll really lay it on the line – that she needs to grow up and start thinking about other people and not just herself.

I stab out Debbie's number and surprisingly, she answers after the first ring.

'Hi, Loz,' she says. 'How's things?'

'Debs, did your Andrew bloke write that piece about Rose in the paper?'

There's an immediate wariness in her voice. 'Yeah, why?'

'Well, thanks to you, William isn't speaking to me. Some of that stuff was really personal.'

'No way,' she says in an innocent tone. 'Like what? Which bits?'

'The bit about the Claymores not getting on with their sons, the bit about William's family suspecting him of being involved in Rose's death.'

There's a short pause.

'I didn't read it, to be honest,' she says finally. 'It looked boring.'

'I don't care if you read it or not, Debs. The point is that you blabbed confidential information.'

There's another silence before Debs speaks; her voice is drawn out and whining. 'I was only trying to help Andrew out. He kept yakking on about needing to make his mark as the new boy on the team. It's so competitive at that place you wouldn't believe it, Loz.' Debs becomes increasingly animated. 'And when it came up that I knew about the Claymores, via you, God knows why but he got really excited. For some reason which I have to say *completely* escapes me, he finds them an interesting subject, so I told him everything I could remember that you'd ever said. And the thing is, Loz,' she adds, 'the way you went on about them, you didn't actually make it clear it was private.'

I don't need to hear any more to be able to picture the scene. Once she'd spotted an opportunity to provide Andrew with something he wanted, she wouldn't have hesitated; William's feelings would have counted for peanuts. I can practically hear the conversation between the two of them because I've been listening to it for years. In her desire to impress blokes, Debs is willing to do, say and promise almost anything.

There's no point even trying to make her understand.

'Well, you know now,' I end up telling her. 'So don't do it again.'

I hear myself sounding exactly like my mother, and Debs picks up on this immediately.

'Yes, Mummy Eagen,' she says. 'Anyway, I believe we've moved on to more interesting topics of conversation than your boring old man.' She lowers her voice to a whisper. 'Andrew's very sexy, Loz,' she breathes down the line. 'I mean *very* with a capital V.'

Adam is furious. 'That fucking girl,' he shouts, launching himself off the sofa. 'When is she going to stop putting herself first all the time? And,' he says, holding up his hand, 'please don't come out with that crock of shit about her parents preferring her brothers and making her feel worthless, because we *all* had crap childhoods!'

'You didn't,' I point out.

'Well, it wasn't fucking perfect,' he roars, practically bouncing round the living room. 'And *your* dad fucked off and left your mum when you were four so you can't get a much bigger rejection than that.'

I catch my breath. 'I've never thought about it like that,' I say slowly. 'Mum always made me feel special.'

He drops onto the sofa beside me. 'I'm sorry, babe,' he says, touching my face. 'I didn't mean to bring that up – I didn't mean anything by it. It just makes me so bloody mad to see her hurt you all the time.'

'But I'm OK,' I protest. 'It's just Debs being thoughtless, that's all.'

Adam shoves his hands through his hair. His brow is furrowed, as if he's hesitating about mentioning something. I reach out to touch his knee and he catches my hand.

'It's not just that.' He looks hard into my eyes, his grip tightens and I feel my knuckles being ground together. For a second, before Ad's expression softens, I'm frightened.

Debs, dressed in black like a spiky silhouette, stood in my bedroom doorway. Behind her, I saw Mum's face, pale with anger before the door was shut.

'That girl,' Mum had said when I turned up at the house, shaking and sick from seeing Debs and Peter together. 'That girl needs a good talking-to.'

I closed my eyes and kept my eyelids pressed down as the bed creaked. I pictured Debbie as a narrow black stripe next to me on the cream duvet cover.

As we lay side by side, face to face, neither of us needed to say, 'Remember?' Our memories had seeped into the mattress like bodily juices, and when I pressed my ear to it I could hear us laughing until we nearly peed ourselves. I could smell the cigarettes we sneakily smoked and the mints we frantically sucked afterwards. I could hear us swapping sex stories and tales of parental arguments, and feel the thump of frustrated teenage feet kicking out against each other.

'I'm sorry, Loz.' Her breath was warm; her fingers cool on my burning cheek.

I bit my bottom lip.

'I won't ever, ever do anything like that to you again. I promise.'

I saw the hurt in her eyes as if she'd done this terrible thing not only to me but to herself. I watched two dew-drops tremble on Debbie's spidery eyelashes and wondered which would fall first.

'Loz?'

I felt as if I was drinking her perfume as I licked tears from my lips.

'Please forgive me.'

'OK,' I said straight away, because I'd known even before she asked that I was going to, that there was so much gluing us together it would be impossible not to.

Adam agrees to go and see William to explain what has happened. For this huge favour I have promised sexual rewards, a foot massage and making dinner for the rest of the week.

From the window, I watch Ad get into the van. In the head-lights, I can see the rain, angled in the wind. Overnight, the temperature dropped dramatically, and walking to an appointment this morning, I could see my own surprise at the sudden wintry weather reflected on the faces around me as everyone battled against the icy rain.

This is the worst kind of weather to run in and my body protests at the idea of getting changed, but I know without even looking in my diary that this is run one hundred and eighty-seven; the two-hundred-day barrier is too close to being broken for me to seriously contemplate skipping a day. Just do it, I tell myself. Just do it.

Only twenty minutes into the run, my ears are aching and my face feels scoured clean. My progress is bone-achingly slow as I zigzag through Brighton trying to evade the bitter wind, but with every turn I take, it seeks me out and blows a numbing mist of drizzle against my bare face.

I take a break, sheltering by the seafront arches. The shops and restaurants around here glow cosily and are busy with customers despite the weather.

When Debs and I were young, a lot of these buildings were derelict and had a bad reputation as a hang-out for druggies and the homeless. Kids were warned to keep away so, of course, it was a popular place to meet up with friends; we'd pass cider bottles round until we thought we were drunk and Debs and I would walk home on our own, giggling and collapsing against each other all the way.

As soon as I get back, I run a deep bath. I lower myself slowly, slowly into the steaming water; the heat a pleasurable pain, my toes prickling as the sensation returns. I only breathe out once I'm immersed. And it's only then that I feel happy I went.

I stay there, topping up the hot water, until Adam returns.

Winter

13

'This weather is shite,' Adam says, looking out of the kitchen window. 'God knows what we're going to do.'

The rain has been relentless. Autumn was the wettest since records began and at almost the end of November, there's still no sign of it letting up. Every day the news bulletins report floods in some part of the country. Footage of people knee-deep in water in the middle of their lounge, possessions bobbing around them, their faces slack with disbelief, is becoming commonplace. There are lengthy discussions on the effects of global warming, the measures that will need to be taken against rising seas and water tables. We are a nation obsessed – and collectively depressed – by the rain. Out running, my vision is impeded by the murky rain-light; the rotted residue of fallen leaves has formed a slippery glaze on the pavements which is as treacherous as ice. Each time I slide and skid my heart booms as I expect to hit concrete. Everyday life has become that bit more effortful: unpacking the shopping from the car, nipping out to the newsagent's, getting washing dry; everything takes on the exigencies of major tasks.

For the hundreth time, I complain about the lack of space to put a tumbledryer as my sodden running gear joins the other damp clothes that festoon every room in the flat, draped from anything which can support a clothes hanger – picture frames, the ends of curtain poles, the tops of doors. The fabric dries out days later, with odours of cooking oil and damp sealed in; and Adam's boots have been banished to the porch which they imbue with a fustiness reminiscent of school sports changing rooms.

At the workshop I ran the other day, none of the attendees would venture out at lunchtime. They watched the rain slashing onto the windows, looked glumly at the pile of still damp umbrellas in the corner of the room and slumped back in their chairs, only livening up when I offered to phone and order a pizza delivery in.

Adam pushes his hands deeper into his jeans pockets and says, 'Might as well have another coffee.'

He has more reason than most to sound gloomy. By now he should have finished all the hard-scaping and construction work begun in the autumn but instead there are Adam-made holes and trenches and footings dotted throughout various gardens in the Brighton area which are full of water instead of hard-core.

Most evenings there's a plaintive call from a client which Adam handles patiently, all the time making faces at me while he speaks.

'What do they expect me to do?' he says, after he's put the phone down. 'Suck it dry through my arsehole?'

Even the wintertime work – the pruning and clearing – is made tougher. Adam can take any amount of heat and cold, but constant rain and damp chap his hands. He comes home with them red raw; they sting and ache and though I rub in moisturizer every evening, by the end of the next day they're just as bad.

Adam paces the kitchen.

'Do you want to smoke in here?' I offer, feeling sorry for him as I look at the sheets of rain on the window. 'It's OK once in a while.'

Adam stops. 'I've no money for tobacco,' he says, and turns abruptly away.

Everything wobbles and clatters on the table as I knock against it in my haste to fetch my purse.

'Why didn't you say something before?'

The garden company is run on such a tiny reserve that if Adam can't finish a job, he can't draw money – but I hadn't realized just how low on funds he'd got.

'You're already paying for everything else,' he says, looking at his feet. 'I didn't like to.'

'It's OK.' I waft the two twenties just out of Adam's reach until he finally meets my gaze. 'You'd do the same for me.' Then I add, 'Besides, I can't have you going cold turkey when it's such miserable weather; it'll drive me crazy.'

Adam grins with relief as he folds the money and shoves it into his pocket. 'Thanks, babe.' He kisses me on the cheek. 'You're a doll.'

Alessandro's is toasty-warm and full of steam; the coffee-machines behind Nat seem to have been transformed into billowing steam-makers, clouding the air and coating the windows in condensation which obscures the world outside.

Nat points to where William is sitting while she makes my cappuccino. 'He's been here ages,' she tells me, and when I glance over my shoulder I see him intent on reading something on the table in front of him. He looks different – unfamiliar, almost – I can't quite put my finger on it; perhaps it's that his hair is wavier in this humidity.

He raises his head a little, stares into the distance before turning his attention again to the papers on the table and I feel a rush of impatience at Nat to stop fussing over the cocoa-powder decoration, to take my money and let me get over there and put an end to his waiting.

'Can I ask you a favour?' Rose asked.

William had just left the house; he'd stopped suddenly in the street as if he'd remembered something before waving cheerily up at us. Rose sipped her breath sharply in, let it out in a wheezy sigh once he'd set off again.

She sank low in her chair, silent for a while, her chin pressed into the blanket wrapped around her. It was a spring day of shifting heat and cold as cloud constantly passed over the sun. It was getting chillier by the minute and it wouldn't be long before we'd need to move back indoors; black clouds were looming low over the sea.

She half-twisted to face me. Under her eyes were bruise-tender shadows, and her skin had a greasy film. It hit me then how ill she looked. Cancer is such a sneaky disease, always doing its devastating work on the quiet. I saw how much weight had dropped off her recently, how her apple-cheeks were shrunken and slack.

'Yes, of course.'

'After I'm – when I'm not here – don't abandon him.' I thought she was going to cry but she didn't. Bony, yellow knuckles poked through transparent skin as she gripped the arm of the chair and it suddenly made me think of gristly meat; I felt sick.

'He's going to need a good friend then, and I can't think of anyone else I'd rather it be.'

William looks pleased to see me. He takes the plate from my hand, sets it on the table.

'So,' he says. 'How are you?'

'All over the place. I've had a madly busy morning.'

'Tell me.' He leans forward, elbows on the table, watching me closely as I reach down to stash the dripping umbrella under my chair. I feel a little unnerved by his attention.

'OK,' I say, unwinding the scarf from my neck. I hook it on the chair-back, shrug off my coat. 'Well, first thing today I had a meeting with a tattooist who wanted to know the implications of letting part of his premises to a body piercer who happens to be his new girlfriend, then I met with five independent sandwich-bar owners who are considering amalgamating some of their food orders to bring down supply costs. After that, I took a working coffee-break with an artists' group who need help budgeting for the renovation of an old outhouse in their studio grounds to house two looms. Then I came here.'

'I'm impressed,' he says, but the patronizing tone he uses wipes away any pleasure I might have felt. I stir my drink slowly, watching clumps of cream collapse under the swirling liquid.

I'm startled by his fingers gently touching my hand.

'Sorry, that came across badly.' His eyes fix on mine. 'I really meant it, Laura.'

I laugh awkwardly and blush deeply. We sit in silence for a moment, not looking at each other.

'As it happens,' William says, tapping the table, 'I shall also be working again shortly. I've received a commission; the confirmation arrived today.' He fingers the corner of what I now see is a typed letter on top of a leaflet and a couple of brochures. I notice the camera bag, hanging under his coat on the back of the chair.

Rose had been right.

She had often teased him about being bored, tried to get him to abandon his line that he was happy sitting round reading, doing crosswords, sorting out paperwork and cataloguing their work. The William she used to describe, the William you glimpsed when he talked about the places they'd travelled to, is now sitting in front of me.

'He jumps straight in,' Rose once told me. 'Before anyone else has finished unpacking, William will be sharing a drink with the oldest resident of the town; by the next day he'll know all the best-kept secrets and local treasures. He just has this knack of getting to the bottom of a place.'

William must have read my silence as disapproval because he sounds a little put-out. 'I needed something to do, Laura. I was going crazy in the house . . .'

'Oh,' I say. 'I didn't – I mean . . .' I start again. 'I think it's great, William, honest. So – what is it? Where is it?'

When he tells me that the assignment is in Brighton, I pick up my cup and hold the rim against my lips. I don't drink; I just needed to do something to cover my surprise.

'The mandate is "Secret Brighton",' he says, and then begins to read off from the letter. *'To encourage tourists to explore further afield than simply the town centre and the pier.'* He pushes his hair back. His face is alive. 'My spec is to create photographs which will entice them to lesser-known places – either interesting or beautiful or . . . quirky.' He grins and looks years younger. 'The woman kept on using that word all the way through the meeting – "we don't mind quirky, Mr Claymore, we don't mind quirky at all".'

He spreads his fingers out across the paper. 'I thought I'd start by re-visiting some of the places my Aunt Dorrie used to take me when I was a boy – if they still exist, of course. There have been a lot of changes since then.'

'Even since I was young,' I tell him.

'You've lived here all your life, haven't you?'

I nod. 'I even went to university here. That makes me sound a bit sad, doesn't it? Rose was always telling me off about it. She used to say that you couldn't settle until you'd tried living in at least one other place. But . . . I know I'd miss it.'

I think about how, when I go out running, I'm always remembering stuff – not just from when I was a girl, but recent events, too; all my thoughts and memories seem interwoven somehow with the streets and places here. If you cut open my brain, Adam swears you'd find a city map inside; like one of those tourist ones, he says, with pop-up cut-outs of my most important places. I look at William and know that I can't explain this very well; not well enough.

'I think if you've been happy somewhere as a child, it's a very strong tie. It is for me, but Rosie could never see the attraction of Brighton.'

'She said you'd go straight back to Barcelona.'

William nods and looks down at his hand. I don't think he's going to speak, so I'm rattling through my head for something I can say to fill the silence when he starts.

'When she talked about it – and you know how much she talked about it – I couldn't think of anywhere else I'd rather be. I'd crave it – I'd feel it, physically, here, burning a hole in my chest.' William glances at me. His face has changed; he looks older again and tired.

'Waiting is awful,' he goes on. 'Waiting for something dreadful to happen is the worst thing of all and I used to latch on to that picture of myself at the airport.' He pinches the top of his nose, a gesture I suddenly think of as being very much William. 'I'd see myself arriving back at the apartment, opening the shutters, walking into the garden, breathing in the bougainvillaea, noting the jobs that needed doing – varnishing the patio furniture, re-potting the palm tree. I remembered that the back shutters would need to be re-painted this year – I rotate the work so they're redone every two years; the sun bleaches them quickly . . .' He peters out. 'Those thoughts kept me going but at the same time, I think I knew that afterwards would be very different – that without Rosie, it might not seem so appealing.'

'So you're staying,' I say gently.

'For a while at least.'

'I'm glad,' I tell him after a moment, and blush as I speak. 'However long it's for.'

We stop at the supermarket a few streets away from William's house. We're in the queue when William remembers he needs a bottle of bleach, leaves his basket of shopping on the floor, and dashes off to fetch it.

As the checkout woman raises her eyes to utter her greeting to me, she looks past me, gasps then pales. I turn quickly to see the source of the horror being played out across her face but the only person in sight is William, hurriedly approaching.

The checkout lady's colouring has risen to a pink flush. Her eyes lock into mine.

'Some people should be ashamed of themselves,' she says quietly, her voice loaded with bitterness. 'Playing God.'

She means William.

I stand speechless. The woman, evidently ignorant that William and I are here together, appears to take my silence as a sympathetic ear and continues muttering invectives as the first of my shopping *bleep-bleeps* through the scanners.

I look at William in alarm. He touches the shoulder of a woman who is joining the line, easing himself in front of her. He speaks to her, holding up the bottle once he's past, and she laughs. 'I know the feeling,' she says.

My instinct is to prevent William – at all costs – from becoming aware of what's happening. I rustle the plastic bags, clump in the tins to make as much cover noise as I can. It is hard to believe that this ordinary woman with her permed, fading blonde hair, her discreet and immaculate make-up, her clothes fresh and neat, can be saying such things as 'murderer' and 'bastard'.

When William comes to stand next to me, I glance at him. His face is blank; he seems far away, not even conscious of his surroundings.

At last, all my items are through. I wait, my face burning

while the woman presses the button and tells me the amount of my bill. The bubble of rage pops inside me, dispersing venom throughout my veins. My hand shakes as I hand over my money. I glare at her as she gives me my change. I want my look to be charged with everything that I'm feeling – disgust, disdain, outrage – but she doesn't pay me any further attention because next up is William who is smiling at her, being charming, chatting about the weather and how busy it is, and the woman glowers, like a demonic child in a horror film. She won't meet his eyes, and when she has to return his card and receipt to him, she does so as if she's handling dog-dirt.

'Thank you, my dear,' William says pleasantly.

I daren't look at him as he guides me outside where humanity swarms on the pavements. Where the street narrows, we're separated in the flow of evening shoppers. I'm losing sight of William. I stretch my neck up to spot him, try to turn round but I'm being carried inexorably on.

'Got you!' Someone pulls my arm, grabs my waist and hustles me into a shop doorway. It's William. 'You're so tiny,' he says. 'I couldn't see you.' He's laughing. 'This is madness,' he says cheerfully.

He holds my arm and we plunge into the crowd again; as it eases, our pace slows. We pass the Salvation Army as they burst into 'Hark the Herald Angels' and I wait for William while he digs out change to put into the charity tin.

We're drawn by the smell to the roast-chestnut stand ahead. We share a bag of them which William holds. They're almost too hot to peel; the tips of my fingers burn, but the pain is worth it. I feed the first one to William, bite into the second. The nuts are sweet, floury – perfectly cooked.

I realize that for once, it isn't raining. The air feels soft. The Christmas decorations along the street glitter and shine in the descending darkness. It looks magical, beautiful.

I sneak a look at William – he seems relaxed and peaceful. There is nothing to suggest that he heard a single word the woman said, and in the cosy, festive atmosphere, I can almost believe that it never happened.

Adam says, 'You've got to remember one thing in this life: most people are weird.'

'But William isn't evil. You've only got to take a look at him to know that.'

Since I arrived home, I've been unable to shift this afternoon's encounter out of my mind. What's burning me up is that I didn't do anything. I wish now that I'd defended William; that I'd told that woman exactly where to get off with her offensive comments and even, somehow, managed to humiliate her, perhaps by loudly demanding to see her manager and reporting her behaviour.

Adam disagrees. 'All you'd have done is embarrass William,' he says. 'Remember, these people have seen his photograph on the news. They've been told he might be a killer, so they're convinced he has a killer's face.' He sucks his cheeks in. 'That sinister, gaunt face, that emotionless expression.' He lumbers towards me with glazed, zombie eyes and outstretched, zombie arms.

I try and push him away but he takes hold of my wrists. I kick out.

'Pathetic,' he says, twisting me round in one move so that I can't escape. 'You're dead meat.'

14

The pattern of daily rain has truly been broken and the last few days have been dry and bright, albeit accompanied by a biting northerly wind.

It's nine o'clock at night so I'm sticking to a route along the seafront where I know I won't find myself alone at any stage. From a distance, it looks cosy down there with the amber glow of the streetlamps against the black water, but as I turn on to the promenade, the force of the wind hits me. This is crazy, I tell myself as an extra-strong gust jerks my head back. I gobble for air. My face is salt-blasted from the spray. I pull my sweatshirt hood up, tie it tight under my chin; all I can hear is my own wheezing, like blood rushing in my ears.

A couple sheltering near the sea wall look as if they're miming hysterical laughter as they hold out their arms to let their puffer jackets fill with air. Their black dog is a cardboard cut-out against the grey pebbles. It charges back to them, tail erect with the wind up its bum, and stops a metre away. I can see its jaws working in a silent, frantic bark.

The other people on the promenade are hunched over, withdrawn into coats, scarves and hats, intent on progress. I startle those I catch up because the wind covers the noise of my approach, but when I try shouting ahead in warning my words get caught and whipped seaward.

I feel as if I'm running on the spot, but I can't give up; I have to do another twenty minutes for it to count. This will be one hundred and ninety-eight days. The two-hundred barrier is tantalizingly close.

When I get back, Adam shuffles into the kitchen. His hair is sticking up all over the place from where he's fallen asleep on the settee. At the moment, he's working like a maniac without a day off, trying to finish up the backlog of jobs from the autumn. At least the daily calls from disgruntled customers have dwindled as all the holes are finally being filled with the rightful material.

For the last couple of weeks he's been coming home and collapsing, with barely enough energy to undo his boots. That's what he says, anyway – to make me feel sorry enough to take them off for him while he lies back and swigs a beer.

'Did you go running?' he asks suddenly.

'Er . . . yeah,' I say, gesturing to my sports kit. Adam shakes his head as if in disbelief. I just grin at him. Now I'm back I feel elated as if I've accomplished a daring expedition.

'Trudy phoned,' he says, yawning and pushing past me to get to the kettle. 'Can you call her back?'

I've hardly seen Mum since she and David returned from honeymoon. She's rarely at the house when I go over to work, although most days there's new evidence that she's been round. There are more full boxes taped shut, more rubbish bags waiting to be thrown out, more gaps appearing on the shelves and in the cupboards. The other evening, when Adam and I went over to David's house to watch the wedding and holiday videos, the tall crystal vase that I'd given her for her fiftieth birthday was on the lounge mantelpiece, and some of the framed photographs of Mum and me were in pride of place on the hall wall.

David's house is very different to our old home; it's modern and very light and spacious. Mum sat with her feet tucked up on the huge white sofa while David fixed the drinks and I tried to identify the subtle difference I felt there was about her. Retirement suits her, being with David suits her, too. She looked much younger than sixty. She seemed elegant and calm and completely at ease, as if she'd grown to fit her new surroundings. And as I thought about it some more, I realized that she looked more at home there than she ever had back at our old place.

'How's the new office coming along?' Mum asks now on the phone, as soon as our opening lines are done, so I know immediately that this is what she needs to talk to me about.

'Slowly,' I tell her. 'Adam hasn't had time to lay the electrics yet.' I pause. 'Why?'

'The thing is, love,' she says, 'they're pushing for a completion date on the house.' I can hear her flicking through papers as she speaks. 'They want to be in before Christmas or they may pull out.'

I had counted on having until the New Year before I'd need to move out. It's not only the delay from the weather that's been holding us up; we haven't enough money to buy the rest of the materials. I look at Adam.

'I can try and put them off a bit longer,' Mum says carefully into my silence.

'No, it's OK,' I tell her, and Adam stops what he's doing. 'We'll just have to fit my stuff into the flat until the shed's ready.'

I watch Ad register my words.

'Fucking hell,' he says.

I raise my finger to my mouth to shush him. He shakes his head and shuffles back to the living room, where the TV comes on loudly.

'I'm sorry, Laura. I know this is tricky for you.'

'It's fine, Mum. It's not your problem. I'm grateful to have had it as long as I did.'

A couple of days later, I go over to the house in the evening to start packing up. I thought I'd cleared out everything when Mum and I first converted my old bedroom into an office. I'd prided myself, in fact, on being ruthlessly grown-up and unsentimental, but when I open the built-in cupboard, I'm alarmed to discover all sorts of stuff — toys, dolls; there's even a bunch of CDs from the 'Peter Period' including a soppy love-song collection, which makes me cringe. There are magazines, a handleless suitcase which is packed with old clothes including my last school uniform. I take it all in with a mixture of curiosity and disappointment. Part of me wishes that Mum had simply thrown it all away without my prior knowledge — and yet at the same time I can't resist picking my way through the items. I find a photograph of me as an angel in a school nativity play. At first glance it's a very sweet shot, but a closer look shows a scowling, tear-streaked face.

My metal halo had gone missing the night before, and someone had fashioned a hasty replacement out of cardboard which wasn't strong enough to stay upright and kept flopping on top of my head. Peering closely, I can just make out the girl behind me, holding it upright as she'd been instructed to do while the shot was taken.

My legs are fizzing with pins and needles from crouching too long. I stand by the window. They've erected glaring lights up in the park now. I know it's supposed to be safer, and I'm grateful for it; as a female and a runner in particular, it makes life much easier, especially the way they've extended the lighting down on the seafront. However, it also seems a shame; it destroys the precious secret space we owned and loved as kids. Next thing, it'll be CCTV checking whether today's children are up to no good, and I can't help thinking that in the relentless quest to make every inch safe and purposeful and pinned down, soon there won't be any more special, private places to escape to.

Over there is where I had my first kiss with a boy whose name I can no longer remember, and where I nearly lost my virginity to someone called Danny; instead, we lost our nerve and chucked each other a week later from embarrassment. It's also the place where Debs and I first met on the swings one summer holiday when her family had just moved in; where a group of us first got pissed on plastic bottles of cider; and where I was playing one day when my mum called me in to tea for the final one of Dad's few brief visits.

My dad, skinny with a shorter, ginger version of my wild hair, was sitting in the living room with a cup of tea and some biscuits. Mum gave me a glass of Ribena and then left us together for what seemed like ages as Dad quizzed me on whether or not I enjoyed school, what were my favourite subjects, and what I watched on TV until I felt sucked dry of who I was. As soon as Mum returned, I escaped back to the park to play.

Debs was waiting for me and I told her my dad was home.

'For good?' she asked.

'Don't know.'

When Mum called me in later to dinner, Dad had disappeared.

'He had to leave, love, I'm sorry,' Mum said, and I could sense her watching for my reaction, thinking that I would be upset. 'He left you a present, though.' She placed a pink teddy bear on the table. 'Isn't that cute?'

'It's all right,' I said, but it meant nothing to me. I didn't want it and I didn't want Dad – I'd known that as soon as Debs had asked that question – was he back for good? I was happy with it being only me and Mum.

But now, strangely, it occurs to me that he'll no longer be able to simply turn up and find us. The house – this solid connection between him and me – will have gone.

I escape from my thoughts downstairs to the kitchen, unlock the patio doors and stand outside, breathing deeply while I wait for the kettle to boil. It's a crisp, clear night with a feel of frost in the air. Christmas is only three weeks away.

'Woolly Head! Hey, Woolly Head!'

A pebble flies over from next door and clatters in front of my feet. Paul's disembodied head, complete with cigarette hanging out of the corner of his mouth, appears over the fence.

'You could have hit me,' I shout, mock angry.

He laughs.

'What are you doing here?' I ask.

'Annoying you,' he says. 'Come round, will you?'

He opens the front door as soon as I'm through the gate, and his smile beams out at me. It's the widest smile I've ever seen – he really does grin from ear to ear. It makes him look as young as when I last saw him, which must be . . .

'Eight years,' he tells me. 'Can you believe it?'

Inside, the heat hits me. He's dressed in shorts and T-shirt and is very tanned.

'Beer or juice?' His voice has an unmistakable Australian twang.

'Juice, please,' I tell him, following down the hall. 'And by the way, nobody calls me Woolly Head any more.'

'Why ever not?' In the kitchen, he folds his arms, considering me. 'It's still appropriate.'

'Ha ha.'

I sit at the table and watch as Paul locates glasses, and then fiddles around in the fridge before removing a carton of orange juice. I feel at ease, as if we are right back to being kids, when we played together all the time.

'How long are you home for?' I ask him.

'A few months. Now the parents are getting on a bit, I thought it was the right thing to do.' He nods in the direction of the living room from where the noise of the TV is coming. 'So what's new? You're still living at your mum's then?'

'No, with my boyfriend, Adam. I've got my office here, that's all.'

'I thought you couldn't possibly be single,' he says over his shoulder as he's pouring the drinks. 'A lovely girl like you.'

I fancied Paul like mad when I was about fifteen, and the

memory of my teenage crush makes me blush furiously. I used to sit on my bedroom windowsill pretending to read while I watched him working on his bike in the garden. I couldn't take my eyes off him – especially when it was hot and he'd pull his T-shirt off. It all had to stop, though, when Debs came over one time.

'What *are* you looking at?' she said, appearing suddenly in my bedroom, Mum having let her in. 'He's nice, isn't he?' she said, leaning across me.

And I made myself say, 'Who, *Paul Yates*?' in this amazed, 'you've got to be joking, he's just the boy next door' tone of voice, because I knew from the way she said, 'Well, I think he's nice, anyway,' that it was going to be easier to pretend I didn't care.

Debs opened the window, yelled down to him, and that was Paul hooked.

Sometimes I'd hear them talking, Debs giggling; sometimes they'd make me join them, call up to my room until I agreed to tag along with them. Debs was always asking me to tag along with the boys she went out with; every now and then, she'd huddle up with me and talk secretly, making fun of them as they stood there, uncomfortable and foolish, waiting for her to finish. Paul put up with it, like the rest of them always did. And the more he tolerated Debbie's behaviour, the easier it got to pretend he was an idiot, to grow out of fancying him.

Paul hands me a glass. 'Well,' he says. 'You look great, Laura, you really do.'

'You too.'

'Yeah? Cheers.' He lights up another cigarette. 'So, what's the gossip? Who's married, dead, divorced, made it big?'

I give him a quick rundown on any mutual friends I can think of, then add, 'And I still see Debbie Forbes. Do you remember her?'

'Remember? You're kidding me, right? That woman nearly broke me. Why do you think I moved to Oz?'

His face looks serious until he winks and grins, but I'm still not entirely convinced he's joking.

'She started a rumour that I had three balls. No girl at school would come near me after that.'

'She didn't! I never heard it.'

'It's true. About her and the rumour, I mean – not about the balls. God, the stuff she came up with.' He stands up and opens the door, wafting the cigarette smoke outside. 'She was the source of a lot of misery, that girl.'

'She was never that bad,' I tell him. 'You boys didn't know how to handle her, that's all. You let her get away with murder.'

'You would say that. You always were the faithful friend. It's cool,' he says quickly, when he sees me open my mouth to protest. 'We're all older and wiser now, aren't we?'

Adam hires a Transit van and we move everything the following Sunday. Packing it into the van is the easy part; finding places for the stuff in our flat seems a near-impossible undertaking.

'So where do you want this?' Adam peers over the top of the filing cabinet which stands between us.

It's an oddly muggy day for December. My skin feels sticky and there doesn't seem to be enough oxygen in the air.

The cabinet turns out to be too wide to fit in the space I'd earmarked, and the only other possible spot is next to the chest of drawers in the bedroom. There's absolutely nowhere for my desk so we carry this – in its dismantled state – to the existing garden shed, and shove it behind the bicycles and Adam's tools. My new work area is a makeshift table – formerly housing the TV – in the left alcove in the living room. I look at it: once I've arranged my computer, printer, phone and fax on it, there won't be enough room to swing a mouse mat.

With all the boxes inside, I give Ad leave to go to the pub while I unpack. I have to be up and running by Monday and I know I'll achieve this much more quickly if left on my own.

I work non-stop and eventually create a satisfactory semblance of organization out of chaos. I have even showered and I'm lying in bed reading by the time Ad gets back.

'Top marks for effort,' he says, standing in the bedroom doorway.

'I won't be able to stand it for long,' I warn him. I've already tripped over a wire which is fed from the hall through to my desk, and my supply of information packs, which are in a box on top of the wardrobe, nearly fell on my head when I had to get one out to post to a client.

'I'll get the shed done really, really soon,' he says. 'I promise. You're my next priority.'

When he slides into bed beside me, his skin is cool and damp from the shower. He pushes off the duvet.

'A lovely sight,' he says as he places a kiss on my neck, before moving down to my breasts, then my stomach. I watch his head bend over my pussy; his fingers hold me apart as he moves his tongue inside. I stroke his hair and when I'm ready, I arch my back so that he will know I want him inside me.

I wake up a short time later because I'm cold. The duvet is

in a heap on the floor. I drag it on to the bed, and cuddle up to Adam's warm back.

Outside, someone bips their car horn and Adam stirs but doesn't wake.

15

It's one of those spirit-lifting, crisp, sunny afternoons and the beachfront is teeming with bladers, joggers, bikers, promenaders, skate-boarders. I keep to a gentle pace, run down into Hove and then come back the same way. I'm reluctant to leave the buzz and the fresh air behind so I find a spot opposite the Green Donut on a bench next to an elderly couple who are hunkered down in thick coats and hats. It's a wind-free day and the sea is flat; the waves nudge against the pebbles on the shore — a treacherous caress before the bullying starts.

There's a fashion shoot taking place on the beach which has gathered a small crowd of spectators. Models in bikinis stand in exaggerated leggy poses, and with expressions of summer-joy stuck on their faces, they throw beach balls to each other, kick up water at the sea's edge, and attempt to stretch languorously on the pebbles, their hair being blown in a machine-generated breeze. The moment they're released by the photographer, they jiggle up and down, hugging themselves, until a woman rushes over to wrap them up in a big towel.

A young girl in a pushchair in front of me lets go of her balloon.

'Daddy,' the girl says, pointing as it floats slowly upwards to come to rest on the telegraph wires above our heads. But her father is rubber-necking the photo-shoot and pushes on without noticing, and she begins to cry – the sobbing of the broken-hearted.

'Shame,' says the old lady next to me.

'Shame,' her husband echoes in a croaky voice, and then they both break into laughter. The woman rocks to and fro with the rhythm of her wheezy cackle and I realize that her feet aren't touching the ground.

I'm in the middle of describing the whole scene to Adam when he says, 'Sorry, babe. When was this?'

'Today. This afternoon.'

'Oh, right, carry on then.'

My story sits heavy on my tongue; I wish I'd never started; I wish I'd just pretended to tell it to Rose in my head.

Adam's cleaning and oiling his garden tools. It's one of his favourite winter pastimes and I enjoy it too. We drink cup after cup of tea in the warm kitchen, thick with the rich scent of linseed and grease. He lays the trowel down on the piece of newspaper on the table. The wood handle glows with oil; he touches it lovingly.

I should keep quiet, read my magazine and let him have this moment.

The doorbell goes. Two long presses, three short ones.

'It's Debbie,' I say to Adam, jumping up. 'She's early.'

'Ta-da!' Debs holds a clinking plastic bag up high. 'I've got the Breezers; chilled and ready to go. I've got the chocolate and the chick flick. Yuk, what's that stink?' She barely pauses for breath as she follows me into the kitchen. 'Oh, hello, Adam. I didn't think you were going to be in tonight.' She doesn't bother to disguise her annoyance. She might as well have said: 'What the fuck are *you* still doing here?'

'Don't worry, I'm not hanging about.' Adam winks at me.

'Another scintillating night down the . . .' She clicks her fingers. 'Remind me again of the name of your local?'

'The Boar's Head,' Adam says, although he knows that she knows.

'Of course. How apt – I don't know how I could forget.'

'Too much chick flickery going on in that pretty little head of yours,' Adam says, and they make faces at each other across the room as I hurriedly put four Breezers into the fridge and give the bag with the remaining two back to Debs while I grab the bottle-opener.

'Don't go spoiling my lovely Laura with your nonsense,' he adds, as I shove Debs out into the hall.

'God, puke. Who does he think he is?' she spits when we're barely out of earshot. 'Who does he think *you* are, for that matter?'

'Leave it out,' I tell her, closing the living-room door behind us.

'But Loz, really. Don't you crave excitement? Don't you want to try something new? Here,' she says, 'look at this.' She yanks up her top to reveal bra-less breasts, and a stud in each nipple. 'Andrew paid for me to have it done. And he watched. He's suggested I have a clit ring next.'

'Is he going to watch that, too?'

'Sure,' she says, flouncing her hair back. 'Why not?'

'He sounds a bit of a perv.'

'Maybe.' She sticks the DVD in the player, stands pressing the remote buttons before turning towards me. 'But Adam's so good, he's bad for you.'

Lately she can't resist a dig at him whenever they meet. To his face, she calls him 'Old Man Adam' and asks him where his pipe and slippers are. Ad never responds, but I know she pisses him off because I see his eyes cloud over as he controls his temper.

'Guess who I saw the other day?' I say to change the subject while the trailers run.

'Dunno.'

'Paul Yates from next door to Mum's.'

Debs shows a total lack of surprise at the news. 'He went to Australia, didn't he?'

'He's back for a holiday.'

'He used to be quite good-looking. What's he like now?'

'He's not bad, not bad at all,' I tell her, trying to keep a neutral expression as her head swivels in my direction.

'Do you fancy him, then?'

'Eye candy, Debs, that's all.'

'Living in Oz,' she says slowly. 'Now doesn't that sound much more appealing than rainy old Brighton?'

'I like my life here, Debs.'

'Just keep an open mind, that's all I ask.' She slits open a bar of Dairy Milk with a ruby-red nail as rapidly and efficiently as a panther disembowelling its kill.

'Whatever happened with you guys anyway? I don't think you ever told me.'

'God, I can't remember, Loz – that was aeons ago. He bored me, I think, or was too clingy. Probably too clingy – that's usually the case,' she says. 'That's what I like about now – being free and enjoying life. You know,' she says, tucking her hair behind her ears, 'I hadn't realized how unhealthy my relationship with Josh was. Too settled, too restrictive. God!' She blows out a sigh. 'All that time I wasted.'

But I'm not convinced by Debbie's talk about enjoying her freedom. She's like a boat in the marina which has come loose from its moorings in a storm and is in danger of being dragged out into the open sea and capsized; or at best gets bashed up a bit on the sea wall.

'Are you OK?' I ask before I can stop myself.

'What do you mean?' she says sharply and scowls a little. 'Of course I bloody am. I've just said so, haven't I?'

A grubby white sock is waved round the living-room door.

'It's OK, the coast's clear.'

Adam presses his chin on top of my head, places his cold hands on the back of my neck, making me shriek.

'By the way, I saw Josh in town the other day,' he tells me as he comes to sit beside me.

'You never said anything.'

He shrugs.

'Why do blokes do that?'

'What?'

'Keep all the interesting stuff to themselves?'

'I forgot.' He grins. 'We had a beer together.'

'Did you talk about Debs?'

'Not much.'

'What did he say? God, I hate the way you make me drag every detail out of you, making me look like some sad, nosy cow.'

'You are a sad, nosy cow.' Adam grins again.

'Come on,' I say, my voice rising. 'Tell me.'

'You won't like it.'

'Come on!'

'He said that he felt as if a weight had been lifted from his shoulders.'

'Oh.'

'See? I told you you wouldn't like it.'

'I'm just surprised. I thought he really cared for her, that's all. I thought he was a nice person.'

'*He* is. It's Debs that's the bitch. She's made no secret of the fact that in less than a week after they split up, she was having the time of her life shagging another man. Josh feels like a complete fucking idiot. So, please, Laura, do me a favour.'

16

Adam leans against the wall in the hallway and watches me perform my stretches.

'Don't go. It's Saturday night. Let's chill out instead, get a bottle of wine. It's too cold for running.'

The sexy look he fixes me with makes my blood fizz, but I'm only briefly tempted. I know how bad I'll feel tomorrow if I miss it. I want to make it a year; I've got that target in my head.

'After,' I tell him. 'I won't be long.'

On the doorstep I breathe in deeply; the cold air is sharp in my nostrils. I start off at a gentle pace. There's a chill winter wind, the sort that drills right into your bones no matter how many layers of clothes you've got on, but once I get going, I forget about the cold as my mind pans across the city, and the feeling of being in my rightful place settles in my chest.

I cut through to a street I like. The houses here are grand, proud-looking; their garden boundaries are tall, established hedges. In the evening light the spines of the holly-bush leaves look like shadow tips, the numerous red berries appear glazed.

When I get home, Adam has gone out. The flat is a disaster area. I make a half-hearted attempt to tidy up while my bath runs, then shut the door on the mess and immerse myself in heat and bubbles.

Adam phones later to say that Matt had needed to discuss some business with him. He'll be back late.

'Couldn't it have waited?' I ask. 'What's it about?'

'Nothing important,' Ad tells me. 'Money stuff, that's all.'

But 'nothing important' seems to require Adam's presence again the following morning, and he tells me at breakfast that after that, he needs to finish off some fencing so won't be back until the evening.

After he's left I stand at the living-room window watching the world go by. Everyone else is doing Sunday things together. The couple across the road are shepherding two youngsters on wobbly bikes down the road, while several people from the flat upstairs descend in a great clatter and cram themselves into a waiting car.

Adam is still working like 'the proverbial dog' as he puts it; from dawn to dusk, still playing catch-up, trying to recoup the losses suffered from the awful autumn weather.

'Whoever said owning your own business was the easy life?' he asked me on Friday evening, before dropping onto the settee and almost immediately beginning to snore. That was our fab Friday night. That's the general state of our social life at the moment; festering indoors – him sleeping while I'm disconsolately flicking through the TV channels.

I continue to spy on the street activities, and when I see the ancient old man from down the road shuffle past with his wife in her wheelchair, out for a Sunday stroll, I decide enough is enough.

'I've bought the Sunday papers and I was hoping that you might be my companion for a lazy afternoon in the pub?'

William looks momentarily nonplussed. 'That would be lovely, Laura,' he says recovering quickly and gesturing me inside.

'It's pretty cold out,' I tell him, so he adds a scarf and a jumper before putting on his coat.

'Hang on,' he says at the last minute. 'I've just got to get . . . um . . . something.'

The wind stings my face as we emerge onto the front. There's spray in the air; I can taste salt when I lick my lips. The seagulls are being hurled around the sky; even their raucous cries make little impression over the roar of wind and sea. My eyes water. I tuck my head down into my scarf.

William shouts something.

'What?' I bellow through the scarf, reluctant to surface from its flimsy warmth even for a second.

'I said I hope the pub's not far.'

It's not far, but it is busy; everyone's had the same idea. Crushed together, the conversation is loud, the air stifling. My ears and cheeks immediately start burning from the sudden temperature contrast. I notice that William's nose is bright red and I tell him so.

'Yours, too,' he responds.

William shrugs his coat off and hangs it over his arm while

we stand at the bar, but I keep mine on, wanting to savour the build-up of heat in the core of my body, to get to that point when it's almost unbearable.

William seeks out two stools and we squash on to the end of a table.

'How's your work going?' I ask him.

He thinks for a moment. 'I'm taking my time, getting a feel for the place. I went on a bus tour the other day. I wanted to do a boat trip too, but they don't run them in the winter.'

'I've always meant to do that – be a tourist for the day.'

'You should.'

I wait, expecting William to elaborate, but he doesn't. He's holding back for some reason and I don't want to push it by prying.

'Which part would you like?' I ask him, gesturing to the paper.

'I should say the travel section.'

'It's the weekend. You can read whatever you want.'

'Well,' he says, a bit sheepishly, 'actually I really would like the travel section, unless you want it first?'

We settle back into silence. I really want to flick through the style and home pages, but don't want to seem a complete airhead so I start reading the news. William is absorbed.

'What do you and William talk about each week?' Rose once asked.

I must have looked surprised because she immediately apologized.

'Forget that – it's none of my business. I was just curious.' She waved her hand around. 'I've always been too bloody nosy for my own good, except now, of course, I haven't got much material to work with.' Then she added, sounding a little angry: 'God! That was really self-pitying.'

'I don't mind you asking, you know. It's not a secret. We just talk about things people usually do: the news, TV, what we're reading. William tells me about some of the places you've been.'

'Doesn't he ever talk to you about how he's feeling?'

I shook my head.

'Never?'

'Never,' I told her, before adding that he sometimes said he was feeling tired, but Rose still looked dissatisfied with my answer.

I sense William watching me.

'I found something.' He reaches behind him for his coat, drags it onto his lap. 'Photos,' he says, pulling two packets out of the inside pocket. 'Rosie's photographs.'

He places them on the table. 'Have you seen them already?'

I shake my head.

'Take a look, then.'

I hesitate. The packets are satiny; cool to the touch. The thought that I'm going to find something important inside has come into my head and now it's there I can't shift it – particularly as William hasn't taken his eyes off me.

I sift through the prints and am relieved to find nothing more than the familiar objects and scenes Rose and I had watched from the top of the house: the buddleia growing out of the wall up on the fifth floor of the hotel, where a butterfly had once teetered on the single flowering stem; the abandoned shopping trolley that the kids had spent a week racing up and down the Crescent until someone took it away; the stained white plastic patio furniture blown about on a neglected rooftop garden. I see, clearly but briefly, Rose's delighted expression as she filled me in on the daily comings and goings of the Crescent.

I hold up a photograph. 'It's Gulliver,' I say, laughing. I stop when I see William is mystified. 'Rose's seagull?'

William shakes his head.

'She made up stories about him,' I explain. '*Gulliver's Travails*, she called them. He was always having to fight his corner – to stay on his chosen chimneypot, to keep the others from nicking his scraps of food.'

As I talk, I feel increasingly embarrassed. I realize, too late, how silly it must sound to someone else. Rose and I could get quite carried away up there in her room where no thought was too bizarre or too puerile to pursue.

'It was just nonsense,' I end awkwardly.

'What about the other packet?' William asks.

It takes me a moment to understand that Rose had been photographing the tops of people's heads as they entered the Claymores' house. Once I've got the handle on the odd perspective, I begin to recognize who they are: there's Mrs Spalding, the neighbour who used to keep an eye on the house for them when they were away and who looked in on Rose every now and then; Ben; Alex with and without Emma; me; William; a friend of the Claymores whose name I've forgotten, who visited several times and who had spoken to me briefly at Rose's funeral; William and Ben together.

The more I study the odd angles and composition of the photos, the more I'm convinced that they were taken hastily and clandestinely – as if Rose simply stuck her hand through the railings and clicked. Otherwise, if she'd shot them openly as people were approaching the house down the front path or as they came across the Crescent, waving to her as I automatically did once I was close enough, they'd have been much, much better.

These photographs are more like products of my untalented efforts, nothing like the standard of Rose's usual work. I remember one of her photos in particular – a landscape of a Greek hillside so starkly real I imagined I could feel the dust-soil blowing against my face.

'Did you know she was taking these?' I ask him.

'No. So you didn't either?'

I shake my head, although I now recall how, a few weeks before Rose died, I had put two rolls of film in for development and collected them for her. I tell William this.

'Ah,' he says. 'I must admit that the logistics of how she'd got hold of them was puzzling me.'

'She just said thank you and shoved them under her pillow.'

'So what do you think she was trying to do?' William asks carefully. 'Or say?'

It hadn't occurred to me that she was doing anything more significant than amusing herself so I study the photographs again and try to picture myself up in Rose's room, hearing people approach the house; I try to imagine what she could have been thinking.

I was very close to Rose then, and it's hard acknowledging that there are already things that I don't know about her, and that I never will have the chance of asking her about. I'd like to put the photos away and forget about them, but William is looking expectantly at me so I urge my brain to come up with an answer. I focus so hard that I forget to blink and my eyes start burning, but in the end I have to admit that I've no idea.

'It's all right,' he says, and he seems relieved. 'It doesn't matter. I thought perhaps she'd said something to you, that's all.'

'Look at this one,' I say, pulling a photograph of me and William out from the rest. 'It's the summer day when Rose packed us off to the beach.' I recognize my sunhat and the loud towel William had bought from one of the tat-shacks down at the seafront.

That day had been particularly hot and Rose was grumpy with tiredness; she was struggling to cope in the heat and hadn't been sleeping well for a long time, though she was reluctant to admit it.

'Take William out,' she'd insisted. 'I can't bear to think of us all being stuck inside in this gorgeous weather.'

I jumped at the chance to give Rose the opportunity to rest. The doctor had been round earlier and given her something to help, but I had the impression she was fighting it because I was there. I went downstairs to find William. He was reading in the lounge and left the room when I told him of Rose's request. He returned a few minutes later.

'It's not compulsory,' he said to me.

'But I'd like to,' I replied, surprised that he suspected reluctance on my part.

It was a Saturday and the beach was packed out. Although the house had felt stifling, neither of us had appreciated quite how fierce the sun was. We didn't have sun-cream or swimming things with us, and in the end we had had to hire a parasol to shelter under. Our conversation was lazy, both of us succumbing to the trance-like state induced by the temperature.

We watched a volley-ball game a couple of metres away on the man-made pitch.

'They're making me feel even hotter,' William groaned as a rally of passes ended with one player landing face-down in a spray of sand while the rest of the team leaped around high-five-ing. 'I'd kill to be out diving right now, down deep in the cool.'

'I've never tried diving,' I told him.

'I'm sure you'd love it; it's got to be one of the best things in the world,' he said, and there was a longing in his voice which made me see, for the first time, how hard Rose's illness was for William too.

'Do you remember that day?' I ask him.

William looks down at his knees. 'Yes, I remember.'

'I've been thinking,' William says later, on the walk home. The wind's dropped and normal-pitch conversation is possible. I feel irradiated from the alcohol; the cold air is refreshing on my warm face. My arm is tucked into William's. Despite the padding of our clothes, I can feel the wiriness of his muscles.

'You mentioned before about how cramped your flat is now – well, why don't you move your office into our – my – house? We've got so much space there. You could use the dining room.'

'Are you serious?'

He squeezes my arm. 'I was going to suggest it before, but I didn't know how you'd feel about it. I thought you might find the whole idea too strange.'

'I don't think I would,' I say slowly, trying not to seem overly eager but already the relief of having a solution is flooding through me. Only now, with the anticipation of space, can I acknowledge how cramped and restricted I've been feeling, how hard it's been to motivate myself to sit down every day at that teeny desk.

'To be honest, I really like the idea,' I tell William as calmly as I can. 'And it would really help me out of a hole; my business is going to suffer if I don't sort something soon, and Ad's no nearer to getting the shed converted.'

We walk along in silence. There's a slight crunching underfoot. I wonder if it's salt from the sea or whether they've been gritting the roads. Freezing weather's been forecast: a rare event for Brighton these days.

'Think about it,' William says. 'There's no need to decide straight away.'

'Thank you. I will.' But I know my answer already.

A gritting lorry passes on the other side of the road. We duck from the shower of salt; granules patter against my coat.

I accompany William to his house to pick up my car.

As I wait for him to unlock the door, I look up at the narrow underside of Rose's balcony and I'm struck again by the strangeness of those photographs.

William ushers me in and shepherds me straight into the dining room from the kitchen.

'I'd clear it out, of course,' he says. 'If you did want to go ahead with the office idea.'

It's quite a small room and not one often used by the Claymores, judging by the pile of boxes and newspapers on top of the table, but it has a nice feel to it with its aspect to the garden.

'What about your sons? Won't they mind?' I ask, knowing the answer. My excitement bursts like a pricked balloon. A clear picture of Emma's suspicious face scoots across my mind; there's no way she'll let Alex agree to this.

'I wouldn't have made the offer, Laura, if I wasn't going to honour it, and they'll see the sense in the idea. They're forever telling me about the dangers of leaving the property unoccupied for long periods of time, and this way there'll always be someone around whenever I'm not here.' He pinches the bridge of his nose. 'To be honest, we've been pretty lucky not to have had any trouble this far.'

Adam lets out a whoop and punches the air. 'Result! I didn't know how the hell I was going to fit in doing that shed for ages. You have said yes, haven't you?' he adds hurriedly.

'Not officially, until I'd spoken to you. But in theory, yes.'

He pulls me to him. 'You won't have to be there for too long,' he says, placing a kiss on my forehead, then my nose. 'I promise the shed is absolutely my next priority.' He frowns at a sudden thought. 'How much does he want?'

'Nothing.'

'Nothing? Bloody hell! Are you sure he's not after something?' He runs his hands up under my top, squeezes my waist. 'There's no such thing as a free lunch, you know.'

'Why did you say that?' I push him away. 'It's not a nice thing to say.'

'It's just a phrase, it doesn't mean anything.' He laughs at my face. 'Don't look so serious.'

'I don't like it. Even if it's just a joke.'

Adam looks at me, then shrugs. 'OK,' he says. 'Point taken. But what a result.'

* * *

'Not bad,' Adam says, looking round. 'Not bad at all.'

Although I'd said there was no need, William has emptied the room. It looks bigger, and with the morning sun pouring through the window, it seems even more inviting. I feel a buzz of excitement. I know exactly where I want everything to go. I'll have my desk facing the garden so that I can look out whenever I want to, I'll have an armchair for when I want to sit and think more comfortably, and I'll always keep flowers on the windowsill. I can really picture myself here.

'What's this door?' Adam crosses the room.

'It just leads to the garden, but I don't know if it opens.'

Adam unlocks it. Cold air rushes in. He stands looking out and I join him there.

There is more greenery in the little courtyard than you first realize. There's a juniper bush, a lilac, and a beautiful bay tree, along with smaller, pretty shrubs, like Hebe and Rose of Sharon – but the rest of the space is crammed with statues and sculptures on various stands and tables, or placed on the paving.

One of my earlier memories of Rose is her dressed in heels, an elegant moss-green silk dress and pink Marigold gloves, washing the statues. There was foam in her hair and hundreds of bubbles were floating around the garden.

'Why not?' she'd asked as William and I came out. 'When else am I going to get the chance to dress up?'

'Everything could do with a good pruning,' Adam says. 'And it's kinda creepy, don't you think? All those eyes. Don't they freak you out?'

'They didn't,' I tell him. 'But thanks for drawing them to my attention.'

Adam puts his arm over my shoulders as William's shadow moves across the kitchen blind.

'You've really landed on your feet here,' Adam says, and I shrug him off, feeling a little irritated.

We join William in the kitchen. He's made tea. We stand up like workmen on a break, nobody getting comfortable. There are still all my boxes and the filing cabinet to be brought in.

'Thanks for helping Laura out like this,' Adam says in his strained, polite voice. 'We really appreciate it.'

William swills his mug out under the tap. 'It's no problem,' he says. 'I reckon I've got the best deal anyway – a pretty young woman around the place and someone to house-sit when I'm away. Isn't that so, Laura?'

I feel myself redden as they both focus their attention on me.

First Adam leaves me to unpack, then William goes out too, popping his head round the door to say he'll be away for a couple of hours.

Once I'm alone, the urge to pay a visit to Rose's room steals up on me until it's my only thought.

I hesitate, one hand on the door, with butterflies in my stomach. When I push it open, the hinges creak. I freeze – guiltily – like a trespasser. The rest of the house is silent, heavy behind me. I tell myself I'm being silly and push the door wide and enter.

The room is gloomy; the shutters are partly closed. It had never smelled like a sick person's room before, but now it does; there's a damp, sour odour. And it's very cold.

The bed, the bedside cabinet, Rose's little desk and chair

and her comfortable armchair are all present but everything personal has been cleared away: her books, the laptop and papers, the big vase William always kept filled with fresh flowers, also the tray with the kettle and cups, the large collection of pill bottles, the lamp, of course, and even the bedding – save for her grandmother's quilt which has been spread over the bare mattress.

I wonder if William did it. It would have taken him ages; he would have had to climb the stairs several times over to do so.

I open the shutters and look around for the big cushion I used to sit on, on the floor, but that's disappeared too. I reject the idea of sitting in Rose's chair and decide the carpet is good enough. Leaning against the arm of the chair, I notice for the first time the mottled green and orange weave of its cover.

Outside seems as flat as inside the room. Nothing holds my interest – there's the same higgledy-piggledy rooftops to the left, the same chequerboard of hotel windows beneath an over-cast sky threaded with watery blue veins.

'Never the same scene twice,' Rose often declared, but today there's nothing special about the view. It all looks – lifeless.

A crash from somewhere in the house makes me leap to my feet, nerves jangling. I hurry to the landing and listen, worried about William returning early, but the house breathes empti-ness below me. I glance over my shoulder and catch sight of an aeroplane about to disappear from view and it suddenly occurs to me why the room feels so different.

Rose never had the window closed and sounds always filtered in: kids shouting in the Crescent, thunder and rain, the tinny buzz of microlights, the raucous calls of seagulls; hundreds of noises that made the scenes come alive, that made the room part of the world.

Adam isn't at home when I get there. The flat looks emptied out and scruffy. I should tidy up but I'm sick of sorting for one day. Instead I go for a run, choosing a circular route. It isn't until I'm past the point of no return that I remember this takes me under a bridge which I hate.

I call it Pigeon Bridge. It's long, like a tunnel, and of brick construction, and because the tiny lights high up on the walls are encrusted with years of pigeon poop, they have only a feeble effect against the gloominess. In the summer it's spookily cool, in the winter, as cold as a crypt.

It echoes with the amplified sound of pigeons – cooing, flapping, rustling. As they fly in, they swoosh low above my head, startling me.

Today in the dusk, it's eerier than ever; dark lumps of matter are frozen to the pavement and there are feathers scattered everywhere as if something has been ravaging the birds up above me. I sprint through and keep sprinting until I'm a long way past.

I stop when I hear the chirpy bleep of my mobile as a message comes through. It's from Adam.

@ boar's head. Join me? got good news!! Xx

I'm in the bath when Adam appears. I smell the beer on his breath as he bends to kiss me.

'You're back early,' I say.

'Couldn't keep away.' He leans against the sink, looking at me.

'Well, don't keep me in suspense – what's your news?'

'You should have come to the pub and found out,' he says, crossing his legs and folding his arms to affect an extra-casual manner.

'I was going to after my bath; you didn't give me enough time.' I flick some suds at him. 'Come on, Ad.'

'We've *only* been asked to give a quote and propose a design for the garden of the stately home outside Brighton, the one which they've been renovating on the TV series,' Adam says, grinning at me.

I squeal and drum the water; foam splashes in my face. 'That is so cool! You might be on TV – you might be famous!'

Adam parades to and fro across the bathroom, posing like a model. 'Oh yeah, I like famous.'

Then he stops suddenly and looks very serious, quite bashful as he speaks. 'You know, babe, this is a really prestigious project and we've been recommended by the brother of the top chap there. He's one of the guys who owned that string of exclusive urban "hideaways" we did the landscaping work for, earlier this year. If we're successful with our proposal,' he says, sounding almost amazed, 'me and Matt will be made.'

I can tell that he's already got his heart set on winning. 'You deserve it,' I tell him. 'You work hard enough.'

I watch him strip off, admire his bum and sneak a look at his cock when he turns briefly in my direction. The water rises dangerously to the top of the bath as he steps in. He crouches down and lets the plug out; the pipes gurgle and knock.

He sits with his back facing me; I rub it with a soapy sponge, then rinse it off. Water sloshes all over the floor.

I lean my cheek against his back and we stay like that for a while without speaking.

Spring

17

One morning when William is out I answer the house phone to Alex. My mouth dries up and for a short beat, I can't speak. I've done nothing wrong, I remind myself. I've nothing to feel bad about.

'William's not here at the moment,' I tell him. 'Do you want me to pass on a message?'

Alex's response is brief and unfriendly. 'No, thanks. I'll call back.'

'Hang on,' he says at the precise moment I'm sticking my tongue out at the phone. 'Actually, could you let him know that I've now taken advice from my solicitors and it's important that I speak to him about drawing up the paperwork.'

'OK.'

'I take it you don't object to putting your occupation of the premises on an official footing, do you?'

I think, Occupation of the premises; what a prat – it's only a temporary arrangement. 'Of course not. William said there'd be some papers to sign.'

'Right, good. Well, the sooner we get this sorted, the better.'

'Absolutely,' I reply, and silently mouth all sorts of rude words at him. After a few seconds of dead air at his end, I say: 'OK, bye then.'

'Oh, and Laura . . .'

'Yes?'

'This is *private* business, you know – not anything for the papers.'

'That's not fair,' I say, but my words bounce off the buzz of the dial tone. Alex has already put the phone down.

'Of course his nose is out of joint,' Adam says later that day. 'Don't be obtuse, Laura. First you were friends with his mum and now he sees you moving in on his dad.'

Adam's come into the kitchen and I've taken the opportunity to talk to him during a rare moment when he's not immersed in his books.

I feel myself colouring up. 'Why does everybody seem to think I've got ulterior motives?'

Adam gives me a strange look. '*I* don't. I was talking about how it might seem to Alex. That house is worth a bomb and he's never got on with his parents, and suddenly you – this kind of adopted daughter – appear on the scene replacing him in their affections. Of course he's going to feel pushed out and resentful, and probably more than a little worried.'

Adam wanders off and I trail after him into the living room, carrying a couple of bottles of beer.

'You know, Ben's been OK about everything.'

'Ben hasn't got a chip on his shoulder like Alex.'

'It's Emma who winds him up about it. I bet Alex would be fine if he didn't listen to her.'

Adam turns round. 'You know what my advice would be? Keep a low profile; don't let yourself get involved in their family business.'

'And how am I going to do that when I'm right there in the house?'

'Your office is there, that's all,' he says, hoisting a heavy reference book onto his knee. 'Look at this, listen to this.' He points to a page, his face lighting up. 'You should see the place; it's incredible. There was a priory on the estate before this house was ever built and the monks worked the gardens for food and medicinal herbs. That means there's been a garden on this site for over four hundred years.' He shakes his head as if the whole thing is simply too amazing. 'Part of the wall still exists and there's this really great circular paving. We're thinking of incorporating it somehow into the design, making it a focal point of some kind.'

He leans back, one arm behind his head, and sucks loudly on his beer while I peer at an indistinct black and white photograph of a patch of ground with some unremarkable stone slabs.

He claps the book shut and hunches over a box on the floor, sifting through papers and documents.

'I'll see if I can wangle you in sometime,' he says. 'But I'm not promising anything.'

'I won't hold my breath.'

The garden renovation is being kept hush-hush because the progress is going to be filmed for a series of TV programmes. Adam and Matt have special passes to enter the premises and they've even signed a legal document to prevent them talking about it. This cloak and dagger approach seems to be the icing on the cake for Adam, who is so fired up by the project that it's practically all he can think about these days.

I pick up the top sheet from a pile of papers that Adam's left on the coffee-table. It's a page showing scary amounts of money for what appears to be cement.

'This can't be right,' I say, flapping the page in front of him. 'Unless you're planning to concrete over the whole garden.'

Adam glances up. He plucks the sheet from my fingers. 'You must be kidding. That's nothing,' he tells me. 'You should see the estimate for gravel alone; we're talking *thousands*.'

I shove some papers aside to make room for my beer.

'Watch it!' Adam barks, and I snatch up the bottle immediately. 'Don't go spilling *anything* on this stuff, Laura. They're my only copies.'

I glance around. This room is far messier than when I had my office here and Ad used to give me a hard time about it. I mention this to him but he chooses to ignore the implied criticism and shrugs.

'Creativity,' he says annoyingly, 'is a messy business.'

It's a similar disaster zone when I get to William's house the next day. I find him in the lounge, kneeling at the foot of one of the crammed bookcases.

'Thought I'd have a clear-out,' he tells me, standing up and dusting himself off. Although the floor's covered in piles of books and there's a bulging black bin-bag beside him, it's hard to see where any space on the shelves has been created.

I sit on the settee and pick up a large book lying close to me with the title *The Aegean Islands*. The cover shows a lone fishing boat moored on the sea at the foot of a mountain. As in many of their books I've looked at, the Claymores are amongst the names credited on the inside cover, and the author has signed the front page: *With much love to my dear friends Rose and William.* As I flick through the pages, the sharp blue of the sea and the stark white cubes of houses pass in a blur in front of my eyes.

I find a couple of loose photographs tucked into the back sleeve. They're of the Claymores when they were probably about my age, dressed in full 1970s regalia. William is wearing bell-bottom trousers and Rose, a white gypsy smock mini-dress. They are both so skinny and perfect-looking they remind me of the mannequins in my client-friend Angus's vintage clothing boutique.

I hold the photos out for William to take.

'This was outside the art college,' he tells me. 'Where we met. A typical story,' he continues. 'Eyes meeting across the student bar.'

I know the story already. I also know that Rose wasn't there that day by accident: she'd spotted William a few weeks before and had been asking around about him. She'd even chosen where to sit so that when he looked up, she'd be directly in his line of vision. As she'd talked I'd felt gripped with the tension of a moment when you know your life is about to change.

William joins me on the settee. 'I thought, Who is that? I just wanted to know her. I couldn't think of anything – or anyone – else.'

I glance down at the photographs in William's hands.

'It's hard,' he says suddenly.

'Yes.'

'You miss her, too?' he asks, but it's really more of a statement than a question.

'Very much,' I tell him, and sadness rushes in, settling inside with a heaviness that threatens to keep me pinned to the settee.

'Rosie looks wonderful,' William says, breaking into the silence. 'Don't you think?' He nods and smiles slightly as if to say, 'Your turn.' I understand then that he's asking to be rescued from unhappy thoughts so I say the first thing which comes into my head. 'You look pretty cool, too.'

I've surprised and embarrassed William. He laughs. 'Well, um, thanks.'

'I don't suppose I could borrow these, could I? I've got a friend who's really into seventies clothing. I know he'd love to see them.'

As William passes them to me, I feel his hand trembling.

'No, sorry,' I say, trying to give them back. 'I should never have asked.'

'Take them.' He stands up. 'It's fine. I'd like you to borrow them.'

I put them in my handbag. When I glance across the room, William is frozen to the spot and his expression is so weird that my heart stops.

'William? What's wrong?' I say cautiously.

He clicks into life. 'Sorry, it's just that I haven't seen one of these for a while.' He bends down and picks up something from one of the piles.

'What is it?'

'It's an anti-euthanasia leaflet.' He throws it at the bin-bag where it lands with a rustle before turning to face me. He looks drained; he pushes his hair away from his eyes and I glimpse the shine of sweat on his forehead. 'When the case hit the news, I used to get them almost daily. Someone was very keen to share their opinion with me,' he says, and his face hardens. 'Like that woman in the supermarket.'

'I didn't think you'd noticed,' I say quietly.

'Oh, I did. I just chose to ignore the bitch.'

The word 'bitch' hits the air like a slap. I sit open-mouthed.

'Sorry,' he says.

'No, *I'm* sorry,' I tell him.

'For what?'

'For not sticking up for you at the time. I felt awful, afterwards. I should have said something.'

William waves his hand. 'There was no point. Nothing was going to change her belief that I'm pure evil — that's why I didn't bother.'

'But she looked so normal, like someone's mum,' I say, but as I do, I have a vision of her eyes glimmering with anger and resentment, and I hear her horrible, spiteful words.

'I received several letters, too, with pretty strong stuff in some of them,' William goes on. 'From both sympathizers as well as accusers, though.' He shrugs. 'Once you're in the public's eye you're a target for every crank and misfit and you just have to sit tight and let it blow over.'

Later that day, when I'm at the cash-point, someone behind me pinches my bum. I whirl round, astonished, indignation all over my face. Paul stands there grinning.

'Haven't we got rid of you yet?' I ask him but I can't help grinning back.

'Another couple of weeks. I can't wait to get out of here,' he says, pretending to pull his hair out.

'Too much of a good thing?'

'Too much cold, too much rain, too much living under the same roof as my parents. Though I love them to bits, they're *driving me nuts*. Don't suppose you've got time for a drink?'

'A quickie,' I say.

He winks. 'Now you're offering.'

I give him a look. 'In your dreams.'

'Frequently,' he counters. 'How did you know?'

'Come on, you lech. Let's go and find a pub.'

'I saw your friend and mine the other day,' Paul says once we're settled at a table.

'Debs? Did you talk to her?'

He shakes his head. 'She was with some tall, dark and hand-some mug – oops, I mean man. She didn't seem very pleased to see me, though; she couldn't wait to rush him away and be alone together. I'd say she's smitten.'

I doubt this but I don't say anything.

'Really,' Paul asserts. 'He looked like a real cocky bastard – all confident and casual, like he had the upper hand – the way *she* always was with whoever she deigned to go out with.'

'I don't believe it,' I tell him, but as I'm speaking it occurs to me that Debs has been behaving strangely recently. I've hardly seen or heard from her over the last few weeks, and usually she won't stop bugging me, especially if there's a new bloke to dissect.

"Bout time she suffered like the rest of us,' Paul says.

I begin to protest but he jumps in quickly. 'I don't know why you always defend her.'

'Duh.' I pull a face. 'Because she's my friend, stupid.'

Paul takes a drink of beer. 'She stole your dress, you know.'

'Yes,' I lie. 'She told me.' I know immediately that he's referring to the dress I'd bought for the Fourth Form end-of-term
Christmas disco, but I'd never in a million years have guessed
it was Debs who took it.

The dress was very different from anything I'd ever owned
before. It was blue satin and quite short, and although I was
nervous about wearing it, deep down I suspected that I looked
really, really good. When I'd come out of the changing room
in Top Shop to show Debs, I'd read in her eyes enough to
convince me that I was right.

After the last class when we went to the lockers to collect
our bags, mine had disappeared.

'I can't go,' I sobbed while my friends searched everywhere.
Debs had put her arm around me.

'You'll be all right in your uniform,' she consoled me. 'There'll
be lots of people still wearing theirs.'

But of course the only ones who hadn't changed were the
weird and the poor – the worst people to have anything in
common with if you hoped to maintain any peer credibility at
all. I wanted to crawl away and die. I felt stupid and conspicuous, and it didn't help that Debs kept drawing everyone's attention to my predicament.

'Guess who got her dress stolen?' she said immediately to
anyone who came up to talk. 'Describe it to them,' she ordered.
'In case they spot the crim wearing it.'

'How did you find out?' I ask Paul, trying to sound unconcerned.

'She confessed – no, wrong word – she *boasted* about it to

me afterwards. She said she was so sick of you going on about your new dress, she couldn't take any more.'

But I know that's not why she did it. I should have realized back then why she'd been so dismissive about the disco, declaring that her jeans were good enough for a stupid school thing. I should have known it was because she didn't have anything new to wear.

'I think I was supposed to have been impressed, but I was just scared,' Paul continues in a joking way. 'It was about then that I began to wonder what I'd got myself into, what she'd do to *me* if the mood took her – bunny-boiler stuff, you know. She was always jealous of you,' he adds, seriously. 'I'm sure that was the real reason she went out with me – to stop us being friends.' He pauses. 'Or something more.'

As if for the first time, I see Paul clearly. I see emerging from the fading tan, a bloated, rather foolish face. I see a puff-necked parading pigeon, hopelessly flirting with me.

'Oh well,' I say as nicely as I can. 'That was then.'

18

Today is officially the first day of spring but you wouldn't believe it. From the raised ground where I'm standing, the Downs stretch for miles and winter still has the country firmly in its grip. It feels as if we'll never be able to prise its gloomy fingers off, and the fleeting sweet scents and tender air which promise warm bright days ahead will remain elusive.

The weather is unpredictable – rain to dry to windy – but always, always there's a dull miasma hanging day after day over the town. It weighs down on me, makes my head feel full of cotton wool.

'Do you want something to eat?' I ask Adam when I'm back from my run and showered and changed. The house feels stuffy, oppressively hot.

'I had a freeza-pizza,' Ad says, not looking up.

He is sitting in his boxer shorts and socks, poring over an immense blueprint which shrouds the coffee-table. I notice that the clumps of mud in the hall are also trailed across the carpet right up to the pile of boots and work jeans which lie discarded by the foot of the sofa.

The whole of the room, like the rest of the flat, is littered with trade catalogues about paving stones and stonework, reproduction garden architecture, reproduction antique statuary. The reading in the loo is all in a similar vein; I feel that I know more about trelliswork and obelisks than it is right for a girl to know.

If it isn't catalogues, it's calculations.

Adam and Matt meet regularly to hash and re-hash figures. They must obtain a loan to support the initial material purchases they would require, otherwise they'll have to pull out of the running. Adam has left it to Matt to smooth-talk their Small Business manager, and they've been waiting on a decision for nearly a week now. I've never seen Ad so tense; he's frantic with impatience at the slow machinations of the bank system.

'Were there any calls earlier?' he asks me.

'I didn't check.'

I leave the room to go and make a brie and rocket sandwich. The answerphone is permanently choked with messages for Adam these days, so I've decided that there's no point in me listening to it any more. I've given up taking the messages down for him – they're so long and detailed: some smarmy architectural dealer telling me the price of x tons of reclaimed bricks or an electrician giving a verbal quote on three options for wiring the three fountains – and to be honest, I don't care that marble plinths cost anything from ten pence to fifteen pounds a cubic inch.

'Don't move those!' Adam yells. The urgency in his voice makes me jump. 'I've got those open at the pages I need.'

I hover, plate in hand, expecting Adam to clear some space

for me, but he continues working as if I'm not there. So instead I go into the bedroom, switch on the portable TV and eat my food, sitting cross-legged in the middle of the bed.

The phone rings and a few minutes later, Adam appears in the doorway. 'That was Matt. We got the loan.'

'Brilliant!' I jump off the bed and give him a hug. 'We should celebrate. How about a beer?'

'Why not?'

But by the time I take a bottle in to him he's returned to the sofa and is absorbed in his papers.

'I brought the holiday brochures back,' I say, sitting down.

It takes a moment for Adam to respond. 'What?'

'Ho-li-day bro-chuuures.' I speak slowly.

Ad frowns. 'Not now, Laura, please,' he says sharply as if dismissing me.

Due to Adam's demonstrative lack of interest, I take it upon myself to decide on our holiday this year. A few days later, William spots the stack of brochures on my desk.

'Where are you thinking of going?' he asks.

'Anywhere cheap and sunny. We can't afford to be very adventurous, I'm afraid.'

He flicks through the pile and pulls one out. 'Cyprus,' he says, 'is a beautiful island. Rosie and I went on an assignment there a few years ago.'

He sits down in the armchair in front of my desk, crosses his legs to support the brochure and begins to flick through it. Watching him, it occurs to me how different planning a holiday must be for William: with all his knowledge and experience he certainly wouldn't be relying on some unimaginative holiday package like I am. All he needs to do is phone up a friend or contact, have a chat and he'd have an instant recommendation of where to stay or maybe even an offer to put him up.

I feel completely deflated: I'm tired of trying to maintain enthusiasm for going away when Adam is too busy even to share in choosing the destination – but also I'm sick to death of Brighton. I imagine myself as an insect stuck on gluey fly-paper; wriggling hopelessly while everyone else buzzes around free to fly off where and whenever they like: William, Mum and David, Paul; even the owners of a handmade candles shop phoned the other day for advice on selling up. When I met them to look at their accounts and business plan, I was surprised because the business was doing fantastically well. 'We know,' they said. 'But we can't stand the weather. We're moving abroad.'

William holds up a brochure and points to a photo. 'There's a wonderful, tiny hotel tucked away in the hills near here. Rosie and I stayed there for a month. They've got natural outdoor pools in the garden – I can't remember the word for them but it roughly translates to "wallow holes". They're only big enough for one person and you have to stand upright in them – well, stand isn't the word really because they're saltwater and you're completely supported – like a flotation tank really but open to the air. You only go at night.' He pauses. 'It sounds creepy,' he says, 'but it isn't at all. Quite the opposite. You walk through the gardens along a lighted path, quite a distance from the hotel, and by the time you get there, you feel completely removed from everything and at peace.'

I look at William and think, I want to know these things; I want to experience these things. From out of the blue, tears spring into my eyes. I quickly rearrange the papers on my desk to hide my face.

'Oh,' William says. 'Sorry. I'm taking up your time.'

'Not at all. I love hearing about where you've been,' I tell him, avoiding his eye. 'And I could honestly do with help making a decision.' I wave at the stack of brochures. 'There's too much choice.'

William gets up. 'Any time – I'd be happy to. Just let me know.'

That afternoon on the internet, I happen upon a site about living and working for voluntary organizations all over the world. Investigating further, it seems that Ad and I – with our skills and interests – would be ideal candidates. I spend the whole afternoon digging deeper, pulling off reams of information. By the end of the day, the idea is bursting inside me: I can't wait to talk it over with Adam.

'What are you going on about?' he asks, his expression a mixture of annoyance and disbelief. 'I'm just embarking on the biggest, most exciting project I've ever had the chance to work on, and you want us to give up a year of our lives and spend it in a mud hut somewhere in Africa?'

He is barricaded on the sofa by papers and books and catalogues. I never get near him, I find myself thinking. We hardly ever touch these days.

More detailed plans for the project have been requested and Adam and Matt are required to give a presentation. The preparation for it is eating into their leisure time, chomping through their budget – and for what? As time goes on, the less convinced I become that they'll get it. Why should they, I think whenever

Adam goes on about it. There must be all sorts of big names after this contract. 'Why *shouldn't* we?' is what he says, belligerently. 'We're as good as or better than the next man.'

'But if your bid isn't successful . . .' I start to say.

'Cheers, thanks for the vote of confidence.'

'And anyway, I didn't necessarily mean right now, just a possible future thing.'

'Everything's a possible future thing,' he says, picking up a piece of paper. 'But if you're asking me whether it's in my top ten list of possible future things to do, the answer would be no.'

The print-offs sit heavily in my lap. 'So you won't even read about it?'

Adam sighs. He places the sheet of paper down with exaggerated deliberateness. This means: I'm being generous enough to listen to you.

'Forget it.'

We sit in silence for a moment.

'Where's this come from?' Adam asks. 'You've never wanted to leave Brighton before now.'

'People change,' I say huffily. 'News flash: I'm not going to want the same things for ever.'

'People don't change overnight,' he tells me.

'Maybe I've been changing for a while but you haven't been paying attention.'

'Whoa.' Adam holds up his hands. 'I'm not getting into an argument right now. I've got too much to do.'

'When haven't you?' I say.

I slam the lounge door, which bounces open again with the force; I stomp across the hall, and slam the bedroom door shut.

I throw myself on the bed and lie face down into the pillow. I'm sure I hear Adam calling my name.

He's going to follow me. I picture him coming in, lying on the bed beside me, throwing his arm round me, pulling me over to lie on my back. He'll look down at me, talk to me, trace his finger across my face, kiss me. We'll get hornier and hornier; our kisses deeper and sexier until we make love. I feel swollen with desire, wriggle my hips into the bed.

But Adam doesn't come. I raise my head and listen; there's not a sound. I tiptoe out, peek through the gap in the door and see that he's sitting exactly where I left him, absorbed and unconcerned.

I go to the kitchen, put the kettle on but never get round to making a cup of tea. I sit at the table with an image in my head of me driving off – screeching away from the flat, bombing through the streets to the outskirts of town. But then what? Where would I go?

19

The North Laines area is buzzing but not as packed as it gets on a Saturday. I make my way down towards Angus's boutique, stopping off at a couple of the stalls to add my signature to a Friends of the Earth campaign and an anti-whaling petition. I think of Peter's scornful comments as I do this and write with a flourish.

'Hey!' Angus waves to me from the doorway of his shop. He's having a cigarette break. I stand next to him with my back against the wall; there's a weak sun, ineffectual against the rapidly moving clouds and sharp wind, and I quickly feel cold.

I sympathize with the human statue who has set up his pedestal across the street; dressed in a thin tux over a dress-shirt, he must be frozen. A little boy shyly approaches and places a coin at his feet. He shrieks when the statue's torso suddenly drops forward and the man's head swivels to peer at him. The boy runs off, half-giggling, half-crying back to his mum.

'I sold him that jacket,' Angus says and stamps his cigarette out. 'Close your eyes, darling, and don't be angry,' he instructs me as he clutches my arm and leads me inside. 'Surprise!'

On the wall behind the cash desk are two life-size images of Rose and William in their 1970s splendour.

'Aren't they great?' Angus asks, darting worried looks at me and jiggling from one foot to the other. 'What do you think?'

'I'm speechless.'

'I couldn't resist such a doll.'

'She does look fantastic,' I agree.

'I meant the guy, sweetie,' Angus says in a put-on camp voice gazing up at the poster. 'Come on, Lorrie, he's irresistible, don't you think? Those wicked eyes, that charming smile.'

'He's fifty-two now, Angus.'

'But he's the kind to age well. Has he aged well, darling? Please tell me he has.'

'Well,' I say, 'I'll bring him in to see if he's OK about these being on display. Then you'll be able to judge for yourself.'

Angus looks alarmed. 'Do you think he'll object? God,' he says, 'I do hope not. I've grown fond of this pair already and all my customers like them. I was hoping to use the image for my business cards, too.'

'Well, don't do anything yet,' I warn him. 'Seriously, Angus, you're supposed to have permission for this kind of thing.'

Angus drops his head. I pat his shoulder and he looks up at me, all puppy-dog pleading eyes.

'Save it for William,' I grin. 'He's the one you'll have to persuade.'

'Bring him to me soon, darling,' Angus calls from the doorway, hamming up a toodle-oo wave. 'Don't make me wait too long.'

'Just wondering if we're still on for this evening?' Mum's voice is tentative. 'As I hadn't heard from you.'

'Yeah, of course,' I say, checking my watch. Shit. It's half past seven and I've just stuffed down the biggest bowl of pasta ever, having completely forgotten we were supposed to be meeting Mum and David tonight at a restaurant in Rottingdean. 'Sorry, I meant to ring.'

I can't even remember whether I'd told Adam about it.

'Uh, no,' he says when I go to find him.

'I'm sure I did.'

'Well, even if you did, you should have reminded me – I've planned work for tonight.'

'Can't you take a break just for one evening? One bloody evening.'

He fingers the plans as if the mere thought of having to leave them for a few hours breaks his heart.

'Forget it. I'll tell them you're too busy,' I say, heading into the bedroom.

'No, it's OK.' Adam follows me. 'I think I'll be able to get done what I need to, if I fit an hour or so of work in afterwards.' He turns a face towards me which says: Aren't I good and clever?

I'd like to tell him that he isn't doing me any great favour but instead I squeeze out a 'thanks' and tell myself off for being so childish.

But halfway into the evening, I regret ever asking him. He's hogged the floor completely so far with the Stately Home Project; no other subject has had a look-in. On and on he goes – renovation this, restoration that. David and Mum politely ask lots of questions, but even their interest must be beginning to wane. Whenever they bring up anything to do with the TV programme, Adam says, 'Sorry, I'm not at liberty to answer that.' And they all giggle as if he's some kind of comedian.

David is very attentive to Mum. For the first time I notice a similarity in their appearance. Both have precise features, slender bodies; there is nothing round, or chubby or overly large about them. They are neat people. If it wasn't for my hair, I could be classed as a neat person these days, too.

I look past them. I watch the drama of a waitress flouncing away from the kitchen, head held high; I watch a couple in the corner jabbing accusatory fingers at each other across the table before the man suddenly reaches out and touches the woman's face, and she puts her hand over his, presses it to her cheek.

'Laura?' Mum says.

'Babe?' Ad says.

'Sorry, did I miss something? I was a million miles away.'

David is holding his glass up. 'Here's to a successful bid,' he says.

'Thanks, yeah, cool,' Adam says, shrugging and going all coy as if he's just realized that he's in the limelight. But he can't leave it at that. 'It's huge. It really is huge,' he says, shaking his head. 'I'll be tied up with it for years – at least three years for the restoration and then there'll be the maintenance afterwards, of course.'

I stare at Adam; he's never mentioned three years before.

'We're not even going to have a chance for a holiday this year, are we, babe?' Adam says.

'I thought we were going to go to Cyprus,' I say. With William's help I've whittled the choice down to three hotels; all Adam has to do is point at the one he prefers the look of.

'Not this year. Maybe next. We'll see.'

I look down, I fidget with the serviette and when I next glance up, Adam is already chatting away to David. I feel the light pressure of Mum's hand on mine.

'I'm just popping to the Ladies,' she says quietly and we get up together.

Once we're alone, Mum turns to me and says, 'Adam looks tired.'

I think, What about me?

She studies me. 'This garden seems very important to him,' she says slowly.

'I should be more understanding,' I state, hearing my own flat tone. I don't want to behave like a sulky child but I can't help feeling that something's not fair at the moment. What do *I* get out of this project except a lot of time on my own?

'There'll be other years for a holiday. But for Adam—'

'Adam, Adam, Adam,' I say, my voice rising, and despite Mum's look of disapproval, I can't help uttering the pathetic phrase I'd thought earlier. 'What about *me*?'

20

For the first time this year, the furniture has been set up outside Alessandro's although there's only one table out there being occupied at the moment: a couple of young women in winter coats and scarves are smoking, keeping their bare hands warm on steaming mugs.

I love people-watching from here. Soon it will be summer and it's not hard to picture the tables lively with colour and chat. That's what keeps us all going at this time of year, I think, imagining that collective sigh of relief as we relax, intoxicated with the sun.

I think I actually did sigh because Nat is peering at me.

'I get the feeling that you've something on your mind,' she says.

I fiddle with my spoon, twizzling it as I turn over words in my head.

'Adam and I can't go two minutes without arguing,' I tell her eventually. 'Each time we do, I promise myself that I won't allow it to happen again, but then five minutes later, he says or does something that completely winds me up, or

I piss him off and snap! In a second we're at each other's throats.'

'Have you talked about it?'

'We never talk; we haven't got time to talk. It's this project of his, morning noon and bloody night.'

Nat looks at me but she doesn't speak.

'Do you know what? I'm such a cow that sometimes I find myself wishing they won't win the bloody tender, even though I know how badly he wants it.'

'But the point is, you don't really mean it. It's only because you're fed-up.'

'I'm lonely,' I say, and tears bite at my eyes. I blink rapidly and force myself to look out of the window. A woman in very high boots walks past, chatting away on her mobile phone.

'Oh, Laura, sweetie.'

'I miss Rose, I miss my mum — I'm glad she's happy with David, I really am, but it's not the same any more. I even feel put out that Debs isn't bugging me all the time like she usually does. But most of all I miss Adam. I know it's stupid but he's hardly there these days, and when he is, he's too busy to even look at me. Sometimes I want to sweep all the books and papers off the table and jump up and down on it shouting, "I'm over here!"' I bounce up and down in my chair and wave.

Natalie laughs.

I lean back in my chair.

'Can I ask you something?' Nat says, and then shakes her head. 'No, forget it. It doesn't matter.'

'What? Come on, you can't leave it there now.'

'I was wondering if you and Adam sleep together much. You know — make love.'

I look at her in surprise. 'Nat! That's a Debs kind of question.'

'You made me ask,' she says, and for the first time ever, she blushes. 'It's this theory I have, that's all. I read about it once and then from listening and watching my customers, it all seemed to make sense.'

'What theory?'

'Sexual estrangement.'

I have to giggle.

'It's a vicious circle thing. You argue so you don't have sex, then you feel even more alienated from each other, so you argue even more. You have to break the cycle – you have to make love – even if it's the last thing *on earth* you feel like doing – to experience that intimacy, to remember who and what you are together.'

'Oh,' I say, and this time it's my turn to redden. 'I guess we – um – don't really do it much any more. He's always covered in a layer of sketches these days,' I add, making an attempt at a joke. 'I can never find him.'

'You should try it,' Nat says, looking pleased with herself and nodding as if she's some wise old bird. 'Seduce the man. God knows, it shouldn't be hard with Adam; he's got a lovely, lovely body.'

'Hey! You're not supposed to say that.'

'Well, it's true,' she says seriously. 'And the fact that you're jealous about him is an encouraging sign.'

'Are you coming to bed?'

'I've got to finish this,' Adam says.

'Will it take long?'

Adam looks up, considers me. 'I don't think so,' he says cautiously. 'Half an hour, maybe.'

'See you in bed, then.'

'Yeah, OK.'

He's got my drift, I'm sure of it. The way he reacted made me feel as if my motives were transparently naughty. Good old Nat, I think as I undress and put on my lacy pink and cream underwear that always gets Adam going.

I try lying on top of the duvet cover but I'm too cold so I get under; it'll be a nice surprise for Ad to discover when he joins me.

Ten minutes go by, then another ten. I listen for sounds of Adam locking up for the night. I check the alarm clock. Another twenty minutes pass and I still can't hear anything. Humiliation flushes through me – I feel like a tart that nobody wants to buy a trick from. I take my underwear off, shove it in a tight ball, out of sight under the bed.

I wake again after three. Adam isn't beside me and I know immediately that he never came to bed. I get up quietly, pull on a T-shirt.

Adam is asleep where I left him.

I shake him awake.

He jerks upright, startled.

'Come to bed.'

He groans, rubs his face and I return to the bedroom.

The next morning, Adam comes into the kitchen.

'About last night,' he begins.

I turn expectantly, my heart softening as I anticipate him apologizing for his failure to come and take advantage of me. I look at his eyes shrunken with tiredness, his face still creased, yet to smooth out to its daytime self, and I think of how I'll respond. 'Don't worry,' I'll say, 'there's always tonight.'

But Adam isn't apologetic at all. He's annoyed, grumpy with lack of sleep.

'You shouldn't have woken me. I hardly got a wink for the rest of the night.'

'Sorry,' I mutter. 'Next time I won't bother.' And I leave the room because I don't even want to know what he's going to say next.

I finally manage to pin Debs down to getting together one lunchtime, although she insists she can only spare half an hour.

For some reason she's gone overboard on her make-up, and instead of masking how tired and ill she looks, it draws attention to the fact. She's behaving oddly, too. She seems hyper, almost hysterical. She keeps clowning around, talking loudly and falsely like someone on stage; almost as if she thinks she's being watched, but the bar is virtually empty. There is only us two and an elderly couple on the other side of the room.

'So what have you been up to then?' I ask her. 'I haven't heard from you in ages.'

'The usual,' she tells me.

'Like?'

'Like the usual,' she snaps. 'Christ, Loz, what is this? A fucking interrogation.'

I stare at her. 'Paul saw you the other day,' I say.

'Paul?'

'Aussie Paul,' I remind her. 'Said you were with some drop-dead gorgeous man.'

Debs brightens. 'Oh yeah, I'd forgotten about that. I was with Andrew.'

'So when am I going to meet this god?' I ask. 'Or are you trying to keep him all to yourself?'

Debs frowns. 'It's hard to arrange anything; he's always very busy.'

'But you're getting on OK?'

'We get on fine.' She makes an exasperated noise and looks challengingly at me. 'We're just not into making a big fuss analysing our every feeling, you know. It's all about enjoying each other's company whenever it suits us both.'

'Paul said you looked love-struck,' I say and instantly regret it. Debbie's face drops, then hardens.

'Paul this, Paul that,' she says. 'Tell me, what does Adam think of you going round with Paul all the time?'

'I only bumped into him in town once and we went for a drink.'

Debs purses her lips as if she's thinking. 'He's not bad though, is he? Grown up rather well, in fact. Better than that gawky teenager he used to be.'

'I don't remember him being gawky.'

Debs scoffs. 'Oh, come on, Loz. He was well gangly — all elbows and size hundred feet.'

I laugh though I shouldn't really. 'He's gone back now,' I tell her. 'To Oz. For good.'

'So, what does Adam think? Is he jealous?'

'I don't think I mentioned it, actually.' Debs has her beady eye focused on me. I shrug. 'Adam's too preoccupied these days for me to talk to him about anything.'

'That's *exactly* why you should make a point of telling him,' Debs says. 'Stir him up a bit.'

'Don't be silly. Besides, I'm not playing games like that. I don't think it's nice or fair.'

'He's taking you for granted, Loz – I warned you he would.'

21

William's *Secret Brighton* assignment has been taking him every-where.

'It's been an eye-opener,' he says, showing me some of his work.

There are photographs of a grotto decorated with scallops and oysters which can be found on the Smugglers' Trail near Hove, there's an ancient yew tree, its trunk grown open wide enough to house a love-seat, there's a museum dedicated to buttons where the walls of one room are covered in thou-sands of individual buttons; it must have taken ages to stick them all on.

William pushes the photographs away from him across the coffee-table as if he's disgusted. 'They just seem flat to me, life-less somehow.' He shoves back his chair and strides across the room. He takes a framed landscape photograph off the wall.

'I won an award for this,' he says, holding it in front of him. 'But it's only because Rosie and I loved the place so much that I pulled it off. We were happy there, we got drunk on the local moonshine, we swam naked in the cove at midnight. It may sound ridiculous, but I think I captured those emotions in the photograph and it's that which appeals to people when they look at it; that which draws them in.'

He carefully re-hangs the picture, returns to the sofa and begins to gather the photos together. 'I hadn't realized the importance of sharing my experiences.'

'Perhaps . . .' I take a breath. 'Perhaps I could come along some time. I know I'm not like Rose or anything,' I add hurriedly, 'but maybe it would help having someone else there.'

When William doesn't immediately respond to my offer but continues to pile up the photographs, I regret having spoken. I'm even considering leaving the room, when he speaks.

'Would you?' he asks softly. 'I'd like that.'

His eyes are filmy with tears and I'd like to give him a big hug but I think action is called for so I leap up.

'How about today? Right now? I haven't got a single appointment this afternoon and with Ad being so tied up in the evenings, I'm even miles ahead with paperwork.'

'Well,' William says. 'Why not?'

'Have you got somewhere in mind?' I ask as William locks the front door.

'Not really, no,' he says. 'I'd planned on a reconnoitre and was hoping inspiration would follow.'

'I know a place that might interest you.'

In the afternoon light, the leaves of the holly tree in the Monkey Garden have a blue-green hue; clumps of snowdrops burst white from the dark soil, their fragile heads belying their spring toughness.

We sit on the bench and I try to attune my ears so I can

identify the noise I'm hearing. It takes me a few moments to realize that it's the opposite — it's silence. Sheltered from the squally wind, the constant buzzing in my ears has ceased.

It isn't long before William starts noticing the monkeys.

'Look,' he says, pointing. Then he spots another and another. His face is a reminder of the same amused delight that I felt when I first discovered the park.

He starts laughing. 'Look at that one.'

It's one of my favourites — a pouchy-cheeked monkey who looks as if he's been caught red-handed with his face stuffed with food.

'This place is crazy — remarkable.'

'I call it the Monkey Garden. I've no idea of its real name.'

William takes his camera out of the case, begins fixing on the lens.

'I don't know if it's well-known or not,' I tell him. 'But I've never yet seen anyone else here.'

He lowers the camera. 'In that case, are you sure you want to risk making it more popular? I sometimes have my concerns that what I'm doing might end up spoiling the very appeal, the essence of these places.'

We both look around. The houses that surround the park have always looked grand and expensively maintained to me, but they also seem to have an unlived-in, almost unloved air, as if they're not real homes — as if they're second homes perhaps, or the occasional residences of visiting ex-pats like William.

'It's probably only coincidental that I've always been here alone.'

William has the same intense, almost secretive pleasure on

his face that I recognize from watching Adam at work; but his physical demeanour is much brisker, more purposeful than usual.

William returns to the bench. 'Thanks for bringing me here, Laura.'

'Actually, it's been nice sharing it with someone else. The world can seem rather surreal when I'm out running; afterwards I sometimes wonder if the things and places I've seen really exist.'

I rub my hands together, only now noticing the cold. William's nose is red over the top of his scarf. A drop of water sparkles at the end of it which he doesn't notice.

'Beer time?' I suggest.

'You're on.'

On the way back from the pub, I take William to Angus's shop. He laughs loudly when he sees the posters while Angus stands anxiously by.

'You hate them, don't you? Oh my God, you hate them.'

William puts a hand on Angus's shoulder. 'No. I'm flattered, really. I just never for a minute imagined that Rosie and I would be fashion icons.'

'Oh, thank the Lord,' Angus says, rushing headlong into high camp, lowering himself onto a chair and fanning his face with his hand. 'Does this mean that I can keep them up?'

'I'd be honoured, but,' William turns to me, 'just don't let Alex hear about this.'

As we're leaving, Angus pulls me back and whispers urgently in my ear. 'Gorgeous and charming,' he says, squeezing my arm. 'You lucky, lucky girl.'

Before I can protest, Angus pushes me out of the shop

towards William, and when I turn back, he winks at me and waves before closing the door.

'William and I went out today,' I find myself saying to Adam that evening for all the wrong reasons. 'We had a drink in the Black Swan.'

I wait. I wait for Adam to ask, 'What were you doing with William? Why weren't you working?' But of course, he doesn't. He continues with what he's doing without a shred of interest in my day.

'Oh yeah?' he says after a considerable pause. 'Nice pub that.'

Perhaps Debs is right. Perhaps for Adam I've simply become part of the furniture. I quiver with anger at his silence.

'We never do anything any more,' I say suddenly, surprising myself.

Adam's head jerks up. 'Right,' he says, slamming down his pen and throwing the papers aside. 'I'm sick of hearing this.' He marches out into the hall, returns and flings my coat and trainers towards me. 'Come on then.'

'I don't—'

'Don't you dare say no,' he warns me before leaving the room. 'It isn't a fucking option.'

We stand face to face in the hallway. I'm trembling. Adam's face is set rigid.

'Where are we going?' I ask.

'Wherever you want; it's you who's so keen to go out.' He folds his arms. 'So?'

'I don't know.'

'Oh, for fuck's sake.'

'I wasn't prepared,' I say. My voice sounds squeaky. 'Because normally I can't get you even to notice me, never mind go out with me.'

'For God's sake, Laura, you're behaving like a child.'

'Oh, fuck you!' I storm into the bedroom. I pull my coat off, throw it down, tug my trainers off and launch them across the room before sinking on the bed.

Early the next morning, when I go running I discover that spring has arrived.

It's as if someone went round the city last night slitting the earth open like an overstuffed cushion and all this yellow filling has spilled out. Roundabouts are cloaked in daffodils, verges are fringed by them, troughs and planters are brimming with them.

There must be thousands of flowers. I think of all those bulbs lying dormant all year round, waiting for their short moment of glory.

There's a sudden downpour. Cars hiss past me, whooshing through the water lying on the road. I keep to the far edge of the pavement but a BMW cuts in tight to the kerb and I get covered in shitty dirty water from the waist down.

'Wanker!' I shout after it, but the man drives on, heedless.

22

I don't intend to mention my birthday to William but it comes out during our mid-morning coffee break in the kitchen. The day so far has been a complete non-event: the post won't have arrived until after I left the flat, not a single person has phoned, texted or emailed me, and this morning Adam kissed me briefly, said, 'Happy birthday, babe,' shoved a card at me and headed off to work before I'd even had time to open it.

He'd written *love and stuff, Ad* as if we were teenagers rather than lovers in a serious relationship.

'Laura, why didn't you tell me? I'd have liked to have got you something.' The disappointment shows on William's face.

'It doesn't matter,' I rush to tell him. 'Birthdays are for kids, aren't they? Like Christmas. It's not so important when you get older.'

'Now listen,' William says, tapping me on the wrist. 'I don't think so, and I don't think you should believe that either. Rosie and I always made a big fuss,' he says. 'We'd dress up, have lots of friends round, drink too much . . .' He stops talking suddenly. 'Sorry,' he says. 'I'm always blethering on about "Rosie and I this" and "Rosie and I that"; I'm beginning to sound like some old sod spouting tales from his armchair at anyone who shows the least bit of interest.'

'I love hearing your stories,' I say immediately. 'Really, I do.'

William smiles and shakes his head. 'So, tell me. What are your plans for this evening?'

I shrug. 'Nothing much. Adam's got a meeting which he says is impossible to get out of.'

'That's a shame.'

'We'll probably do something at the weekend instead,' I tell him hurriedly, even though Adam hasn't mentioned anything as such.

At five, as I'm packing up for the day, William knocks at my door.

'Would you mind popping into the kitchen before you leave?' he asks, and disappears before I've had a chance to reply.

My heart sinks. It's about my birthday, I'm sure of it. William's been unusually absent for the whole of the afternoon and now I could kick myself for bringing it up. It'll be awkward and embarrassing. I feel my face setting into a false smile of thanks just at the thought.

William is lurking outside the kitchen; he ushers me inside.

On the table there's a vase of sunflowers, the heads sagging forward with the weight of their heavy, brown fuzzy-fur centres. There's a bottle of wine and two strawberry French pastries, one with a candle lopsidedly stuck in the fondant topping.

'Sit down, sit down,' he orders, pulling out a chair. He ceremoniously places a large envelope in front of me. I open it — it's a photograph of the Monkey Garden mounted on card.

It captures the atmosphere perfectly. At the heart of the picture, the ghostly snowdrops phosphoresce in near-black soil at the foot of the ancient holly tree. The orang-utan shines silky smooth. As if I'm actually in the park, I begin by spotting first one monkey peeping out at me, then another, then another.

'Came out pretty well, don't you think?'

'It's beautiful.' I lean across, kiss him on the cheek. 'Thank you so much.'

'I'll get the wine flowing.' William expertly uncorks the bottle and pours two large glasses.

The wine tastes fruity and clean.

'I haven't had a surprise for my birthday for a long time.'

'I'm glad you were OK about that,' William says. 'Not everybody likes surprises.'

'Rose did, didn't she?'

'She claimed not to – she said it was a wasted opportunity to buy a new outfit but of course, really, she adored being the centre of attention.'

The following silence conjures up Rose's absence more than any words.

'Do you ever go up to her room?' I ask. It must be the wine giving me the nerve; after only a couple of sips I'd felt it going straight to my head.

'No. I couldn't even face clearing it,' he says. 'Ben did that.'

'I do. I should have asked if it was OK. Do you mind? I'll stop if you do. Please tell me.' The alcohol has pinked my cheeks; my lips are sticky from the cake. I lick them quickly.

'What do you do up there?'

'Think,' I tell him. 'Sit and watch the world go by. Sometimes I remember stuff we used to talk about. Sometimes,' I glance away, then back at William, hold his gaze. 'Sometimes I ask her advice or her opinion.'

William smiles. 'Rosie was never shy about giving either of those. Does it help?'

I nod. 'Usually. I feel calmer, clearer about whatever's going on.'

He hesitates. 'I'm glad.'

I'm overheating; I press the cool wine glass to my burning face.

'God,' William says, jumping up. 'I forgot I'd cranked the boiler on to max. No wonder we're frying.' He opens the back door and there's a rush of sweet, damp air from the garden.

'I don't want you to think I go nosing all around your house while you're out,' I say.

'I'd never think you'd do anything like that, Laura.' He speaks so quietly I find myself leaning in to hear better. He looks hard at me for a moment before suddenly sitting up straight.

He picks up the bottle. 'We're being far too serious, and one thing I do know is that birthdays aren't meant to be serious.'

I've drunk too much to drive so I take a taxi home.

I turn my mobile back on, hoping that someone will have sent birthday wishes, and there's an immediate flurry of beeps and buzzes as a stack of voice and text messages pile in. I catch the eye of the taxi driver in the rear-view mirror and grin foolishly when he winks and says: 'Someone's popular.'

All the texts are from Ad. They don't say much, just: *where r u?* and *pls call immed* and *r u ok?*

There's a cheerful 'Happy birthday, love' voicemail from Mum and one from Adam saying, 'Hi, babe, I'm at home, just wondering where you are and what time you'll be back. Give me a call, babe. Speak to you later.'

There's something odd about Adam's voice – it rings false despite how casual he sounds; it's as if he's *trying* to sound normal. I look at my watch; it's gone ten. Adam wasn't supposed to be back until late and yet the time of that message is seven o'clock.

Alcohol sloshes from side to side in my stomach as panic rises. I look out of the window – I'm only a few minutes away from the flat – I stare at the mobile lying in my sweaty hand. I don't want to ring Adam. I know something's happened. I'll be home soon; where I will see for myself.

Every traffic light is against us. Every minute is elongated. I resist the urge to get out and start running.

I burst into the lounge. Adam scrambles up from the sofa and stands blearily in front of me.

'What is it?' I ask him. 'What's happened?'

'It was supposed to be a surprise,' Adam says flatly, rubbing the side of his face.

It's only then that I register the room: candles, burned low, sit on every surface, the coffee-table has been cleared of all paperwork and laid out like a restaurant table with a cloth, place settings and a champagne bucket in the middle.

'Oh God, Ad. I'm so, so sorry. I thought you had a meeting.'

'I lied,' he says. 'Rather too convincingly, evidently.'

I reach out towards him as he turns, but he doesn't notice; he walks away from my outstretched hand.

'We could have the champagne,' I suggest, following him into the kitchen. 'Take it to bed.'

'It'll be warm now. Besides, I've got to get up early tomorrow.'

Adam's opened the back door. He's leaning against the frame smoking a cigarette; wisps of smoke drift inside, over his head. The smell reaches me by the sink as I run the tap for a glass of water.

'I'm really sorry. I never for one moment imagined you'd do this.'

Adam doesn't reply. There's a weird uneasiness in the air. I sense that Ad isn't just upset about me coming home late. I shiver; the heat from the alcohol has dissipated, leaving me clammy-cold and tired.

'Debs came over,' he says. 'She left you a card and present.'

'Cool,' I say. 'Did she say anything?'

Adam twists round. 'Like what?' he asks sharply.

'I haven't seen much of her lately,' I explain. 'I thought she might have bored you with the latest gossip.'

'Not really.' He flicks the cigarette butt outside, blows the smoke into the garden, over his shoulder.

I have a clear image of poor Adam, desperately trying to get rid of Debs before she scented something was up, before she saw the living room all done out and me absent. Before she got the chance to rub his nose in it.

'Who's Paul?' Adam asks suddenly.

'Paul?'

'Debs asked if you were out with Paul.' He crosses his arms trying to look angry but I can tell that he's worried. 'And I'm just wondering who he is, seeing as you've never mentioned him before.'

'Oh, Ad,' I say, stepping towards him. 'It's OK. Paul is a childhood friend, he's Mum's old neighbour's youngest son, back from Australia for a few months. I saw him when I was over there, packing up my office. He isn't even in the country any more – it's only Debs causing trouble.'

'He's in Oz?' Adam looks puzzled.

'Yes.'

'She told me you'd been out with him the other day,' he says, and his voice breaks a little at the end.

'I bumped into him in town one lunchtime a couple of weeks ago; we had a quick drink, that's all.'

'Do you fancy him?'

'No!'

'Does he fancy you?'

'I don't know. No. Possibly. What does it matter even if he did? He's on the other side of the world, Ad.' I take a deep breath. 'We talked about Debs mainly, in fact. He used to go out with her – one of her old victims. We talked about school, being young. That's all.'

'Why didn't you tell me about him before?'

'I don't know. You were too busy or something.' I throw the accusation out and instantly regret it. 'Sorry,' I say, putting my hand on his arm. He stiffens. 'The moment passed and then I didn't think of it; it didn't seem important.'

I slide my arms around his waist; tuck my hands into the back pockets of his jeans so that he has to press close to me. 'Debs wanted to get you worried, to make you jealous, Ad. I wouldn't do that to you, you know that.'

He grimaces. 'I knew it was that cow making trouble really but I couldn't stop thinking about it when you didn't come home, when you didn't answer your phone. I was imagining all sorts of shit.' He pulls me tight.

'I'm sorry to have spoiled the evening you planned. I stayed at William's,' I tell him hurriedly. 'He gave me a little party, because I told him you were working late.'

'At least you had a nice time. At least one of us had a nice time.'

'It was very sweet of him,' I say.

'Let's look at the sky,' Adam suggests after a moment. It's something we often like to do. We turn round, lean against each other without speaking. There are thousands and thousands of stars. The screech of a vixen makes us both jump. We laugh and our breath comes out as opaque puffs. Adam pulls me closer.

Debs is on the phone first thing the next morning.

''Fess up,' she says immediately. 'What happened to you yesterday?'

'Oh, hi Debs. Thanks for dropping me in it.'

'Why? What *did* you get up to?' There's an undisguised eagerness in her voice.

'Nothing,' I tell her and I try to sound stern. 'And you know it. But Adam was really upset.'

'Great,' she says, undeterred. 'Mission accomplished.'

'Debs, this isn't a game.'

'Oh, come on, Loz. He needed a kick up the pants, the way he's been treating you lately. And I bet one thing: I bet you made mad, passionate love all night.'

My moment's hesitation is enough to convince her.

'You did,' she crows. 'You did. You can thank me later.'

'I'm not thanking you for anything,' I tell her, but the truth is, last night we had made love and for the first time in ages,

I'd felt like we really connected. 'I know you meant well, but it could easily have gone disastrously wrong.'

There's no response from Debs so I continue talking into the silence. 'All I'm saying is, please don't try that kind of thing again.'

'Whatever you say.' She gives an exaggerated sigh. 'Where were you then? With your mum? Nat?'

'No.'

'You weren't really with Paul, were you?' Her interest immediately flares.

'I told you he's gone back to Oz.'

'Oh yeah, I remember now.'

'I was at William's.'

'William?' Debs repeats, disappointment ripe in her voice. 'God, for a moment there, I thought you'd finally gone and done something exciting.'

23

Alessandro's has been really busy today, Nat said as she flopped down opposite me, leaving Becky to carry on cleaning the machines. Every now and then we have to raise our voices as a roar or hiss interrupts the flow of our conversation.

'At this rate, I'm going to have to think about employing more staff before the summer season.' Nat sighs. There's a smudge of tiredness under her eyes. 'I hope I get another Becky.'

Nat's summer staff are often a source of amusement, despair or frustration. Some of them are disastrous; one repeatedly failed to fill the espresso machine with water and burned the motor out; another had an eating disorder and couldn't resist the cakes left at the end of the day. Nat sacked them both with barely a blink of an eye. 'I can't afford to be soft,' she said.

'Now where were we?' she asks me.

'Debs,' I say, resuming our earlier conversation. 'I was saying it was lucky for her that it turned out OK in the end. If Paul hadn't moved back to Oz, Ad might have taken a lot more persuading.'

Nat emits a tiny snort of disbelief. 'I'm not convinced she didn't know exactly what she was doing.'

I shake my head. 'She's been going on at me for ages about making Adam jealous; she just seized the opportunity without thinking it through as usual.'

'Then how do you explain the other Adam episode?'

'What other Adam episode?'

Nat looks stricken. Her mouth is a big 'o' of horror. I feel sick. Not my Adam, I think. Not my Adam.

'Oh God, forget it,' she says, pressing her fingers into her forehead. 'Forget I ever said that.'

'I can't,' I whisper. 'You know you have to tell me now.'

'I'm sorry, Laura,' she says. 'I swear I've been spending so much time here that my brains have turned into cappuccino froth.' She reaches out, touches my hand. 'Don't look so worried – Adam's done nothing wrong. He came to see me for advice, that's all.'

'What about?' I ask slowly.

Nat's hair hangs down, framing her face as she fiddles with her cup. 'I feel terrible. It was supposed to be a secret, but you might as well know, now I've let the cat out of the bag.'

I nod because I can't speak.

'Debbie turned up one evening at your flat, saying she was looking for you.' Nat's tone is soft at first, then harsher as she gathers momentum. 'She came on to him, and when he didn't respond, she told him she'd tell you he'd tried it on with her.' She finishes with a gasp as if she's shocked. As if there's something to be shocked about.

I hear the click and gulp in my throat as I try and force away the dryness. My voice sounds as if it's miles away. 'But she doesn't even like Adam; she says he's boring.'

'Did she ever really like Peter, or does she just need to have whatever you've got?' Nat retorts, and immediately follows it up with an apology. 'Look, I'm making it sound much more serious than it was,' she says. 'It was only because Adam was worried about your reaction – after what happened with Peter – that he needed to talk to someone about how to handle it.'

I watch my hands trembling on the table in front of me as if they don't belong to my body. When I lift them to place them in my lap out of sight, they feel heavy and numb as if I'm suffering from a severe case of pins and needles. I wonder why Adam couldn't have talked to me.

Nat continues, 'We both decided it was better if he kept quiet because nothing had happened, Laura – absolutely nothing on Adam's part, and although Debs is a devious little cow, we agreed that she was probably only calling his bluff.'

'His bluff?'

'Yes. Which is why I think she behaved like that with Adam on your birthday: she acted out of spite to get back at him.'

I'm trying to let Nat's words sink in, but before I can hold on to them, Becky calls out to Nat and breaks my train of thought.

Nat twists round to talk to Becky and I let my attention slide away across the room. I wonder where they sat, Adam and Nat, when they were discussing all this. Did Ad have coffee? Did he eat some of Nat's cake while they talked about me?

'When did this happen?' I ask her, when she turns back.

'A while ago. You were out running, I think.'

'I'm always out running.'

Nat thinks for a moment. 'Some time last summer because it was hot and I'd been really busy.'

'Last *summer*!' I find it hard to believe that Adam could have kept the whole thing quiet all that time.

'It definitely was then,' Nat says, 'because he turned up when I was closing and fixed the ice-cream machine for me which had just died.'

'He's good at fixing things,' I say automatically.

'He loves you so much, that man,' Nat says. 'The way he talked about you, it was special, you know?'

I try to nod.

'You won't say anything to him, will you?'

'I don't know.'

'I think it's best to leave it, now that nothing's happened.'

'I suppose so.'

'There was nothing in it,' she says. 'At least, not as far as Adam's concerned.'

'I know that, it's just . . .'

As the car gets closer and closer to home, my shaking gets worse. It's so bad it feels as if the steering wheel's vibrating in my hands.

'Calm down,' I tell myself. 'Don't be so stupid. Calm down, everything's going to be fine.' I repeat it out loud, over and over again.

I reach our street and pull up against the kerb. I breathe in deeply, count to ten before I look.

Adam's van is there, which means he must be home, but the flat is in darkness. The window in the flat above is black too; the gold orb of the streetlight is reflected in the blank pane.

I hold onto the front door until I hear the click as it settles into the frame. I stand absolutely still and listen. Under the silence I hear a murmuring coming from the lounge. Adam's dead to the world; flat out on the sofa, illuminated by the TV's blue haze.

I get changed, make a cup of tea and sit on the two-seater opposite. The TV is on too low to make proper sense of the words.

I watch Adam.

Usually his feelings are written all over his face, so how can I have missed that he was keeping such a secret from me? I look closer. He suddenly seems appallingly self-contained.

My eye is drawn to Adam's crotch where one hand has strayed. I fight to control the images in my head. I don't want to imagine Adam's thick, erect penis advancing towards Debs, towards anyone else but me.

I focus hard on the TV. I switch to a news channel where I watch a journalist mouthing words while in the background smoke pours from a bombed-out car and people dash to and fro.

Adam groans and pushes himself upright. 'How long have you been back?' His voice is husky from sleep. He scrubs at his hair, making it stick out at all angles. He looks like a big kid.

'Not long. Half an hour or so.'

He stands up, switches the light on. We squint at each other, wincing from the brightness. I don't follow him into the kitchen. Let him have his cigarette, I think, before I talk to him. Give him a few minutes to come round. I feel strangely calm, and adult-like in my approach.

Adam appears suddenly in the doorway. 'Fancy a stir-fry tonight?'

'Yeah, great,' I reply, although we've eaten the same meal twice this week already. He disappears almost immediately. I carry on sitting there. Adam marches back in.

'We're out of bloody noodles,' he says, dropping to the settee. 'Any other suggestions?'

I remember now that I'd said I would pick up some shopping on the way home. I shrug.

'Are you all right?' he asks, staring at me in an accusatory way.

'Yeah, why?'

'You're behaving like a fucking zombie, that's why,' he says, launching himself up again.

My mobile starts ringing in my bag in the hallway. I don't move. Ad comes back, clutching the phone. He hands it to me.

'It's your friend and mine.'

I stare down at Debs's name.

'Aren't you going to answer? You were only moaning the other day about her never being in touch.'

My face is burning up. 'I don't feel like talking to her right now.'

'Can't say as I blame you,' he says, before leaving the room.

24

One evening, Adam suggests we go out for a walk. Without discussing our route, we make our way down to the beach.

'We haven't been here for a while,' Adam says, echoing my own thoughts. In the first months when we were going out, we'd walk for hours talking, talking, talking – and somehow always end up here.

This time, with our hands stuffed in our pockets, we exchanged barely a word the whole way.

The sea is a slick black, with only the occasional thin frill of white disturbing its uniformity. The pebbles hiss as the waves touch the shore. It sounds sinister, as if it's waiting for a victim.

To our left, the pier is lit up, and all along the front, neon signs flash on and off: *Hot Dogs, Fish 'n' Chips, Amusements*.

'Why didn't you tell me about Debs?' I ask Adam.

There. It's asked. The question I've been holding on to for over a week.

'What about her?' he says, half-listening; neck bent as he concentrates on rolling a cigarette.

'That she tried it on with you.' My voice wobbles. I keep my shaking hands deep down in my pockets and play with a thread my fingers have discovered there.

He's slow to react; he's just licked the Rizla paper and his mouth is still hanging open when he turns towards me.

'What?' he drawls before my question hits home, then he straightens up. His whole body tenses. 'What's that cow been saying now?'

'Nothing. I heard about it from Nat.'

'Great,' he says. 'I thought I could trust her.'

'It came up by accident.'

'Right,' he huffs. He cups his hand over the cigarette, his lighter flares. He takes a deep drag.

I don't like the concerned way he's looking at me, and it's only at this precise moment that I realize I'm very unhappy about him thinking the best way to protect me was by keeping me in the dark.

'Ad, I need to know what happened.'

He sighs. 'Debs came round, you weren't in, she started on some flirty shit and at first I thought she was just behaving oddly, like she might be drunk; then I got the message and asked her to leave.' He steps towards me, but I edge away.

'I need to know *everything*,' I tell him. 'I need to know all the details so I don't start filling in the gaps . . .'

'Laura, this is exactly why I didn't tell you. You're getting upset over nothing.'

I dig my feet down into the pebbles and face him. 'Please.'

Adam takes another drag. 'There's not much more to add,' he says. 'I opened the door and it was Debs. I said you were out running. I was cooking pasta and I had to rush back to the kitchen because I could hear the pan boiling over. She followed me in and said, "Do you always answer the door in your underwear?" or "half-naked" or something like that.'

'What?!'

'I'd just got my boxers on,' he explains.

'For God's sake, Ad.'

'Look, it was hot and I was hassled. I wasn't expecting anyone and I didn't know she was going to follow me inside, did I? She asked me how long you'd be. I said at least an hour because I didn't want her hanging around – and she goes, "What can we do to fill the time?" and I'm thinking *we're* not doing anything. And I turn round and she's right here, right up close.' He gestures with his hand. The red ember of his cigarette glows briefly an inch from his body then is gone. 'So, she reaches out, puts a finger on my chest, looks at me all googly-eyed and then I get it. So I step away and say, "I'll tell you how I'm going to spend the time – eating my dinner on my own watching TV, that's how. And I don't know what you're going to do, but it won't be here".' Adam looks at me. 'And that's it.'

'That's it?'

'Well, after that she acted all put-out, saying there was no need to be so defensive, it wasn't like she fancied me or anything, but then she went on about how easy it would be to tell you that I'd tried it on with her. She said she'd be particularly convincing now that she could describe my – er – underwear – in detail.' He pauses. 'It sounds stupid but I didn't know if she was joking or not. I can never tell with her, she's so bloody weird, so that's why I went to see Nat – to see what she thought about the whole thing.'

Adam blows a long streak of smoke over his shoulder away

from me. The wind sends it straight back, shrouding his face momentarily. 'So, babe? What do you make of it?'

'I don't know.'

'But you know you can trust me, don't you?' he asks. 'You know I'm not another Peter?'

I nod, but I keep thinking about Ad in his boxers and Debs up close to him, touching him.

'Is this why you've been acting strangely?' Adam asks suddenly.

'What do you mean?'

'You've been so jumpy and distant; I thought you must be getting your period.'

I scuffle some of the stones with the toe of my trainer. 'Why do blokes *always* presume that?'

Adam stands in front of me, legs wide, his hands held palm up in front of him. He's grinning. 'Well, I didn't have much else to go on, did I?' He throws his cigarette down and leaps forward, catching me as we stumble together on the uneven ground. Adam clutches me hard, pins me to him until we find our balance. My startled breathing whistles in my ears.

We make love that night. We kiss. Adam murmurs into my ear, his hands hot on my back. He holds my waist, lifts me over so that I'm sitting astride him. I push back, my hands on his chest. I push down. Adam groans and grips my waist again as I begin to move. I close my eyes because I don't want to look at him; something feels wrong about this but I don't want to stop. It seems important to continue.

Afterwards we lie face to face; our features are visible but distorted in the shadowy light.

'Anyway,' Adam says softly. 'She's not my type.'

'Who is?' I ask, knowing that whatever words he's about to choose, he'll mean me.

'Wild-haired sweet women, who are fanatics about running.' He fumbles for my hand.

'That's lucky.'

He squeezes my fingers. 'Isn't it?'

Later, Adam, heavy in sleep, has pinned me in an uncomfortable position. I don't want to disturb him so I lie there, wide-awake.

Months after I'd severed as many ties as I could with Peter – packed in my job where we both worked, moved back in with Mum, withdrew from contacting most of our mutual friends – I was still raw from the humiliation.

I felt dirty and stupid and ashamed.

But everybody told me that I needed to go out: Mum, Nat, even Debs dared to say it. It would do me good, they said, though it seemed to do the opposite because most nights I'd return and cry for hours in my room.

I hated myself. I hated the way I flirted with blokes but if any of them dared to make a pass, I'd run a mile. I could imagine what they thought of me: pricktease, frigid, although none of them were nasty enough to say it to my face. Some of them were really nice blokes and I wished I could behave differently but I couldn't imagine having sex with any of them, or with anyone ever again. I didn't even want to touch myself; I pushed all sexual urges down and away.

Then I met Adam at a party.

'I like your dress. It's different,' he said.

I was wearing one of my favourites – a 1970s dress that I'd bought from my new client, Angus – and four-inch stilettos.

Then Adam saw my face. 'Oh, have I said the wrong thing?'

'No, it's only . . .'

It was only that as he'd spoken he'd gently touched my shoulder, and instead of recoiling in alarm, my flesh had gone zing: immediate goosebumps all over, and all I could think was how much I wanted him to touch me again.

I think I gawped, but Adam says he doesn't remember it that way. He remembers me smiling – that's the first thing he liked about me, he always says: that I had an honest smile.

Ad stirs, slides away from me. Released, I shift across the bed, startled by cold on my skin. At first I think it's the sticky patch of semen but that's long since dried and it's just the coolness of the sheet.

We never make love when we're happy these days, I suddenly think; it's always after an argument or confrontation of some sort. I can't stop going over the last few weeks, to winkle out whether that's true – one, two, three occasions spring immediately forward.

So that's what was wrong.

25

'I hope this is important, Loz,' Debs says as she comes in. 'I may have given up the chance of an evening with Andrew to be here.'

'Won't he ring you?'

Debs shrugs. 'Nah, he just turns up. Spontaneity, Loz. Ever heard of that?'

But her eyes shift away as if she's hiding something. She's dressed up again as if she's ready to go out clubbing for the evening: her make-up is immaculate and she's wearing the skimp-iest of clothing. As she shrugs off her coat I notice how thin she is. Her collar-bone is so prominent, it looks as if it could pierce her skin.

'Ad told me,' I say. 'He told me about that time you came on to him.'

There's a split-second delay before Debs bursts out laughing. 'Oh Loz, you should have seen his face.' She can barely speak properly she's laughing so much. 'He was terrified – he looked like he was going to wet himself. I'm sorry, Loz,' she says, wiping away tears. Her mascara hasn't smudged one little bit – the stuff she uses must set like concrete. 'That's one hell of a drip you've got there, though nice bod, by the way – lucky you.'

She looks at me and her face instantly changes. A flush rises up her neck and disappears underneath the layer of make-up on her face.

'I promised you, Loz,' she says quietly. 'I made a promise I'd never do that to you again.'

'I – just – needed to . . .'

'I meant it.' Debbie's gaze is unflinching. 'Everything was different then – we were both different.'

I nod, nod, nod. Tears are gathering, spilling over. Debbie's face is a blur.

She sits next to me, rubs my back. 'You big baby,' she says. 'What's this really all about?'

But how can I explain to her? All I know is that I sense something is happening, and everything is changing, and I don't know what to do about it.

From the kitchen, I hear the impatient sound of cupboards and the fridge being rapidly opened before Adam reappears. We look at each other and chorus: 'Indian takeaway!'

When the delivery arrives I hoist myself off the settee into the kitchen. As I'm walking back with my over-full plate, sauce spills off the edge and onto my favourite T-shirt; the funky ice-blue one with an eyeball print.

'Oh, shit.' I point the mustard-coloured stain out to Adam. 'It's ruined,' I tell him.

'Shame,' he says. 'I always thought you looked pretty sexy in that one.'

'Not fucking helping, Adam.' Irritation spurts inside me. I

resist the urge to throw my food against the wall, to watch it splat on the white before sliding down in a greasy ochre lump.

Chomp, chomp, chomp. I keep on eating past the point of comfort, until my stomach feels bloated and heavy, like an appendage stuck to my body. I burp – a pungent, curry burp. I want to run. More than anything in the world. This morning's run seems like days ago. I need to feel my muscles stretching, to experience the sensation of movement but of course I can't do that now.

'You all right, babe?' Adam asks and I'm about to snap, to vent my disgust and anger on him when I realize how ridiculous I'm being.

'Fuck it, fuck it, fuck it.'

Adam throws the phone down. There's a thump as he flings the back door open so hard that it makes contact with the fridge behind it and sets the empty beer bottles on top rattling.

'Ad?'

He strides back and forwards on the patio, puffing frantically on a roll-up.

'What is it?'

Adam stops pacing. There are tears gathering in his eyes. My heart stops; I've never seen Adam cry. He fights it, sucking in air, grits his teeth.

'That was Matt,' he says, squashing the dog-end viciously under his foot. 'There's a problem with the fucking figures. The loan won't kick in immediately and we don't have enough capital to cover the first outlay before payment starts.'

'What does that mean?'

'It means that even if we got the fucking contract, we

couldn't afford to do it. What a waste of fucking effort. Shit.' He sways from side to side, his hands clenched as if he's looking for something to punch. I step back and he resumes his pacing.

'I'm sorry,' I say.

His head jerks up. 'Funny,' he says, his voice loaded with sarcasm. 'Because I thought you'd be pleased. Isn't this what you wanted?'

'That's not fair.'

'Oh, forget it.' He pushes past me into the house. 'I'm going for a beer.'

I get quietly out of bed when it's light enough for me to see what I'm doing. I don't want to wake Adam. I was half-asleep when he made it home, but I know it was late.

I pee, clean my teeth and pull on my running clothes. I've been running in the early mornings for over a week now. I can't sleep past five o'clock and it's the only way to stop my mind churning over and over.

In the two weeks since Ad and Matt learned of the problem with their finances, the frantic paperwork and meetings have resumed but with an increased frenzy and intensity.

I'm not sure Ad even has the energy to shower these days; he often falls asleep on the sofa where I leave him for the night.

I can't talk to him about it; his eyes warn me off. 'Leave me alone,' they say. 'I don't want to hear it.'

When I look at him, I see hurt and anger. He blames me, I'm sure of it. He's got it into his head that I've somehow jinxed the project because I never believed that they could pull it off. I can't even be the voice of reason. I can't say what I think someone should say to them, which is: 'Admit defeat, write it off, move on.'

I don't know how much more I can stand.

As usual, I head for the Monkey Garden. It still amazes and delights me that it opens at dawn and shuts at dusk. This strikes me as something otherworldly, an almost magical arrangement left over from a different time. I'm intrigued by the enigmatic park attendant too. Even though I've been arriving here very early recently I've yet to witness the unlocking of the gate. I'd like to catch him but part of me fears the disappointment of discovering a disagreeable, grumpy man who hates his job.

I'm alone in the park again, although today there are signs of previous visitors. There's a cluster of cigarette butts next to one side of the bench, and a can of Stella leaning against the front leg where I'm sitting. When I pick it up, the dregs slosh in the bottom. I reach over and drop it, with a clang, into the old, black iron bin.

Leaves are emerging all over the trees; these tentative pale-green sproutings look as fragile as ricepaper. On the magnolia bush there's been a sudden unfolding of pink flowers; they remind me of decorative wax candles and I can imagine the tree flickering with light in the mysterious dark once the garden's been locked up and its inhabitants have regained their solitude.

Overhead, the harsh cries of a squall of seagulls tear through the quiet. Antsy jackdaws rise off the rooftops to bombard and chase them away. The sky is momentarily chaotic with raucous, wheeling birds; then, just as quickly, they're gone.

The image of Adam asleep beside me this morning comes unexpectedly into my head. He looks even more handsome when he's asleep; when he's awake, his chin can appear almost cartoon-like in its heftiness, especially when he juts it forward if he's annoyed or sulking. And that's all I seem to see these days, that jaw stuck out at me, his face blanking me.

I'd like to screech and chatter my frustration loudly like a monkey, curling my lips back in anger, but I fight it down — and when I focus again on my surroundings, the first thing my eyes settle on is the gentle, wise face of the Hanuman monkey.

One more chance, I think. I'll give Adam one more chance.

26

The shutters in Rose's room clatter with the through-draught as I open the door. I've grown to like the emptiness up here. I've moved Rose's chair back to its spot in front of the windows and covered it with her grandmother's quilt. I'm certain Rose wouldn't mind me using it; the satin is cool but soft and I like to rest my cheek on it sometimes.

I open the shutters to rain-splattered glass. A gust of wind rattles a fresh batch of drops against it.

When I took a walk to the beach at lunchtime, the strength of the wind was astonishing. I felt that if I'd leaned backwards, it would have supported my weight. The waves were so big that spray was arcing across the promenade, and the salt stung the tender skin under my eyes. Even the seagulls were struggling. Every time they flew up, they were hurled across the sky, their squawks and screeches a feeble protest.

Inside, the wind whistles down the chimneys and gusts under the doors, and at this height, the house creaks and shudders so that I feel as if I'm aboard a galleon ship being buffeted and rocked as it rides a rough sea.

It's freezing, too; the heating system is totally inadequate. All morning I've had to keep my sleeves pulled down over my fingers against the numbing icy draught coming from the window in my office. It would have made using the laptop tricky if I'd been able to concentrate for one moment and do any work, but my thoughts were constantly turning to warming food – bowls of steaming vegetable soup, jacket potatoes split open, oozing melted golden butter.

And to Adam.

Last night he didn't come home at all. It was gone twelve by the time I plucked up the courage to ring Matt's house. Matt answered.

'Uh, yeah – sure, Laura, he's here. I'll get him to call you back.'

But Adam never phoned.

This morning I got a text message from him saying: *soz 4got 2 call u til woz 2 l8. slept @ matts. we r getting sumwhere @ last! call u l8r. X*

My fingers had been trembling as I'd accessed his message; after the long, worrying hours of his silence his casual text seemed almost insulting.

I flop into Rose's chair feeling wrung out and empty.

The sounds of William entering the house echo up the stairs; the force of the front door being sucked closed by the wind, reverberates in this room. By the time I reach the kitchen, William is already huddled next to the oven with all the gas rings alight.

'I've just remembered why I lived in Barcelona,' he jokes, rubbing his hands above one of the dancing circles of pinky-blue flames.

The skin on his face looks almost transparent; his tan has completely disappeared – sloughed off by English weather.

His smile wavers as he looks at me.

'Laura, is something wrong?'

27

'Where's all this come from?'

Adam's face visibly pales. He lowers himself onto the settee opposite me. He clasps his hands, holds them down between his knees. 'Did I miss a conversation?' he asks, and he sounds angry. 'We seem to have gone from experiencing a bit of a rough patch to some kind of trial separation. What happened in between?'

'You were out,' I tell him. 'Or too busy.'

He shakes his head as if he's dodging my nastiness. 'I don't understand,' he says. 'Is there someone else?'

'Of course not.'

He raises his eyes to meet mine. 'Well, what then?'

'We've been miserable for months now,' I repeat. This seems so obvious that I don't understand why Adam's behaving as if it's all news to him. 'I thought you'd have jumped at the chance to have some peace.'

'Well, you got that wrong.' He holds my gaze. It's me that finally looks away.

'It's like my head is full of cotton wool,' I try and explain after a moment. 'The simplest things seem incredibly difficult to do.'

'Like what?' Adam says. 'What things?'

'I don't know,' I reply, my voice shrill. 'Just things.' I picture the spare room at William's, which he's said I can have if I need it. My own room. I'm counting on it. Panic shifts inside me that somehow Adam will prevent me from getting there.

'It's extreme,' Adam says finally. 'Your reaction is way out of proportion, Laura. I don't get where it stems from.'

I sigh with frustration and that seems to trigger something in him. I see it flash in his eyes and crystallize there.

'Is this about Debbie?' he asks suddenly, and leaps up. 'Oh God. It is, isn't it? It's all about that.'

'No.' Unbidden, an image of Debs pressed up to Adam's chest comes into my head. 'Although I don't think there was any need to parade around in your underwear in front of her.'

'I didn't *parade*. She barged in. How many times do I have to say it, Laura? I didn't do anything!' he shouts. 'I don't even like her.'

I let his voice settle into silence and then say, 'Anyway, it's not that.'

'Then what? You've got to give me a better reason than you have.' He stands in front of me with his hands on his hips, his chin thrust forward. Just looking at him makes me angry.

I count the reasons off on my fingers: 'We don't have fun, we don't have sex, we don't even have conversations any more. All we talk about is bills and food and whose turn it is to empty the dishwasher, and shout at each other when we're tired.'

'That's what happens,' he says, raising his eyebrows and gesturing to the room, as if he's appealing to an audience for their support against the idiot he's having to deal with. 'Come on, Laura – every couple goes through this at some point. It's a normal, temporary glitch.'

'How long can temporary last? It's been months, Ad. Months.' I take a deep breath. 'And I have been trying all that time, but you haven't been listening, you haven't been paying any bloody attention to me. You've been so wrapped up in that garden of yours . . .'

'Christ, you're jealous of the fucking garden.'

'I'm not.'

'You are. You've been anti the project from the start.'

'I have not!' I shout. 'And I'm not jealous, because I don't care any more. Do you hear me? I don't fucking care!'

Adam recoils. As I register the hurt in his eyes, a hard kernel of detachment settles inside me. There, it says, see what you make of that.

Adam sits next to me and I tense.

'What about the other night,' he says softly, 'when we made love? Do you imagine it could feel like that if I didn't care about you, if it didn't matter about us?' His voice is shaking. I can sense his panic now.

I think of that bittersweet lovemaking. Adam hasn't realized that it's only arguments that bring us close these days.

'Look,' he says, taking my hand. 'We need to work this out together – here.' He tugs at my hand, pulling me against him and though I resist initially, I give in. 'You're being silly,' he murmurs in my ear. 'My silly girl. You know I love you.'

I feel an overwhelming sadness. My tears drip onto Adam's shoulder. 'I love you, too.'

In the morning, Adam is up first.

'I couldn't sleep,' he tells me, but he has a determinedly cheerful air about him. He makes me toast and tea and then sits at the table; with his chin propped on his hand, he watches me eat. A lump of bread sits high up in my throat, I force it down.

'I've been thinking it over,' he says. 'You're right, I have been putting you – us – on hold and letting lots of other things take priority.' He rocks back in his chair, rat-a-tats the tabletop. 'So I'm going to make it up to you – starting today. How about we do something this evening?'

Over Adam's shoulder, the morning sun highlights the cloudy glass of the window. I can even make out the greasy smear of Adam's handprints above the sill outside where he supports himself when he's pulling off his boots to come in from working in the garden. I know the rest of the flat is in the same neglected state – the bathroom is grubby, there are piles of clothes in the bedroom in various states – unwashed, washed but unironed – and as for the lounge, it's like the nest of an old reclusive professor with its dusty stacks of files and papers and books.

A few days ago, William had shown me the guest room: clean and neat, with its twee, floral wallpaper and brass bed.

'I'm sorry, Ad, I can't.'

'Prior engagement?' he asks jokily, but his eyes flick away and back.

That emotionless kernel inside me is growing shoots, taking hold. I shake my head.

'I'll ask if Matt can put me up for a while,' he says, and this time when I meet his eyes, I see they're empty, his face is closed down; all the fight's gone out of him.

'No, this is your flat. I'll go to William's. He said it's OK.'

There's a second's pause.

'You mean William knows about this? How come he knows?'

'I was upset the other day and we just got talking.'

Adam blinks hard. He drags the pouch of tobacco towards him, opens it, lays out a Rizla paper; his fingers clumsily pinch together a heap of tobacco shreds.

'It makes it sound like you've been planning this for ages,' he says quietly.

I push my plate away and get up.

'Laura,' Adam calls after me. 'What's this really about?'

I stop at the door. 'What I've said, Ad.'

We stare at each other across the room. I think, He cried when he thought they'd lost the project, but he's not crying now.

The first night in William's house reminds me of a time years ago, when Mum left me to stay overnight at the house of an aunt I didn't really know. When Mum waved goodbye, her repeated warning about minding my manners rang in my ears. Everything had to be judged against that edict – was drinking my cocoa quickly bad manners or did it show I liked it? Should I refuse a second biscuit? Was I right to say I wanted to watch *Dr Who*, or did that mean my aunt was forgoing the programme of her choice? I felt confused and overwhelmed by each petty dilemma.

Earlier tonight, a similar awkwardness had descended on William and me. I was trying so hard to be sensitive to sharing William's home that I had probably ended up making us both feel uncomfortable, and by the time I escaped to bed, my head was pounding from the effort.

Now, inconveniently, I desperately need to pee. If I hold on any longer, I risk disturbing William by wandering round the house just as he's dropping off to sleep, but equally, if I go now, there's a chance I'll bump into him as I haven't heard him come upstairs to bed yet.

Tomorrow, I must definitely buy a full-length towelling bathrobe; my bedtime shorts and vest-top suddenly seem ridiculously teeny and indiscreet.

I can no longer ignore the pressure in my bladder. I slowly open my door, tread quietly along the corridor to the bathroom, unfamiliar shadows and creaking floorboards spooking me all the way. Once I've peed, I dash back to my room as quickly and silently as I can.

My mobile says I've got a message. I feel a jump of happiness; I know it's going to be from Adam. I snuggle down in bed before reading it, fingers crossed that he's said something nice.

nite nite babe, miss u bad xxxxx

I feel my hardness dissolving. I think of the way Ad helped carry my bags to the car and how he hugged me goodbye. He's trying to understand, he's trying hard for me. I feel an old ache of missing him.

I quickly tap out: *thinkin of u. xx* and press Send.

I remember the eve of Mum's wedding which I had spent at her house, apart from Adam for the first time since we'd been living together. That night, Ad and I exchanged a flurry of texts; my mobile furtively *cheep-cheeping* under the duvet until the early hours. Our messages got ruder and dirtier, so that by the next day we were totally lusting after each other. In the register office, I felt my face heat whenever I caught his eye, and at the reception we drank a bottle of wine as we devised elaborate and fantastical schemes for engineering moments alone.

'Laura, I got your message, love. Whatever's happened?' Mum's voice is rushed with anxiety. 'You and Adam seemed fine the other evening.'

'We did?'

'Yes,' she says, her voice high with surprise. 'You were both so happy and excited.'

'Adam was happy and excited,' I tell her. 'I was fed-up.' The speed of my anger surprises me; it surges through my body, fizzing in my veins. 'And that's exactly the problem – nobody noticed. You obviously didn't, Adam certainly didn't; it was as if I didn't exist.' I break off and then add, 'And that's how it's been for a long time.'

There's silence. I'm trembling but I tell myself to wait. I'm not going to back down; it's about time Mum knows that living with Adam isn't the paradise she seems to consider it to be.

'Why don't you come over and we can talk about it?'

'OK.'

'What about this evening?'

'No, I can't, thanks. I'll ring you,' I say.

'You know David and I would be happy to put you up,' Mum tells me after a brief pause.

'Thanks but I'm fine at William's.'

'Look, love, do you really think it's a good idea, you staying there?' Mum says slowly.

'What do you mean? Why wouldn't it be?' I ask her. 'I'm OK here, Mum, honestly.'

'Oh my God,' Nat says, her hand stopping in mid-movement. 'You can't stay there.'

'Why ever not?' Her reaction puzzles me.

She presses the plastic top down onto my takeaway cup. 'It's part of the problem – can't you see that?'

'I don't know what you mean,' I tell her. And I don't. I really don't have a clue what she's on about.

'How is Adam?' she asks.

I shrug. 'He's OK, I think.'

Nat sweeps an assessing eye over the queue. 'Give me five minutes and I'll get Becky to cover for me.'

I glance at my watch and shake my head, stepping out of the way of the next customer. 'I can't, I'm sorry. I've got an appointment to go to now.'

She looks flustered then brightens up. 'Come and see me later, then.' She calls over the roar of the milk frother: 'Come over this evening.'

'What's this crazy message about you living over at Gramps's place?' Debs asks as soon as I answer the phone.

'I thought you'd approve. You're always going on at me about making Adam jealous.'

Debs isn't impressed. 'I hardly think shacking up with an OAP is going to do the trick.'

I don't bother to remind her that William is far from a

pensioner. 'It was the best I could do at short notice,' I say, making a joke of it. There's a brief pause as if Debs is busy with something.

'So how long are you going to make him suffer?' she asks eventually.

'Who, Adam?'

'Duh – yes. Of course.'

'I don't know.'

There's another pause which is odd because Debs and I are never usually short for words. Adam's always saying, 'You two can talk for Britain.'

'This isn't a permanent thing, though, is it, Loz? You are getting back with Adam, aren't you?'

'What does it matter to you?' I ask half-lightly, but testing the waters, too. 'You don't like him, anyway.'

Her response isn't what I expected to hear.

'Well,' she says slowly. 'He's OK, really. In the scheme of things.'

In the corner on the floor to the left of the windows, there's a daddy-longlegs which has been mummified in white wispy threads, its wings clamped to its sides, its legs bunched together. On the ceiling above it I can just make out the remains of an old web, but there's no sign of the spider that is responsible for the handiwork.

'Where are you?' Debs asks suddenly. 'It sounds very echoey.'

'I'm in Rose's room – it's pretty empty.'

'What on earth are you doing in there?'

'I'm thinking.'

'You're weird, Loz. Seriously – you need to get out more.'

'Thanks.'

'You didn't do this because of what I said, did you?' Debs asks and I'm surprised because she sounds genuinely concerned.

I think about this for a moment. 'There were lots of reasons,' I tell her.

'I mean, this may come as a bit of a shock to you – but I'm not always right, you know.'

'Now she tells me,' I joke back, but I feel strangely light-headed. I have a sudden overwhelming desire to end the call and lie flat on the floor.

I'm running in the middle of Tottington Woods when it starts to rain. At first the trees provide shelter but as the rain gets harder, it breaks through the canopy until it's streaming over me: strands of wet hair flick across my face, water runs in my eyes making it difficult to focus on the track. I slide on the slippery ground; in some places where the path is furrowed, I sink in mud. My trainer catches on an elevated tree root and I go down, landing in a slimy puddle.

Not hurt, I think, checking myself. Just covered: *in fucking mud.*

Back at the car, I contemplate the single fleece top that I have with me. I can either keep warm or use it to wipe myself down. I choose warmth; I'm already shivering and besides, once the mud's dried it'll vacuum off the seat easily enough.

I get in the car and turn on the ignition. The radio blares into life. I turn the volume down a little and watch the rain. I never vacuum my car, I think. Adam does that for me. Like he changes the oil and checks the tyres.

That's girly, I tell myself. It's about time I did that kind of thing for myself; I'm not some useless bimbo. But the next thing I know, I'm collapsed against the steering wheel, crying my eyes out.

28

Mini-heatwave. Mini-heatwave.

It's a crazy spell of boiling May weather and the media can't get enough of it. There are photographs in the newspapers of old people paddling at the edge of the sea in Eastbourne; video shots on the news pan across dozens of milky-white, bare-chested bodies covering the grass in London parks. Records are broken daily: for ice-cream sales, for lager; barbecues are sold out, and because of Delia Smith's fruit barbecue recipe, sales of bananas, pineapple and maple syrup have hit an all-time high.

The big question is: Will it last until the Bank Holiday? William Hill have stopped taking bets because they say it's a racing certainty but a lot of people aren't willing to take the risk and wait. There's an epidemic of so-called bad backs and migraines – companies are already reporting dramatic peaks in the number of people phoning in sick for this time of year. Nobody wants to miss out. We think it's our right after being subjected to the misery of the long, long, long winter.

The air in my office is completely still; the angle of the sun makes a direct hit on my desk, causing me to overheat and making it impossible to concentrate. I stand in the doorway to the garden to cool off. William calls through the open kitchen window: 'That doesn't look like work to me.'

'I'm not getting on very well,' I shout back.

'Take some time off,' he suggests. 'How about an afternoon on the beach?'

We take my car and drive to Camber Sands. The traffic trundles along; I picture the cars as multi-coloured segments of an infinite snake, winding its way through the roads. The heat builds in the car; I accelerate whenever I get the smallest chance to gather speed, to let the breeze blow through and refresh us. Our conversation palls and unfurls with the highs and lows of temperature.

Even though it's a weekday the car park is overflowing and the beach is packed. There would be rich pickings for any managers seeking their missing employees down here, I think, as we make our way towards a free patch of sand.

A sudden shyness makes me reluctant to strip down to my bikini in front of William, but he doesn't hesitate to take his clothes off.

'God,' he says, standing bare-chested. 'This feels good.'

I sneak a look at William and am surprised at how good a shape he's in for fifty-two – his body's more toned than quite a few of the younger blokes around – but I have to look away when William's swim-shorts are revealed.

'Obscene object alert,' Debs hisses whenever she spots a culprit wearing a similar pair of short, tight Speedo trunks, and I blush at the thought of us cracking up at William's expense.

The temperature continues to rise throughout the afternoon. I doze, and when I wake up, the sea has receded to a silver line on the horizon. Only a few people are braving the long walk across sand which regular visitors know is alternately hard as concrete or soft with viscous green-tinged mud which squashes up between your toes. Kites, grounded by the still air, lie like a washed-up shoal of garish rays.

I look in the direction of Dungeness Power Station, but heat-vapours distort my view.

Steady streams of people arrive over the dunes. It's the evening crowd – those that have just finished work bringing their families, and groups of teenagers who are here for the night. The smell of barbecues lighting up begins to taint the air.

William pays a visit to the refreshment kiosk and returns with a feast: chips, Coke and a hot cheese and onion pasty each. I'm suddenly starving. The pasty's flavour is intense; it's the cheesiest, most onion-y pasty I've ever tasted. I devour it.

Afterwards I lie flat on my back, my stomach stretched with food.

On the drive home, we stop off at a country pub and sit outside. The air temperature has dropped but my skin feels hot and tight, my face warm to the touch.

'You look really pretty,' William says suddenly. 'The beach life suits you.'

In the Ladies, I contemplate my reflection. My face has caught the sun and my hair has formed thick ringlets from the salt. My reflex is to rake my fingers through to free it, but then I stop. I step back. William's compliment sits inside me.

A girl comes round, setting an oil lamp in the middle of each table. The atmosphere changes; everyone's voices become hushed, couples lean in closer. I can imagine secrets being divulged, hearts being opened out, promises being made.

'Do you miss Adam?' William asks softly, startling me from my thoughts.

'Yes.' It's true, I do miss him very much but at the same time, even though it's only been a few weeks since I moved in with William, I'm finding it increasingly hard to remember our life together.

'Have you spoken to him?'

'We agreed not to for a while.'

'I see.'

A moth flutters towards the lamp. I wave it away and it lands on the back of my hand. I feel it tickle as it creeps along my skin before flying off.

'What do you think I should do?' I ask. 'I'd appreciate your opinion.'

William shakes his head slowly. 'I don't think I could say . . .' He breaks off.

'But you must have formed some impression – from the things I've said.'

'Well, from what you've said, Laura, I'd say that Adam probably loves you very much.'

I digest this for a moment. 'Rose never thought that Adam was the right person for me,' I tell him.

William looks up; his eyes are glittering black in the flickering lamplight. His skin has deepened a shade already; he looks fitter and healthier than he's done for a long time, since maybe back when I first met him. He pinches the top of his nose.

'What makes you say that?' His tone is off-key and he clears his throat before asking: 'Did Rosie say something to you?'

'She wasn't going to – I had to drag it out of her – but in the end she admitted that she thought I'd be better off with someone more adventurous, a bit more challenging.'

William frowns then speaks gently. 'Rosie wasn't always right, you know, Laura. Only *you* really know what you want.'

Too late to stop it, I witness the immolation of a moth as it flies straight into the lamp. There's a crackle and spit, and the flame gutters a deeper blue for a second. Another moth begins to circle, then another, then more. William and I attempt to fend them off, but they drop, like planes hit by gunfire, into their death.

When we get home, I check my mobile. I have a voicemail and a text message. I listen to the voicemail first. It's an urgent call for help from one of my clients, a woman who owns a hand-made gift paper and card shop.

I wait until I'm alone to read the text. Intuition tells me it will be from Adam again. It is.

I can't stop thinkin bout u. miss an love u lots an lots. xxxx

I lie in bed and read Ad's message several times. My head feels woozy from the sun; my ozone-saturated body is heavy with sleep which I succumb to, sinking deeper and deeper before I've decided what to text Adam in reply.

Summer

29

Nat's angry – and I don't know how to handle it. This isn't how Nat is; not with me. She gives me advice, she'll speak her mind, but in the end, she's always, always on my side.

'I'm sorry, Laura, I still don't understand why you had to move out.'

'I couldn't see any other way.'

She sighs. 'It seems such a risky thing to do.'

When Nat finally meets my eye, it's with a long, searching gaze and her face looks troubled and dejected. It occurs to me that there's something excessive, almost melodramatic, about her behaviour. After all, this is happening to me, not her. Irritation pinches at me. I've admitted that it was a gamble to have taken such a huge step but it does seem to be paying off. Not only am I regaining the peace and strength I badly needed but Ad and I are closer than we've been for months. Every evening, we spend ages exchanging text messages. I lie on my bed, browsing a magazine, looking forward to the first *beep-beep* which signals that Ad is ready to chat.

One time, I asked him to describe what he was doing at that

precise moment, and ever since I picture him sunk low on the sofa with a bottle of beer balanced on his stomach as he taps out his words. I'm convinced we're able to talk more openly and sexily than we would ever have managed face to face. Our text messages are living love letters, and I save my favourites to re-read over and over again.

I'm briefly tempted to tell Nat about our messaging to allay some of her worries but I feel protective towards this new, cautious connection between Adam and me. I'm concerned about spoiling what we've created by casually revealing it to others.

'I always envied you and Adam,' Nat says slowly.

I sit back in my chair. Never for a minute have I imagined Nat envying me about anything.

'You hardly ever saw Adam.'

'But he was evident in you. Since you moved out, it's as if there's something missing about you.'

I catch my breath. I look at Nat and suddenly read in her face not concern but the same expression that I see in my mother's — a disappointment, a judgement — as if Ad and I together are worth more than as separate people.

It's not fair to say that. It's not that something is missing, it's just that something about me has changed.

A few days later, Ben pays a surprise visit. It's the first time since I've moved in that I've been present when one of William's sons has come over. Although William has said there's no need to go out, I've made a point of being as unobtrusive as I can to avoid any awkwardness.

I make more of a fuss over preparing the tea than is required in an attempt to cover up my nervousness. William has gone out to buy the Saturday paper which leaves me feeling uncomfortably like a cross between a host to Ben and an intruder in the house.

Ben leans against the work surface, watching me.

'Are Alex and Emma coming too?'

I must have looked worried because Ben steps towards me and places his hand on my arm. 'It's OK, Laura,' he says gently. 'Not today.'

'Oh, thank God,' I say, and then flush deeply. 'Sorry, I didn't mean it like that. It's only that I know Alex wasn't happy with me having my office here and, well . . . William hasn't said as much, but I get the impression your brother is really put out now I've moved in.'

Whenever Alex and Emma have paid a visit I always get the feeling afterwards that my office and bedroom have been given the once-over. Both rooms feel disturbed somehow. There's a subtle change in the atmosphere, too vague to identify; the lingering scent of aftershave or perfume perhaps.

Ben grins. 'Yeah, he isn't exactly chuffed.'

'The last thing I want is to cause trouble between you all. I just needed somewhere to go quickly and William offered, and it *is* only temporary until . . .'

Ben prompts me. 'Until?'

'Until we decide what to do, I suppose.'

'We?'

'Me and Ad.'

'Actually,' Ben says, and I see a fleeting reminder of his father in the way his hair falls in front of his face when he inclines his head, 'I'm kind of pleased Dad's got company at the moment, but I hope you can work it out with Adam – I really liked him.' He glances at me. 'Or is that comment insensitive, in the circumstances?'

I shake my head.

'So it's not over between you two, then?'

'No,' I say, but my face feels hot under the spotlight of Ben's scrutiny as if he's caught me out lying.

As soon as William returns, I escape.

I start my run off a little half-heartedly even though it's lovely to be out on such a soft summer morning. I'm having to learn all new routes from William's house and I miss the knowledge I'd gained of my old area, where I could vary my run depending on any contingencies – the weather, how strong I was feeling, even the time of day.

William's house is close to the centre of town and only a short distance from the beach, so that no matter how I plan ahead, I always, at some stage, end up in the middle of crowds of shoppers or get caught on a busy part of the promenade. My new landmarks are Brighton's famous tourist attractions: the Pavilion, Victoria Fountain, Churchill Square, the Green Donut, and yet I feel strangely dislocated from the city I know. I'm forever stopping to get my bearings, veering off whenever the area starts to look unsuitable or changing course if the wind is strong – only to find it's head-on for the last mile. I rarely achieve a good rhythm as my body's always battling for its equilibrium, and I can't remember the last time I truly enjoyed a whole run.

Today I tell myself it's just a phase to be worked through and try to shove any negativity out of my mind by concentrating on my posture and focusing on maintaining a relaxed pace. For a while adrenalin purrs in my stomach but after I've stopped at a junction to decide which direction to take next, the rest of the run is pure slog.

As a final effort, I sprint the last few metres into and across the Crescent – to boisterous cat-calling from the boys playing on their skateboards and bikes.

'Go, girl,' one of them shouts, and, 'Your tits are bouncing!' calls another.

I stand on the doorstep and catch my breath. I wave to the lads; they're cheeky, but inoffensive really. Sometimes when I've walked past, I've listened in on their conversations and have been touched by how tender they are with each other. I recognize it. It's the same rough kindness underlying the banter between Adam and his mates over the pool table down the pub.

I miss that, I suddenly think. I miss Ad.

30

The good weather in July is holding on by the skin of its teeth; all the forecasts are predicting that it will break next week.

William has dragged a couple of old deckchairs out from the recesses of the basement. The wood is bowed and the cloth has perished along the seams so it's only a matter of time before they give way, but the dip is so deep it's as good as lying in a hammock. The afternoon sun is fierce, filling the courtyard with intense heat which makes it impossible to move without breaking out into a sweat.

Minutes trickle by. I watch a blackbird rustling industriously around in the mulch at the foot of the laurel bush. A bee comes zizzing across the patio from nowhere; it meanders towards me, then shoots vertically up as if it's being sucked skyward by a giant vacuum cleaner.

I wake when the sun has moved behind the taller bushes and the cool shadows have dowsed the heat in my scorched skin; I rub at the goosebumps on my arms and stretch.

The young couple in the ground-floor flat two houses along are having a barbie. Wisps of smoke carry the smell of cooking in my direction. Someone turns the music up and a woman yells above it: 'Who's looking after the sausages?'

A bloke bellows back: 'Me.'

There's a pop of a champagne bottle and a whoop, some laughter.

'Fucking catch it,' another man shouts and there's more laughter.

I have a sudden vision of me as an old woman, stuck away on my own, watching and listening to the world getting on without me.

William's in the lounge hunched over the dining table, his hand clasping his chin; he's in deep concentration looking at photographs which he's spread across the top.

I know as I speak that I'm disturbing him, but it doesn't stop me.

'William, would you like to go out?'

He reacts slowly.

'Sorry,' I say. 'I can see you're busy.'

He gestures me to approach; to stand next to him. He smells strongly of sun cream mixed with the peppery scent of his aftershave.

William's taken a small commission from one of the big diving schools who want shots for their promotional brochure. They're not paying much but William's happy to do it for sentimental reasons, as this area was where he first learned to dive. For a fortnight or so now he's been accompanying divers in the practice pool; he's also been to a couple of the local wrecks and dived on Brighton reef. I'd been amazed to hear that Brighton even had a reef.

I look at the array of the spiny-edged, the frilly-headed,

the tentacled and filamented. I look at the bulbous face of the glummest-looking fish, and the squat tousle-topped tubes which have a startling resemblance to the gaudy pink- and green- haired plastic gonks Debs and I used to try and win in the Penny Arcade. I find it hard to believe all these weird and colourful creatures can exist in our cold, murky waters.

'Are you feeling cooped up?' William asks.

'A little.'

He glances out of the window. 'It's a beautiful evening. It would be a shame to waste it.'

We stroll along the promenade. There's a gentle sea-breeze which is warm against my bare legs. Our intention is to sit outside somewhere for a drink, but everybody's had the same idea and all the tables we pass are full. We walk the length of the 'street of a thousand restaurants' where the air is completely still and sodden with odours of food and alcohol, and double-back when we reach the end.

We decide to stop at the next pub we come to.

William goes to the bar while I wait outside to grab any table which comes free. When he returns, he scans left and right, left and right, completely failing to see me. I wave at him, then have to shout to attract his attention. A couple of girls who are watching giggle.

We lean against the pub wall, our drinks in our hands, saying nothing. It should feel companionable, but somehow the silence weighs a little on me. I sense a sinister undercurrent threatening to undermine the heightened happy mood of the others around me, to bring drama crashing down at any moment. It's already started, I notice, with one of the giggling girls who is now sobbing on her friend's shoulder.

The wine tastes sharp. I would, I realize, have preferred a lager.

'I have a feeling you're bored,' William says and I hurry to deny it. I tell him of course I'm not, which is true – but I do feel left out; though this may be just because everyone else seems drunk and I'm not.

A few days later, when I meet up with Debs at Starbucks, the first thing she asks is: 'What's happening?'

'Nothing,' I tell her.

She studies me. 'God, you're serious. You've gone from boring to mega-boring with a "Do Not Pass Go".'

'Thanks.'

Debs sips at her drink, pulls a face. 'God, I hate this stuff.' She looks longingly at my mocha with extra cream.

'Why did you order it then?'

'Diet. Andrew likes them skinny.'

'Well, if you don't count as skinny, then he must like them skeletal.'

'Give us a spoon of cream,' she says. 'Just for a taste.'

I scoop up a big heap and feed it to her. She licks her lips appreciatively. 'Mmmm.'

'Isn't it?'

'I had my clit pierced,' Debs announces loudly and wriggles on her seat. I pretend not to notice that everyone has turned to stare; it will only make her worse. 'Andrew's very experimental; he wants us to do foursomes and stuff.'

'You're not going to, are you?'

'Here we go – lecture time.'

I shake my head. 'I couldn't do it, that's all,' I tell her. 'I love that intensity between me and Adam; I couldn't share that.'

'But you've left him,' Debs says casually as she fiddles with the tag of her teabag. 'So it can't have been that good.' She has a faint smile on her face as if she's teasing me. But I know it's what she really thinks – it's what everyone thinks, even Adam.

'It's only temporary.'

'Until when?'

I hesitate. Debs holds my gaze. I shrug. 'I don't know. The right time, I suppose.'

I can't explain to her. All I know is that I've started to think of every message Adam and I send as a pulsing, electrical synapse connecting one to the other like lines being pencilled in on a join-the-dots puzzle. At some point, the picture will be revealed.

'Earth calling Loz,' Debs says, waving a hand in front of my eyes. She shakes her head. 'What's got into you? I've never known you like this.'

'Like what?'

She shrugs. 'Odd, you just seem odd.'

Alessandro's is crowded, both outside and in. As I wait in the queue, I watch Nat at the far end of the serving counter chatting to a customer. When she catches my eye, she frowns before she smiles.

I wish I hadn't come now but it's too late to walk out.

There are four staff working today. Becky is with Nat behind the counter and two other girls – students, judging from the piercings and colourful hair – are clearing the tables.

'Hi.' Nat leans across the counter and kisses my cheek. I

sense the collective sigh behind me of all red-blooded males who caught the moment. 'The usual?' she asks.

'Yes, to go, though, thanks.' I glance around. 'Bombed out again, I see.'

'It's non-stop. But I'm not complaining.'

I hate hearing Nat's polite voice used with me. I hand over a fiver, take my drink and change in silence.

'Hang on,' Nat says as I turn away. She calls to Becky. 'Two minutes,' she mouths across at her and lifting up the flap of the counter, she steers me to a quiet spot near the stockroom door.

'Adam says you've been texting messages to each other.'

'Oh.'

'That must mean you still care about him?'

'Yes, of course, but . . .'

She holds my arm, leans in towards me. 'Then why not go back now?'

'We agreed three months.'

'But who's making the rules? Adam would have you back today, you know that. This self-imposed exile is stupid.'

'I can't.'

'But it's Adam, Laura,' she says softly. 'He's crazy about you.'

As her fingernails press gently into my flesh I have a powerful feeling that she would like to shake me. I look directly at her.

'You've made your point now, so what's stopping you?' Her face says it all: I'm being unreasonable, I'm the bad guy here. 'Is it pride or do you just want to punish Adam even more?'

'Punish? It's not about that.'

'Then what is it?'

I wish everyone would stop asking me the same question.

'I don't know.'

Nat drops my arm and sighs with exasperation. Behind her, I catch Becky's eye; she's flushed and harassed. A long, long queue is forming.

'You're needed,' I tell Nat and I walk away.

My text alert sounds. I stretch across to pick up my mobile from the bedside table. My heartbeat quickens when I see Adam's name but it's from nerves, not anticipatory pleasure. Since I've discovered that he's told Nat about them, Adam's messages no longer seem so special.

This time, however, there are only three words: *can we talk?*

I text back: *ok.*

No sooner have I replied than Adam rings.

'Babe,' he says. 'Hi.'

The sensation of his physical presence washes through me: I picture him tanned and strong and hungry. Hungry for food and for me; he always feels extra horny from the sun. These thoughts tug at my stomach.

I roll over on my back. I look out of the open sash window and catch sight of the domes and minarets of the Pavilion. The sun's setting and they're gleaming in the mauve and pink sky.

'How are you doing?' I ask Adam.

'All right, and you?'

'OK, I suppose.' Out of nowhere, tears start.

'Are you crying?'

I can't answer him.

'What are we doing this for?' Adam asks, and my heart swerves at the 'we'. No finger-pointing and blame from him.

'I don't know.'

'Let's meet,' he says. 'Let's go on a date on Saturday. And talk properly.'

'OK,' I tell him. 'OK. I'd like that.'

The Crown is one of those ancient pubs with inglenooks, cosy corners and soft gold lighting. Adam and I have been here a few times, for birthdays and anniversaries, and I always feel as if I'm stepping into history.

We've arranged to meet up quite early, to give us plenty of time to talk, and there aren't many other customers here yet so I get the pick of the tables.

Adam's late. I sit there, sipping my beer too quickly, with butterflies in my stomach, trying not to fiddle with my hair. It took ages to get it looking OK so I don't want to ruin the effect this early on.

The pub starts filling up but there's still no sign of Adam. I get out my mobile to see if he's left me a message but there's no reception inside. I don't know whether to wait or walk out and try to phone him. People keep glancing across at me – the greedy sole occupier of a table for four. In the end when someone asks if their group can sit down I get up and leave them to it.

Outside, my phone comes to life and I listen to my voice-mail, received only a few minutes after I'd arrived here.

'Babe, I'm really sorry but an emergency meeting has come up and I can't make it – I'll explain later.'

I let the words sink in. I know what the emergency meeting is about – the stately home garden. It seems strangely apt and yet disappointingly banal that Adam has let me down for that. An emergency meeting.

Fuck you, fuck you, I say in my head, but my heart isn't in it. It's just a way to stop myself from crying.

'Fuck you, fuck you,' I whisper, and a passer-by twists his head, glances furtively at me before carrying on.

It reminds me to start walking myself.

I sit in the car and listen to the message again before trying to phone Adam; my call is immediately diverted to his answering service. The long, aimless evening stretches ahead of me. There's nothing else for me to do other than head back to William's.

'You're back early,' William says, hurriedly pushing himself more upright. Perhaps he'd been dozing.

'Adam couldn't make it.' The material creaks as I lower myself into the deckchair.

'Oh, Laura.'

'I don't want to talk about it,' I tell William, not looking at him. I don't want to see what I know will be a pitying expression.

'Good,' he says. 'We can be quiet together.'

In the dusk light, the garden is full of shadows. I'd like to dissolve into the background and disappear for a while.

'How about a drink?' William offers some time later.

'What I could do with right now is a big, fat spliff.'

William sighs. 'God, yes, but unfortunately I can't help there.'

I can. My usual supply from Angus is in my room, untouched for ages because I hadn't thought it was right to smoke grass in William's house.

On the way upstairs, I pick up my handbag in the hallway and look at my mobile. Adam still hasn't called back. I switch the phone off. I'm unavailable. I'm in an emergency meeting with William.

William watches me intently as I roll the spliff. I try not to hurry even though I have the same urgent desire for the effect that I sense in him. When I lick the paper, I feel him straining not to lick his lips.

I watch him drag deep with his eyes closed. We don't speak, we just pass the joint to and fro. Tension seeps away until all my edges are softened.

I roll another spliff while William fetches candles and wine.

'Did I disturb you when I came back?' I ask when William returns, remembering his odd reaction earlier.

'No, I was just thinking and remembering.'

I suddenly feel terrible. I'd forgotten about Rose.

'Good memories,' he tells me. 'In fact, I'd been laughing out loud and was embarrassed you might have heard me and thought I sounded crazy.'

I find myself considering William's profile; he's caught the sun from being out on the diving boat and looks very tanned in the subdued lighting. With his linen trousers and flip flops on, he even manages to look sophisticated, sunk in the tatty deckchair, his bum millimetres from the floor. 'I'd never think you were crazy,' I say.

When he catches my eye, for no good reason I find myself blushing and out of nowhere I start giggling. William looks surprised, but then he too catches the giggles.

We shush each other several times as we try not to wake our neighbours. It's later than I'd realized; all the houses around us are in darkness. The moon briefly appears in a tarnished pewter sky. There's not a single star to be seen.

The candles have burned so low the flames are beginning to flicker as the wicks reach the melted wax. Soon we'll be in darkness but I no longer need to achieve invisibility.

Suddenly, William sits forward, leans his elbows on his knees. 'You know, I really enjoy your company,' he says; his speech has acquired a wondering tempo. 'I've just realized that.'

I absorb William's words slowly. The cold wine has dazed me. I think I say thank you.

31

I'm tired. I've not been sleeping well for the last few days. It's so hot and humid at night that even a cotton sheet feels heavy and coarse on my skin.

This morning I'd come up to Rose's room hoping that at this height there'd be a breeze to alleviate my headache but the air is stifling, and when I look upwards, the fierceness of the sun takes me by surprise. I look down quickly, but glaring spots remain in front of my eyes for several seconds. It's a relief finally to be able to focus on the gentler colours in the Crescent below, where the hanging baskets on the old-fashioned street-lamps froth with pink and purple and red flowers.

A man with a plastic tank strapped to his back and a long pole is watering them; hearing the excess water splashing to the ground makes me want to stand underneath and let the cool water flow over me. It reminds me, too, of playing games in the garden with Adam last summer; running around with the hose pipe, squealing and laughing like kids until my stomach hurt.

Thinking about Adam fills me with anger. Despite all his

calls and messages, I haven't spoken to him for a week since he stood me up. I simply can't bring myself to talk, and any text message that I start to compose sounds too bitter and resentful to send, so that I end up abandoning the attempt.

This morning, it seems my silence has finally pissed him off. The message he sent was terse: *I get the point.*

I wish I could talk to Rose. I wish I could hear her calm voice, just for a few minutes – just a whisper – but her soothing presence eludes me.

Something is happening in the Crescent. I lean forward and spot William walking towards a group of boys.

Like a hunting pack of animals, more boys appear from every direction; some on skateboards skim past William, a couple on bikes do stoppies right in front of him, another nudges up to his heels. Someone shouts and my heart lurches. I want to run down, beat them away and protect him.

But there's no need. I watch as one lad gets off his bike and offers it to William. It's so low to the ground that when William sits on it, the boys and I laugh. He looks hilarious; his knees almost reach his chin.

William navigates a wavering passage through the boys and they cheer as he picks up speed and tracks an uneven circle. As he performs a second loop, he looks up at the house and spots me. Tears of laughter run down my face when he waves and wobbles violently, almost falling off.

I go to see Angus. I tap on the shop door, even though it says Closed, as I can see him in there – enjoying his 'winding down' time as he calls it. This is when he potters around the store, hanging up clothes that shoppers have knocked from the hangers and not bothered to pick up; tweaking the displays; noting – and mourning – the loss of any 'special treasures' which have been sold.

He waves me away when I press my face up against the glass door but he's only joking. He lets me in and gives me a double *mwa-mwa* greeting on each cheek.

'How's business?' I ask.

'Fantastic, darling. The best summer yet.'

It's hot inside and the air is heavy with the mustiness of second-hand clothes. While Angus goes upstairs to get my weed, I go through the racks and discover a lurid pink satin puff-sleeved blouse.

'Oh *yes*, Laura,' Angus calls from the back of the shop as I hold it up against me in the mirror. 'You have to buy it.' He hands me the white envelope. 'Are you developing a bit of a habit? It wasn't that long since your last lot, was it?'

'Me and a friend had a bit of a major session,' I explain. 'Him,' I say, pointing to the poster of William. 'We'll be a bit more restrained with this lot.'

'I should think so, too, lovey,' Angus says and winks. 'He's no good to you doped up to his eyeballs, you know.'

Much to Angus's amusement, I go bright red.

A few days later, William knocks on my office door and hovers there.

'Can I talk something over with you?' he asks.

'Of course.' I put aside my work, and as he's still hanging back in the doorway, gesture to the armchair in front of my desk that he usually sits on without my needing to invite him.

He doesn't normally knock either, I realize, and my stomach tips.

William pinches the top of his nose, clears his throat. Then he looks directly at me. 'I've just heard that there's a possibility I'll be offered a big commission in a couple of months' time,' he says. 'I'd be based back in Barcelona, although the work is actually further south, in the Valencia region. It's through a friend of a friend,' he continues. 'Someone I've worked with before.'

'Oh,' I say. I'm not sure what's most surprising: the news of the commission or that he's obviously been in constant contact with friends. Sometimes I feel as if William knows everything that goes on in my life and I know next to nothing about his. I'd been surprised the other day to find him hooked up to the internet in the lounge. Emails, I think. Of course he'll have been using email.

'Are you going to take it?'

'I'm in two minds. It sounds pretty interesting and I'd see my friends, of course, but I'm not sure about going back to our – my – old apartment.' William falters. 'To be honest, I'm a bit nervous about the idea.' He gets up and walks over to the window. 'And I'm not sure if I want to leave Brighton right now.' He turns around. 'I'm getting to quite like it here. I've established some roots for the first time and there are people that I'm reluctant to walk away from at this point.'

'Your sons.'

'Yes,' he replies slowly. 'Yes, my sons. It's good to think that I'm getting to know them both at last.'

Silence settles in the room when William has gone. A few minutes later, something bangs somewhere in the house, making me jump. I'd have to get used to being on my own here if William went away; I'd officially be the house-sitter.

The thought of being alone here grips me. I'd hate it. I'd hate living here without William. Panic swells. What would I do without him? I hardly ever see anyone else these days. Mum and Debs are both getting on with their lives. Nat thinks I'm horrible, and Adam and I aren't speaking any more.

That thought crashes into me.

It's a big mistake to rely on William, because he can – as he proved a minute ago – just up and leave, without worrying about me. And there's no reason that he should care. After all, I'm only his lodger, a friend at most – dispensable when you have plenty of them, as William has.

William suddenly opens the door and walks straight in.

'There's something else,' he says, then stops. 'What's wrong, Laura?'

He squats by my chair, spins it to face him, taps his fingers on my knee. 'Laura?' He makes me look at him. His face is deadly serious. His eyes take in the telltale tears which have gathered in my eyes. He holds my gaze, unflinching.

'There was someone else I didn't mention who is keeping me here,' he says. 'You.'

And then a moment later, he's gone.

32

I walk down to Alessandro's. Nat is on the phone. She makes a yakkety-yak gesture, which means her mum's on the other end and Nat could be a while so I sit at a table outside to wait.

There's not much activity to nose at. The street is quiet as it's that in-between time of day, after the shoppers and workers have gone home, and before the evening crowd appears. I take out my mobile from my bag to check if I've got any messages. Nada. I tap through the menu to the *write messages* option. My thumb is poised – who do I want to send a message to?

I think of William. When I'd left the house, he'd been working on his laptop, putting together a portfolio of recent work. I think how much he'd enjoy receiving a message from me. His mobile is a recent acquisition which still holds novelty value for him.

I ponder over what I should write. I tell myself not to think about it, just to do it: otherwise what's the point? It's only a friendly message. So I tap, tap, tap away.

@ *Alessandro's – wish you were here*

I know when I read it over that sending this message will alter everything.

I don't want to change anything, I tell myself, but even as I'm thinking that, even though my hand is trembling, even though I can hardly breathe I select *send*, then select William's number and then – before I can stop myself – I press OK.

I am instantly swallowed up by fear and embarrassment. I feel the heat rising through me and put my hands to my cheeks to try and cool them. I jump a mile when Nat plonks herself down at the table in front of me.

The first thing she says is: 'Have you spoken to Adam?'

'No.'

Nat sighs. 'I thought not. He came to see me again.'

'Why?'

'Because you won't speak to him.'

'He was the one who didn't turn up that day. I need time to think about what that means.'

'He had to go to an emergency meeting for the project.'

'Oh yes, the project.'

Nat gives me a searching look. 'He said you'd react like that. Don't you want to know? Don't you care that they won the contract? It's an amazing achievement.'

I bite my lip. 'Of course I'm pleased . . .' I start to say.

'I think you're being unreasonable.' Nat shakes her head. 'I don't like to say it, Laura, but I don't think you're treating him right at all.'

I don't speak, but the voice in my head says, *He hurt me.*

'I don't recognize you any more,' she says in the end.

I wonder if I should tell her that sometimes I don't recognize myself but just then my phone on the table between us goes *bip-bip* and the message envelope flashes away. Nat leans over, looks at my phone, then at me.

'Aren't you going to read it?' she asks and I colour up immediately. 'Go on,' she urges, not taking her eyes off me.

I slide the mobile towards me, press *read* and there is William's reply.

I wish I was there with you too. I miss you

I stare at it.

'Laura?' My head jerks up. 'It's William, isn't it?'

We both know that Nat isn't simply asking me whether it's William's message which has just come through.

I say, 'Yes.' And my answer is loaded with implications, too. But up until five minutes ago, I swear I hadn't known it. I hadn't known it was William.

As I'm approaching the house, I feel as if there's grit in my eyes. I keep blinking but I can't get rid of the blurry vision. It must be nerves; my mouth is parched though my hands are sweaty.

William's at the end of the hall, by the kitchen.

'Hi,' I say.

'Hi.'

When I'm a couple of steps away from him, I have to stop. I can't go any further. We haven't exchanged another word but we haven't broken eye-contact either. Time freezes then blips to life again as William steps forward, reaches out and pulls me close into a long, long hug. His body feels new but familiar; slim and strong as maybe I've always imagined he would feel.

Wow, I keep thinking. Wow, this is William.

Our faces are so close, we're all eyes. I tip my head back to try and read the emotion in his, but all I make out in the dingy light is that they are more grey than blue. I move my attention to his mouth; his lips look soft as if they're ready for kissing.

I'm sure we're going to kiss, but we wait too long. The mood shifts and William draws away. He squeezes my hand briefly before he turns and walks into the kitchen.

I stand in the hall. Realization is dawning: that was a pity hug. William was *consoling* me. I feel cheap and stupid.

'Aren't you coming in?' William's head appears. 'Are you all right?' He takes my hand again. 'Come and have some wine. I think we need it, don't you?'

An hour later, when we're way down our second bottle of wine and more than a bit drunk, he pulls me up from my chair and kisses me.

'Is this OK?' he asks.

I nod.

'You're so beautiful,' he tells me. He holds me around the waist. 'Your hair is completely lunatic,' he says, winding a strand through his fingers. 'I love it.'

He leads me out of the kitchen, down the hall, to the foot of the stairs. Each step seems harder to take; all the energy has been sucked out of my legs. I am filled with horror at the thought of being led to his bedroom, the room where, until she was ill, Rose would have slept with him. Rose, my friend, William her husband. I'm losing my nerve. William senses me hanging back. He turns round.

'Your room,' he says in a hoarse, low voice.

I perch on the edge of the bed. I'm shaking again, but I tell myself, If you didn't want this, then you wouldn't be sitting here.

William kneels in front of me. He pulls off my top, undoes my bra, runs his hands across my breasts. He pulls me closer, bends to suck my nipples before lowering me onto the mattress. He undoes my skirt, pulls off my knickers, eases me further up the bed and sits beside me, not speaking, just looking.

I reach for the duvet to cover myself up, but he stops me. 'Don't hide yourself.'

So I lie on my side and undo the buttons of his shirt, one by one. When he shrugs it off, I start undoing his trousers. He stands up to remove them, but hops around, getting in a pickle. It's funny, but I don't giggle. William's so serious that I don't want to put him off. So I avert my eyes.

When he presses his body on top of mine, I say, 'Oh,' because it's somehow surprising to feel his cool skin against mine, but nice. A nice surprise.

He runs his hands all over me, kisses me all over, and I close my eyes and concentrate on the sensations drawn down my body when he enters me. I open my eyes once and catch sight of William's intense expression, his determined mouth before he buries his face into my neck.

33

I collapse against my pillows and look at William. I'm washed through with sex. I reach out, curl some of his chest hair in my fingers; it's damp with sweat and greyer than the hair on his head. I ask him if he uses hair-dye and he appears wounded by the suggestion.

'Do you think I should?' he asks, turning onto his side so that he can see my face more clearly. 'Is that what you mean?'

'Of course not,' I say. 'I think you look gorgeous as you are.'

He humphs his disbelief.

I smile to reassure him. 'You look fine, Wills, honest.'

'I've been wondering,' he starts, then stops. 'I don't know how to put this, without it sounding awful.'

I tense immediately. Don't say it, then, I think; there won't be a good way. My mind leaps ahead. He's going to say he's made a dreadful mistake. These past few days when we have done nothing but live in this bed, when it's seemed as if he can't get enough of me; when he's sucked me, bitten me, done one hundred and one things to me, stopping only to eat a little, to sleep even less, to wake and start again – these days have been wonderful, dreamlike, but now, well, he's emerged from the fantasy. Sated and ready to acknowledge the foolishness of our actions, he wants out.

Suddenly, our cosy bed feels sordid. The air in the room is stale, it stinks of bodies which have lingered too long inside; the sheets are grubby, my skin feels filmy. I poke morosely at a spot on my chin, induced by William's unshaven chin.

Don't hurt me, I want to tell him. *Don't say anything cruel.*

'I think we should consider keeping quiet about us for a little while.' William pushes the hair away from my face. 'But I don't want you to think I'm ashamed of you.'

'It's all so sudden. Of course we need to take our time.' But as I speak I wonder if that's true. I'm not sure either of us can pinpoint the moment when it all began. It seems to have been creeping up behind us for a while and it's only now, by chance, that we've looked round and discovered it's there.

I lie on top of William; his cock fidgets between us.

'Our relationship won't be easy, Laura.'

'I know,' I tell him, but the relief of hearing him say the word 'relationship' has left me feeling carefree. Just to make sure, I ask him: 'Do you – you know – see this as . . . going on, then?'

'Why? Don't you?' William immediately looks crushed.

'Of course, Wills.' I quickly press my lips to his mouth in an attempt to blot up his fear. Our love is like a newborn baby, I think, plump with life but so fragile, too.

'There'll be a lot of people who won't be very happy about it, who'll be quick to point out everything that's wrong,' he says.

I remember Nat's numb shock at just the thought. I picture

Debs's reaction: *'You've got to be kidding me?'* and I can't even begin to imagine what Mum will say.

William continues, 'I think Ben will be OK, but I'll need to find a way of handling Alex.'

And Emma. The memory of her words at Rose's funeral chills me whenever I let myself think about it. I press my face into William's neck. Emma will never let Alex like me; she'll always think I'm trying to come between them and William. Panic rises as scenes of family arguments and rifts pile into my head.

'You do think we'll get through it though, don't you? You do think that?' I whisper, and hold my breath waiting for William's reply, silently urging him to be strong.

'Oh yes,' he says, stroking my back. 'I'll make sure we do.'

I've an urge to shower, so I get up. I feel William watching me as I open a drawer for a clean towel. I straighten up and turn round. He's lying with his arms behind his head. I blow him a kiss.

'You haven't ever said much about your father, Laura,' he says out of the blue.

'No.'

William is waiting for more but I've nothing further to add.

'Is it difficult to talk about?' he probes gently.

I shrug. 'People expect me to be hurt but I really don't feel like that. Mum more than made up for him,' I say. It occurs to me that this is his secret fear – the reason I'm with him.

'Dad has a place in my history, not in my present,' I tell him, taking off my bathrobe and getting back into bed. 'And I'm certainly not looking for another father.'

William's body is hot and sticky.

'I'm glad to hear it,' he says, as he pulls me tight and bites down on my shoulder. 'Because I don't feel a bit fatherly towards you.'

'It's happened,' I whisper to Nat as she pushes my cappuccino across the counter.

She looks at me uncomprehendingly.

'Me and William.'

She recoils as if I've struck her. 'Oh, Laura.'

'Is that all you can say?'

She casts her eyes down.

'You should be happy for me.' I try a smile out on her. 'Aren't you happy for me?'

'I am if you are,' she says, but her voice is flat and she won't meet my eyes.

'Don't tell anyone,' I remember. 'For now,' I add.

I find Rose's photographs when I'm tidying up the coffee-table and sit down to look through them. I'm unaware of William until he reaches from behind and takes the one I'm holding from my fingers.

'Wills, did you realize that there's a lot more of us two than anybody else?'

He drops the photo onto my lap; it skims across my knee and slides to the floor.

'We weren't even friends then really, but looking at them now, you could almost think otherwise.' I bend forward to pick it up. 'Oh my God. You don't think Rose suspected something, do you? Do you?'

I turn round but William has already gone.

I re-examine the photographs. Of course Rose didn't suspect

something; there had been nothing to suspect. I feel stupid for having spoken my thought out loud and grateful that William had been out of earshot. The simple explanation is that he and I spent more time at the house with her than anyone else.

Besides, Rose would never have remained my friend – she wouldn't have encouraged me and William to go out, she'd have kept me away from him – if she'd had the tiniest suspicion about us.

I gather the photos together. Around me, all the unspoken concerns, all the unanswered questions, shift and stir in the house like fractious ghosts who have been woken up when they'd rather be sleeping.

It's pointless to keep trying to understand what Rose was feeling when she took these shots; the same way there's no point trying to imagine what she would make of William and me now. It's a subject we're probably wise to avoid; it's a long road to nowhere.

I check that William is busy preparing dinner in the kitchen then I shove the photographs back into the packet and push it to the bottom of a pile of books on the bookcase.

I go shopping for nightdresses because my bedwear is embarrassingly teenage and I feel cheap in front of William if I'm naked when we go to bed.

There appear to be three categories of women's nightwear: frumpy, frilly and floaty – in varying degrees of transparency. I almost walk out but force myself to return to the floaty section, gather several and head for the changing rooms.

I fling one after the other aside, my reflection sniggering, 'You look ridiculous, just ridiculous.'

In desperation, I re-try a pale brown satin one from the

discarded heap and suddenly it dawns on me what these clothes are about. They're sexy in a subtle, grown-up way. This time my reflection whispers: 'You're a woman.'

I buy that one and the same style in cream, and a third, a shorter, lacier black one which I think could be classed as a negligée. I imagine telling Debs of my purchases when I meet her later and her shrieking, 'Didn't you have a negligée already, you bloody tomboy? I've got one for every night of the week!' But then I remember our relationship is a secret so I have to cram my shopping into a decoy W.H. Smith's carrier bag so that Debs doesn't truffle out the goodies.

In the middle of lunch, my mobile bleeps with a message. I freeze. Debs looks at me expectantly, then narrows her eyes at my discomfort.

It turns out to be from Angus, not Wills at all but Debs has scented something is amiss.

'Who was that?' she asks, her eyes glinting.

'A client,' I tell her.

'Clients text you these days, do they?'

'The ones that are more like friends do.'

We resume eating. I think of my secret as a mouse huddled in the grass, its heart pattering away as the hawk circles above. Sun, shadow, sun, shadow.

'I'm stuffed,' Debs says, clattering her cutlery down, even though she's barely eaten a third of her pasta. She leans back in her chair, pulls her hair round to hang over one shoulder and looks at me.

She'll never guess my secret, though; she won't be expecting this at all. And somehow, I like that idea.

*   *   *

One night, when we are getting ready for bed, William seems quiet.

'Is something wrong?' I ask.

'No,' he says. 'It's just – I feel so happy.'

'Me too,' I say.

But the face William turns towards me reflects my own uneasiness, and once more, the knowledge that I haven't ventured into Rose's room for weeks nudges at me.

William holds his hand out to me and the touch of our fingers drives deep into me; I instantly feel wet. He draws me into bed, lies me on my back. He tugs my nightdress up to my thighs, gathers the material in his hands, begins to rub the cloth across my pussy, both hands, all his fingers pushing and pressing; he squeezes my swollen lips together, then folds me open, rubbing and pressing.

I take hold of his cock; he moans softly, and I try to pull him towards me. I'm greedy for him, greedy to feel him inside me.

He bites on my bottom lip so I can't speak, holds my hips down with one hand while he slides silk-covered fingers inside me.

Afterwards, in the loo, I feel William's sperm dribble out of me. I watch the pearly liquid coil and sink in the water. On my return to the bedroom I stop at the foot of the stairs, but I don't go up. I still haven't dared to ask him the question: 'What would she think?'

34

William stands in the bedroom doorway. 'Um . . . bad news. They're on their way down – Ben, Alex and Emma. We've got a couple of hours. Three at the most until they get here.'

It's Saturday and we were having a leisurely morning in bed; William had only taken the call because he happened to be in the kitchen making fresh coffee.

I launch myself out of bed and start charging round, manically trying to straighten up the disaster area of the room, recalling with a wave of horror the state of the rest of the house. What if William hadn't answered? They would have caught us red-handed. The thought makes me feel sick.

'Why now?' I ask, my voice high with nerves and indignation. 'Is this what they always do? Give you short notice, like some inspection squad?'

'It's just a family visit.'

'Do you think they suspect something? Do you think Ben noticed something when he was down here last time?' I tug the duvet into place and plump up the pillows. 'They're coming to check up, Wills. No doubt about it.'

'You're being paranoid, darling,' he reassures me. 'If you remember, there was nothing to be noticed at that time.'

I scoop up the clothes that are lying around into a heap on the floor and yank out all items of William's before shoving the bundle into his arms.

William's calmer now; he regards me with amusement.

'It's not funny,' I tell him.

'It does have a certain comedic appeal, you have to admit.'

I find myself smiling back. William drops the clothes he's holding and pulls me to him. 'It'll be fine.'

'But we're not telling them today, are we?'

'I don't think that's a good idea, do you, darling?'

'Then you'll have to stop calling me darling – it's a bit of a giveaway.'

We spend the next hour whizzing through the house, cleaning and tidying. I go to take a shower while William pops out to fetch some milk.

We meet back up in the living room; it's definitely tidy but a quick scan is rather disheartening. Everything seems to shout out our secret: the candles on the mantelpiece, the way our magazines are all mixed up in the same pile. It wouldn't surprise me if the two mugs of coffee on the table sprouted cartoon little legs and arms and danced around singing, 'They're lovers, they're lovers.'

I remind myself that as a lodger here, my presence would be evident, that it wouldn't be odd for us to share a bottle of wine, to have a coffee break together.

'Perhaps I should just go out like I usually do,' I suggest. 'Wouldn't that be better?'

'Please.' William looks bereft. 'I need you here. And anyway, where would you go all afternoon?'

'To see a film.' I've no idea what's on, but frankly a Disney movie with a room full of hyper, screaming kids would be preferable to enduring Emma's hostility. My whole body is trembling, my hands are clammy – I'm surprised that William hasn't noticed.

He puts his arm round my shoulder and sucks on the side of my neck.

I push him away. 'You mustn't. You can't leave any marks.'

He holds me still and pulls my T-shirt off over my head. 'I want you with me, I need you.' He kneels on the floor and sucks on my stomach; heat runs through me. He pulls me down to him, he squeezes my breast and sucks on the flesh that he's pushed up from my bra. I feel the bruise blossoming as I lean my weight into him.

He kisses me on the lips. 'And besides, you can't avoid Alex and Emma for ever.' He picks up my top and helps me put it back on.

I sneak a couple of swigs of whisky while William's out of the room to steady my nerves. It'll be better, I try and convince myself, once they've arrived. It's the waiting that's the worst.

And it is better: it's easier than I thought.

Wills sets the tone. He openly mentions that we've been out for a drink a couple of times; he doesn't try to hide that we know each other's business. I admire his tactic and take my strength from it, but I still feel as if I'm walking on a tightrope. If I look down I'll fall, but if I just keep my eyes on Wills and focus on the end of the day, I can do anything – cartwheel, balance a tray, juggle.

I chat to Ben on my own for a while – he's easy to talk to. He tells me about mountain biking, and in his funny descriptions of haring down hillsides and ending upside down in a muddy ditch, I hear the same entertaining style of story-telling as his father has.

'Dad seems so much happier these days,' he says suddenly, in a hushed tone and I can't stop myself from blushing deeply. I glance at Emma, who happens to be watching me. In a panic, I look first at William and then back to Emma. She frowns and then, to my horror, I see realization cross her face. We stare at each other for what seems like forever until she turns away to respond to something Alex has said.

I'm totally freaked out. I have to get away. I escape to the kitchen and collapse against the work surface. Sweat is pouring out of me.

William follows shortly. He breathes onto my neck, 'You're doing great.'

I spin round. 'Emma,' I manage to say. 'She knows.'

William's standing very close. Lust is written all over his face. It seems completely naïve of us to think we could ever have hidden it.

He is unperturbed. 'You're imagining it. Everything's fine.' His body tilts involuntarily towards me. 'Christ,' he groans, stepping back. 'Soon,' he says, as if making a promise.

A few seconds later, when Alex opens the door, my heart pounds as much as if he'd caught us.

'We're off now,' Alex says.

I think: We've made it. Thank God. We've made it. Relief makes me delirious. I am super-friendly, super-cheerful. I say, 'Great' and, 'Lovely,' and, 'Really wonderful to see you all again.' I am effusive with my goodbyes before I disappear to my room, leaving William to wave them off.

I fall onto my bed, completely drained.

A few minutes later I hear someone coming up the stairs. I call out, 'Wills?'

Emma opens my door without knocking and stands in the doorway with her arms crossed and her skinny legs set in a wide stance, like a bouncer's skeleton.

I raise my head. She steps into my room as if she has every right to do so and stands looking round; a human CCTV camera registering every corner, scrutinizing every inch.

'What do you want?' I stand up. I swallow hard and taste her perfume in the back of my throat. It makes me almost gag.

'Just wanted to make sure you're comfortable,' she says, as she turns to leave.

'I'm great, thanks, Emma,' I tell her, hustling her out as fast as I can. 'Everything's just fine.' As I start to push the door closed behind her, my fingers touch soft material. William's bathrobe is hanging on the hook.

My face gives it away. Emma yanks the door towards her and peers round. 'Oh, my God,' she says. 'Oh, my God. So it *is* true.'

William and I sit side by side on the sofa and face the jury. William clasps my hand in his; I can feel the pulse in his wrist bumping against the heel of my thumb.

'Just when were you planning on telling us?' Alex thunders.

'When it was appropriate,' William says calmly. 'This is all so new and sudden . . .'

'Not for her it isn't,' Emma butts in. 'She's been planning this for months.'

'I haven't!' My forceful denial ends in a high-pitched squeak.

'Oh, come on, Laura,' she spits out. 'Give up the pretence – you've been found out now, for God's sake.'

I burst into tears. It's horrible, horrible, horrible.

I hear Emma's voice detailing the evidence against me, recreating me as a heartless, scheming cow, a gold-digger, a family-breaker. I hate her for making me feel wrong and dirty. William is no longer holding my hand; I'd be surprised if he ever wants to touch me again after this.

'Shut up, Emma,' William says suddenly. His voice is low and insistent. 'Shut up. You're clearly being ridiculous.' He stands up and places a hand heavily on my shoulder. 'Laura's incapable of such behaviour. This is as much of a surprise to her as it is to the rest of us.'

Silence blossoms.

I stare at my knees; I can't look at anyone. All I can feel is the pressure of William's fingers gripping tightly.

'Now,' he continues, 'I suggest we talk about this some other time, once tempers have cooled.'

35

'*William?*'

'Yes, William.'

'You're kidding, aren't you?'

'No.' I sip my wine.

'You gave up Adam for him?'

'I didn't *give up* Adam for anyone,' I protest. 'This happened afterwards.'

Debbie, in a pretence of indifference, produces her compact and begins to start applying lipstick. 'You can't possibly think William is a good idea,' she says after a moment, lowering her mirror slightly to look at me.

'Why not?'

'Oh come on, Loz. I mean, where do I start?'

'Why are you always so rude about the men I fall for?'

'Uh – could it be because you always have appalling taste?'

'Listen,' I tell her, half-joking. 'I'm not the same as you – I have to like the people I sleep with, OK? It doesn't matter to me how good a job they've got, how loaded they are, how big their dick is, or how bloody old they are.'

'So he's not hung like a donkey then?'

I nearly choke on my wine.

She hooks her little finger up. 'Oh God! Don't tell me – Mr Peanut?'

'Actually, it's mindblowing, the sex with him. He's so intense; I've never known anything like it.'

Debs pretends to cover her ears. 'Uggh, please, no more details. I'll vom.' She clicks shut the compact, places it on the table. Her lips look wet with gloss. She frowns. 'Seriously though, Loz . . .'

'Don't say any more,' I tell her, somehow feeling suddenly more grown-up. 'I know it's a bit of a surprise. Talk to me when you've got used to the idea.'

'It's just I feel I'm somehow to blame, that I should have stopped you ages ago.'

'Stopped me? Stopped me from doing what?'

'Leaving Adam.'

Mum insisted that we meet at her local golf club, which is where she and David spend most of their time these days.

'I'd like to treat you to a meal,' she'd said, sounding delighted with the idea of seeing me. 'We'll have a good catch-up and then David can join us after he's finished his round.'

It's an overcast day, but muggy – warm enough to sit outside. Nothing on the menu appeals to me: my stomach is tied in a knot. I wish now that I'd been more forceful about seeing Mum at her house. This place suddenly seems far too public to be breaking personal news. Groups of people trudge past pulling golf bags on wheels, and most of the other tables are occupied by people wearing either pastel-coloured jumpers or business suits.

I look at Mum. Her lips are pursed in concentration as she vacillates between spaghetti carbonara and salade niçoise. When we hugged hello earlier, she'd held me tightly for a long time, and I'd felt like crying. I wish I could forget about the reason I'm here and simply enjoy her company, but I want to be straight with her. I want to be honest.

'Have you heard from Adam recently?' Mum asks, glancing up. 'I was wondering if they got that stately home contract in the end?'

'Yes. There was a picture of him and Matt in the local paper.'

The waiter brings our drinks and we both order the salad.

'Oh,' she says, 'I must have missed it. Did you keep the cutting? I'd like to read it.'

'I threw it away.'

'You should have hung on to it for posterity; to show your kids.'

My heart is thumping. I feel sure that if Mum looked over, she'd be able to see it pressing up through the skin on each beat – bam, bam, bam. I rest my hand on my chest.

'Mum – me and Adam are finished. I've found – um – I'm with someone else now.'

Her mouth hangs open, her eyes search mine.

I press on, stumbling over the words. 'It's William,' I say. 'Who would have believed it? I know, I can hardly believe it myself – but there we are. I've fallen for him and he has too. I mean for me.'

Mum looks as if she might cry. She stares over my shoulder, her lip trembling, out across the green, as if willing David to come and rescue her.

'Mum? Say something.'

'I'm sorry, Laura,' she says after a while. 'I can't pretend to be pleased. Adam was such a nice young man.'

'But William's a nice man, too. Once you get to know him, you'll see.'

'Oh, love,' she says, and a tear escapes and begins a damp track through her foundation. 'He's nearly as old as me. He's old enough to . . . and it, well . . . it doesn't look very proper, does it? In the circumstances.'

'What on earth do you mean?'

'Laura, his wife *has just died.*' She leans forward. 'She was your friend, he was arrested . . . What do you imagine people are going to think?'

'What are you suggesting?' I hear the shrill agitation in my own voice. 'God, Mum, what are you saying?'

'I'm not saying anything.' Mum is flustered. She begins picking at her serviette. 'It's so unexpected,' she says quietly. 'I don't know what to think.'

'William was completely cleared, Mum. All this – we – started after Rose died.'

Mum frowns and reaches out to take my hand. 'Come and stay with us, please. Just for a while until . . .'

'No.' I ease my hand away. 'Thanks, Mum, but I want to be with William. We're happy together. Don't worry about me. Everything's going to be fine.'

There's a bustle of voices and Mum looks alarmed. Behind me, David is approaching with his golfing buddies. He waves cheerfully and I wave back.

'Laura,' Mum says in a hushed, urgent tone, 'please don't say anything about this to David. Not here in front of our friends.'

She fixes everyone with a bright smile as the group crowds round the table; animated from their game, they throw compliments at us both. I listen to myself replying, to me laughing. I'm conscious of Mum doing the same. Perhaps to others, she seems normal, but to me her distress is thinly disguised and when I catch David looking quizzically at her, I decide to leave.

Mum doesn't try to dissuade me. For a brief moment, she clutches my arm, but she doesn't speak.

At the door, when I turn back, David is already seated beside her with his arm round her.

'Let's get out of here,' William suggests. 'Let's get out of the house.'

We stop and sit on a cold, damp bench on the promenade looking out to sea. There's been a flash of heavy rain and the water, unable to drain away quickly enough, is lying in puddles. In them you can see the reflections of the seagulls as they wheel above us. If you look up and down rapidly, it's disorientating. You can no longer differentiate between the sky and the ground.

I point this out to William and we lift and lower our heads time and time again until we feel dizzy and have to desist.

I catch him frowning. 'What is it?' I ask.

'We've never talked seriously, have we?' he says. 'About the future.'

He's been watching a little boy with his parents down on the beach. They're playing a slow game of football, the mum and dad whooping and clapping every time their son succeeds in making unsteady contact with the ball.

'You mean children?'

'I'm nearly fifty-three,' he says.

'Think of Picasso.' A photographic image of the elderly Picasso on the beach with his young child and wife has jumped into my mind and I describe it to him. 'I can picture us like that. Just like that.'

'Picasso! How flattering.'

I hear the smile in William's voice. He rubs his chilled fingertips in circles on my palm before clasping my hand tightly.

'The last thing I want to do is cause trouble between you and your mum; I know how important you are to each other.'

Each time I remember that afternoon last week, Mum's embarrassment and disappointment slap me in the face.

'Is there anyone who's pleased for us?' I say, half-joking.

William doesn't reply; he simply squeezes my fingers.

'Do you think we've done wrong?' I ask William. 'Do you think we're bad people?'

'Of course not. I don't think you're bad at all. Do you think I am?'

'No,' I say. 'I think you're wonderful.'

The little boy has fallen over. His father gets him upright but the boy immediately thunks down on his bum. He's having a temper tantrum; his angry wails are a pitch higher than the cries of the gulls.

'What about Rose?' A rush of bravery whips the words out of me before I have time to pull them back. 'Do you feel guilty about her?' I whisper.

'Rose would be happy – for both of us,' William tells me very firmly.

'What makes you so sure?'

He kisses me on the neck. 'I just know she would be.'

36

Inside the pub, the harsh afternoon sun illuminates the ash and dust lurking in crevices and corners. An aura of despair and loneliness hangs over Adam. He's intent on reading a newspaper and doesn't see me until I reach the table.

He turns a hard, closed face towards me, folds the paper in two and leans his arms on it.

'Hi,' I say.

'Laura,' he says, frowning. 'Hi.'

When I return with the drinks, I am suddenly filled with impatience to escape from the gloomy atmosphere and from Adam's hang-dog expression.

'Congratulations, by the way,' I say. 'On winning the contract.'

Adam lets loose a bark of laughter and shoots me a hostile look. 'Yeah, right,' he says. 'Thanks.'

I'm shaking. 'I have to tell you something,' I say. I push my hair off my face, though what I'd really like to do is use it as a curtain – shouting the words through it before scuttling away.

'I know,' Adam says. 'Let's get it over with quickly.'

This pulls me up short. 'You know?'

'Debs kindly let me in on the secret. That's why I kept ringing to try and see you. I wanted to know if it was true. You know what she's like – she makes up so much.' His face is set rigid.

'Debs? What right—'

'She did me a favour, actually,' Adam says, trying to sound casual but there's an icy edge to his voice. 'Otherwise hearing about it first from the newspaper might have been a bit of a blow.'

He unfolds the newspaper and pushes it towards me.

'Top right,' he tells me, needlessly – I couldn't miss it. The name 'Claymore' leaps off the page. I feel the blood drain from my face.

NEW LOVE FOR FAMOUS PHOTOGRAPHER WIDOWER

William Claymore, the Brighton-born award-winning photographer, has found love only months after losing his wife, Rose, to cancer. The new woman in his life – a twenty-nine-year-old business adviser from Brighton called Laura Eagen – was his wife's close companion in the last days of her illness.

A family friend informed us that they'd been keeping their relationship a secret until now because of the difficult times following William Claymore's questioning by the police over the suspicious death of his wife. And although they are living together, there are no plans to marry as yet.

'You didn't know about this, then?'

I shake my head, dumbly, and place the paper out of sight on the spare seat.

'I'm so sorry, Ad.'

'It's the speed of it I can't get to grips with,' he says, shoving his hand through his hair. 'One minute we were fine and the next . . .' He looks appealingly at me. 'What happened, babe?'

I search for what I can tell him. 'We got disconnected, somehow.'

He repeats the word 'disconnected'.

'I'm sorry,' I whisper again. I bite on my lip; it's not fair to cry in front of Adam.

'Look,' he says suddenly. 'There's something I'd like to ask you, and I want to know the truth.' He pauses. 'Was this always about William? Is that why you moved out?'

I try and read in his face what he wants me to say.

'No,' I answer. 'I don't believe that it was.'

'You don't "believe"?'

'Oh Ad, I don't know any more. William and I have fallen in love – it just happened from nowhere. And the truth is, I don't know when it began.'

Adam blinks. He swirls the last inch of beer round and round the glass. The muscles in his cheek are quivering, his jaw is clenched so tight.

'Ad?'

He shakes his head and blunders up abruptly, sending the glass spinning. Beer flies everywhere. I leap back away from the table. By the time I look round, Adam has gone.

Debs hesitates before letting me in; the hesitation makes me think that she already has company but there's no one inside.

She disappears into the bathroom without saying a word and I stand there counting to ten over and over again.

Debbie's flat is incredibly untidy, as usual. It's piled up with clothes and magazines and just lots of stuff – like a rodent's nest.

'You seem stressed,' she says now as we squash onto the sofa, the only clear space in the room.

'I've just seen Adam.'

'Oh yeah?'

'You told him,' I state, trying to keep my voice calm. 'About William and me.'

Debs gives me a long look. 'It came up,' she says.

Something inside me snaps. 'So, you just happened to call him and mention it, did you?'

Debs sighs. 'No, I rang Adam to see if he'd give an interview to Andrew about that stately home garden thing and I asked how he was doing.' She picks at her thumbnail. 'I didn't realize he didn't know. I assumed you'd have done the decent thing and told him first.'

'You've got a cheek, talking to me about doing the decent thing.' My anger's been waiting for this moment; I hear my voice rising as it unwinds. 'And what's your excuse for telling your boyfriend all about me and William?'

'Uh-uh. *I* didn't say anything.'

'Doesn't our friendship mean anything to you? After all these years – you think you can just offer my life as bait to keep a bloke interested?'

'I didn't offer anything, if you want to know. They already had the story.'

'You sleep with my fiancé, you flirt with my boyfriend, you steal my dress. From day one when I met you, you've been causing me trouble. Everyone's always telling me what an awful friend you are – no, what an awful *person* you are – but I kept on making excuses; I always defended you. But I can't defend you any longer.'

'Newsflash,' Debs says, standing up. 'I've never asked you to defend me. In fact, I'm sick of you expecting me to be grateful because you condescend to be my friend while all you do is talk about me and laugh about me behind my back. Well, not fucking any more!' She jabs her finger viciously at me. 'I have fucked up, I admit it. I've done lots of things I'm not proud of. Yes,' she holds her hand in the air, 'I shagged Peter – along with the rest of Brighton's female population. I tried to tell you, others tried to talk to you about him, but you didn't listen. We thought you must have got some kind of open relationship arrangement going on – I didn't know that you were just too much of a simpleton to see what he was up to – but as for trying it on with Adam . . . it was meant to be a joke.'

'A joke! There's something wrong with your head,' I tell her.

'No, your heart. If you've even got one. You need help.'

'*You're* the one in need of help. After all, *I'm* not shagging an old man who knocked his wife off only a few months ago – a woman who was supposed to be your friend. Where's *your* heart, my little frizzy-haired gold-digger?'

I think I'm going to hit her, but the instant I imagine the sting of my hand slapping against her cheek, I know the desire to act has passed. I stumble up, my legs threatening to fold underneath me, but I manage to make it out of the door.

Ben and William are in the lounge, talking. William hustles me to sit down while he pours me a whisky. I huddle on the settee, clutching the glass. He sits next to me, draws me to lean against him.

'I'm afraid I've got bad news,' William says. 'That's why Ben's here.'

As Ben bobs his head in acknowledgement, the phone starts ringing.

'I suppose we can turn that off now Laura's back safe.' Ben kneels on the floor to pull the phone connection out.

I look at William. 'What's going on?'

'Journalists,' he tells me. 'They've been ringing all afternoon.'

'Emma's really come up trumps this time,' Ben says, brushing his jeans off. 'Even Alex thinks so.'

'Why? What's she done?'

Then I see the newspaper open on the coffee-table in front of Ben. William turns to me, brushes the hair off the side of my face and says, 'I'm sorry, darling. She's told the press about us.'

'I rang a lawyer friend,' Ben says, 'and basically, there's nothing you can do about it. They've been clever – not actually saying anything slanderous but juxtaposing phrases which could give a negative impression. *Could* being the operative word.'

'It wasn't Debs?'

William looks puzzled.

'I thought . . . I accused my friend Debs of being responsible for the story.' I'm struggling to speak clearly. I swig some whisky; it burns in my throat. 'I said some hateful things to her. I told her I never want to see her again.'

William rubs my knee. 'I'm sure she'll understand,' he consoles me. 'Once you've explained everything.'

I turn to Ben. 'That article makes us sound despicable, doesn't it?'

He smiles apologetically. 'It's not great,' he says.

'And it's not important,' William rushes to add, placing a kiss on the top of my head.

'No,' I tell him. 'You're wrong. Of course it is.'

Autumn

37

A well-spoken, charming man contacts me on my mobile about the initial stages of setting up a small business which, he informs me, is to be the commercial side of a non-profit-making organization. The concept of the project sounds right up my street and my business head switches in. I talk to Andy for nearly an hour and then go and sit in the kitchen while William is making dinner, to get down on paper the ideas which are buzzing in my brain.

Garlic- and rosemary-scented steam clouds the window. William opens the back door and fresh air weaves in.

'I'll move,' I say when William once again gently bumps into my chair as he angles past on his way to the cupboards.

'No.' He squeezes my shoulder. 'There's no need.'

It's because my proximity pleases him; as it does me, too. I like the way he reaches out and touches me every now and then. I like the way he stops for a breather and a chat – like now, bringing his glass of wine to the table.

He has tomato paste on his nose. I wipe it off, lick my finger clean.

'So, what's it all about?' he asks, but before I have a chance to tell him, the house phone rings.

Even though we've had the number changed and are ex-directory now, the way William freezes, just for a split second, shows that like me, he still feels vulnerable to unwanted calls.

It's Ben, and I can soon tell from William's tone that there's nothing wrong; that he's just calling for a chat. I wriggle my back to ease the tension in my shoulders.

'Yes, she's here, working. I will. Yes. You don't say! Yes, I certainly will.'

William chuckles. This is a special laugh he uses only with Ben, and the funny thing is – Ben sounds exactly the same. When they're in the room together, it's like hearing a boom and chortle in stereo. And what's funniest of all is I don't think they have any idea.

'Good news,' William says, replacing the handset. 'Ben was over at Alex and Emma's a couple of nights ago, and apparently they seem to be coming round to the idea.'

Of us, he means; he doesn't need to say it.

This is great news even if it's hard to keep my face neutral at the mere mention of Emma's name; even if part of me immediately gets jittery about her motives. William has put a lot of effort into talking to his sons and I'm grateful that he hasn't once made me feel that I'm not worth it.

The air's turned chill, a brief prelude to a sudden downpour. I watch drops bounce up from the paving slabs and others burst as they hit the statues. William massages my shoulders from behind. His hands seek out my breasts, he dips his head to kiss my neck.

'Shit,' he says, abandoning me when the sauce starts to spit and bubble over.

I take a sip of wine. It tastes good.

William has his back to me, already absorbed in what he's doing and I'm suddenly aware how normality has crept up on us: we're nothing but an ordinary couple sharing a bottle of wine, discussing the ins and outs of family life.

My enthusiasm for work is re-ignited; over the next week I embark on a wave of calls to clients. Now the summer rush is over, it's cheering to discover they've time to talk again, and it's encouraging when they are receptive to some of my new ideas.

My mood is buoyant on the day I'm due to meet Andy.

It's beautiful weather and I take my time walking to the restaurant. The air is warm and juicy with the scent of mown grass. The sun is out, but it's no longer that harsh summer light. Everything seems calmer, more muted. The town is less frantic; you can walk at a slower pace without someone swinging a bag into the back of your knees or catching the heel of your shoe. The shop windows are dressed in their subdued autumnal uniform of greens, aubergines and browns.

Andy is waiting for me when I'm shown to the table. He greets me enthusiastically and jumps straight in about the project. He is witty and animated, and the discussion takes us through three courses with hardly a pause from either of us.

'I like that,' he says appreciatively to one of my suggestions. He sits back and contemplates me. 'I heard you were good,' he continues, 'but I didn't think you were going to be this good.'

I'm amused by his flattery, but I can also tell he's impressed. My desire to clinch this contract spirals.

'Who told you?'

He taps his nose. 'A little birdie,' he says and grins. 'So,' he continues. 'Tell me a bit about Laura, the person not the businesswoman.'

This pulls me up short. 'Such as?' I respond warily.

'What do you like to do? Do you have a love-interest? That kind of thing,' he shrugs.

'I like running and yes, I have a . . .' I hesitate '. . . a partner.'

'You mean a boyfriend?' He winks at me and I nod and leg it to the Ladies where I consider my strategy.

Either this is Andy's rather clumsy way of getting to know the person he's dealing with, or – possibly – this is the start of a come-on. If that's the case then I'll need to handle the situation sensitively without risking losing everything. I want this work, I realize, very badly.

I dry my hands and tidy myself up. Or perhaps Andy is just one of those blokes who, encouraged by our lively meeting and a few glasses of wine, likes to try his luck but takes being turned down with good humour.

Not to worry, I tell myself. Whatever he's about, I've dealt with more complications than this before.

Andy cuts off talking on his mobile as soon as I sit down. 'Sorry, Loz,' he says. 'Do you want another coffee?'

I stare at him. There's only one person who ever, ever calls me Loz.

'You're *Andrew*. You're Debbie's journo,' I hiss. 'You bastard! You conning, lying bastard!'

'It took you long enough,' he says, unperturbed.

Stupid, stupid, stupid.

I start shoving paperwork haphazardly into my files. I just

want to get out and away from his smirking face. I can't believe I didn't cotton on before now. He even looks exactly as I'd imagined him – a trendy, arrogant, good-looking bastard.

'I've a good mind to bill you. Do you know how much time I've wasted on this?' I am appalled that I might cry in front of him; tears press hotly in my throat, burn at my eyes. I swallow hard.

'Hang on a minute,' he says, gripping my wrist. 'Calm down a bit. The project exists. I'm on the board and I'll recommend you get the contract – you've proved you know your stuff.'

I pull away from him. 'Gee thanks, that means the world to me.'

'I'm serious. I thought I'd write a feature on the project, and put in a plug for your business at the same time. What do you think? It would be kind of cool, wouldn't it?' He looks eagerly at me.

'Oh yes, it would be great – if there wasn't some great huge catch to it all. Like I'm supposed to spill the beans about William assisting Rose's suicide, or maybe bumping off his terminally ill but oh-so-in-the-way wife before she's really ready.'

'Is that how you see it?' he says too quickly.

'Oh, get lost.'

'I'm disappointed,' he says, and I almost laugh at his arrogance. 'I would have thought you might welcome the opportunity to put across your side of things,' he continues. 'Euthanasia is always a meaty, controversial subject and maybe bringing these cases to the public's attention can help get the laws changed.'

'Aren't you ever going to leave us alone? Do you know what it feels like to dread every phone call? Do you have any idea what it's like, reading those hurtful things? Doesn't the unhappiness you cause bother you at all?'

'It's important, what we do.' Andy sits back. 'Admittedly it may not be nice sometimes being on the receiving end, but without us, society would be far worse off.'

His unflinching self-importance and conceit is too much. I stand up.

'Do me a favour and at least be honest and admit that you get off on dishing dirt and creating drama. You don't give a shit about the greater good.' I pick up my briefcase. 'But let me tell you one thing: William and I are stronger for all that you've put us through, so if the aim was to wreck what we have, then you've failed.'

I turn to leave. 'Here's your scoop,' I say, stopping for a moment. I find it pathetic how quickly his head lifts, his eyes fasten on mine; he can't help himself. 'There was nothing sinister about Rose's death – as the autopsy proved if you'd like to check your facts. All William and I have done is fall in love.' I hold his gaze. 'Now that's something I'd be interested in seeing – whether you've got the guts to write a feature about love?'

The house is empty when I get home. I stand looking out at the garden. Leaves have begun dropping. A green film covers the paler statues, and the patio looks oily.

The house feels oppressive; our peace seems so flimsy and shortlived. I feel sick at the thought of my life being pried open once again and being powerless to do anything but watch everyone have a good poke around inside.

I catch sight of the Monkey Garden photograph on the wall

and decide to run there. I want to be cheered by their cheeky faces; I want to sit in that quiet and be able to breathe.

The light is dying as I turn onto the street. My legs are heavy; it's a much longer run than I've attempted for a while and the temptation to ring William to pick me up in the car at the end is growing increasingly strong.

Ahead, near the park, I can see dark pools on the pavement. I try to figure out what they are as I run closer; they're too dense for water and have a shiny appearance which is reflecting and holding the light from the evening sun.

It's red paint – dried but still slippery underfoot. I stop running. More red and yellow paint is daubed and streaked across the iron railings of the park. As I push the gate open, I notice that the original lock is broken and a replacement padlock has been added. I know then to expect the worst but I'm still not prepared for the sight.

Paint is everywhere – smeared over the bench and across the paving; slopped on the fallen leaves, splattered up the bark. Branches of some of the trees are split away from the trunks – their raw white insides look like torn flesh. The newly planted saplings have been snapped in two, flowers have been trodden down on the beds or ripped out and lie sagging on the ground. A lurid yellow mask obliterates the features of the orang-utan's face; a crude penis has been painted on its belly.

I look around in a panic for the other monkeys. I push aside the lilac branches, rummage in a couple of shrubs, peer up into the darkening canopies, seeking out all their favourite spots. But it's futile. All the monkeys have disappeared. Every single one.

38

William is out when I get up. He must have left early, as the post is still lying in a heap in the hall. I shuffle through what is mostly junkmail, and find amongst it a pink envelope addressed to me. I don't recall ever receiving a personal letter here before – everyone I know usually uses the phone, texts or sends emails, and so I can't imagine who it's from. The postmark is local but I don't recognize the writing which, though carefully done, is quite fancy with loops and curls. I wonder if it's from William. I'm not sure I've seen enough of his handwriting to recognize it, but sending a love-letter in the mail is the kind of romantic gesture he might make.

I defer the pleasure of opening it until I've made my tea and toast and Marmite. It's raining outside and the kitchen is snug – William must have put the heating on before leaving. I take the first bite, savouring the salty rush in my mouth, and slurp my tea for that salt-sweet contrast. The bread is soggy in my mouth and I picture William shuddering in mock distaste.

The envelope sits next to my plate. I wipe my hands and slit it open with a clean knife. I can see as I pull out the paper that it isn't a letter; there are a few lines set in the middle of the page, like a poem. I smile: William.

When I unfold it, the first line jumps out at me.

Murdering whore

The toast sticks in my throat.

Murdering whore
You won't get away with it.
I'm on to you. I'm on to both of you
You'd better watch out.

I drop the paper as if it's scalded me. Fear crawls across my body. I muster up the courage to check the window, certain that I will see a face looking in, but of course there's no one.

I abandon the kitchen and go to my office where I pace around, sit down, then pace again before returning to fetch the letter. I study it with as clinical an attitude as I can muster. I manage to stir up a little anger and indignation, but these are shortlived; what stays with me is its disturbing, menacing tone.

Minutes stick, then twitch forward.

When William comes back a couple of hours later, I don't have to tell him something's up – he takes one look at my face. *What's wrong?* his eyes say. *What's happened now?*

He steps towards me and I draw the letter out from my pocket.

'Oh no,' he says.

I watch him grow pale as he reads it.

'Darling,' he says finally, 'don't take it to heart. The people who do this kind of thing are messed up.'

'They hate me,' I say. Sobs jolt my body. William holds me tight and rocks me. I feel torn apart. All I can think is, I have never been hated before. I have never known what it is like to be hated until now.

'They don't know you,' he says. 'It's not about you, Laura, you know that. They're mixed-up, fucked-up people.' He takes me to the living room, supplies me with a large whisky.

'Can they do this?' I ask, now that I'm calmer. 'Isn't it illegal?'

'The advice I was given when the letters came before,' William tells me, 'was to ignore it, because unless someone actually starts being threatening in person, or sending broken glass or bombs, it's pretty much all bark and no bite. But we could tell the police if you want, just to keep them in the picture.'

Another thought comes into my head. 'What if it's someone we know?'

'I doubt it will be. The police told me that it's almost always from a complete stranger.'

'Emma?' I suggest hesitantly.

William lets out a bark of laughter. 'She's screwed up, that girl, but even she's not as over the top as this. I mean – "murdering whore"!'

'The ones you got before, Wills – were they as bad as this?'

He doesn't answer immediately; he pinches the top of his nose. 'No, but pretty horrible all the same.'

For the next couple of days, I steel myself to receive another letter – but the post brings nothing more distressing than bills. I begin to relax again; my heart no longer races whenever I hear the clang of the letterbox. I tell myself that the weirdo has vented their anger, and that is the end of the matter.

Then, five days later, another arrives. I spot it from down the hall, the candy pink standing out against the other brown and white envelopes. I force myself to go forward.

'There's another one,' I call out to William in the next room, as if this will make it seem less sinister, but he doesn't appear to have heard me.

I pick the envelope up and I'm aware of a scent. I sniff the paper. It's a floral perfume. I inhale again – it's familiar but I can't place it.

I think: a woman. A woman writes these.

I open it hurriedly, standing in the hall.

It begins like the other:

> *Murdering whore*
> *I won't ever let you forget.*
> *What right do you have to be happy?*
> *Whenever you're happy, I'll remind you what you did*
> *Then we'll see.*

I can picture the kind of woman who would write these words. She'd be fifty or sixty, her sour-looking appearance reflecting the bitterness she feels for her disappointing life. I suddenly remember the woman in the supermarket and I'm hit with the certain knowledge that I have solved it. Her face was ordinary but her eyes had poured out a lifetime of resentment towards William.

She must have spotted us in the shop again, or perhaps she sees us most days walking hand-in-hand past the window. The sight of us makes her blood boil so that she is driven to write, egged on by this powerful, though misguided emotion.

'It's her!' I say, barging into the kitchen, waving the letter. William looks up, startled. 'It's the supermarket checkout woman.'

'How do you know? What does she say?'

'It's anonymous again. But I can feel it.'

The next day, when I'm not expecting another so soon, one arrives. My guts immediately start churning; I have to rush to the loo before I can read it.

> *Murdering whore*
> *How can you sleep at night?*
> *Take a look in the mirror.*
> *A long look.*
> *Do you see what I see? Aren't you ashamed?*

Later, when I'm alone in the bedroom, I examine my face in the mirror. I am pale, with dark shadows under my eyes. My hair is dry and frizzy – it's missing the deep wax treatments I used to put in every week when Debs and I went to the sauna.

But these are external signs, and what I'm searching for is deeper than that. I lean closer. I think of William this morning. Before he left, he was humming. He started from the moment he got up, continued into the bathroom, while he dressed, and all the way downstairs without breaking off once. When I joined him for breakfast, all the curtains downstairs had been drawn and sunlight was filling the house.

As I'm remembering this, I'm trying to read the emotion in my eyes. Can I see love? Tenderness? Or something else?

I blink hard.

All I know is that William was happy, and as I watched him, I felt a lightness travelling through my veins.

Before I have time to deliberate, I have picked up my coat and am striding down the street ready to confront the cow of a woman who is not going to spoil another minute of my life.

The few tattered leaves which remain on the trees shiver in the wind; the rest have fallen and been blown to rest in soggy piles against the kerb except for the odd crunchy escapee which I crush underfoot as I march along. I feel powerful, like Superwoman, I joke to myself. I am Superwoman going into battle against the evil Supermarketwoman.

As I near the shop, my pace slackens as I consider my method of attack. I stop a few metres away to weigh up my options. I imagine playing my letter-writer at her own game – the hunter becoming the hunted – by leaving a disturbing sinister note. But almost immediately, I reproach myself for even considering stooping to her level. I shall tackle her face to face – with dignity.

I spy on the checkouts from the safety of an aisle. There are only three open and all are manned by young people – the tall girl I saw when I came in, an appallingly spotty lad, and a woman with a brush of peroxide hair and bright blue eye-shadow. I circulate through the shop several times to ensure she isn't around somewhere, stacking shelves, but there's no sign of her. I think back to that day when she served us, and remember that it was late afternoon so I buy some peanut butter and a carton of milk and go home, determined to return tomorrow after four, to catch her on the later shift.

The woman doesn't appear the next day, or the following one. There are all sorts of possible reasons for her absence. She might be on holiday – I picture her tagged along with a sibling's family, the strange spinster aunt they feel obliged to invite every year – or it could be she's off sick, or simply that my visits haven't coincided with her hours.

Each time I go there, I dawdle round the shop for as long as I can before I start feeling conspicuous. I'll have to be patient, I tell myself. But I will see her.

At least I no longer feel like prey. Instead, I am energized, hyped up with a purpose. William notices my change in mood. 'You seem chirpy,' he says one time, and once when we're preparing a meal together, I catch him smiling to himself.

I've decided not to let on what I'm up to until it's over, since he'd be sure to worry or advise me to not waste my time, and I want to finish the matter properly. I am determined to be the cause of and witness to the cessation of these letters, rather than have them dwindle out of existence because she's got it off her chest, or is bored, or has decided to torment some other poor soul.

Nearly a week goes by without another letter, which makes my preferred theory that the woman is on holiday even more likely. But as each uneventful day passes, the more nervous I feel as I approach the supermarket.

I still haven't decided exactly how to handle the confrontation. I guess I'm hoping that my materializing in the flesh in front of her will provoke such a profound feeling of shame in Supermarketwoman that she will stop writing. I will speak to her, though; I'm clear about that. I think I'm going to say: 'I know it's you who's been sending the letters.' And then take it from there.

I practise the delivery of this sentence out loud at home. I want the tone to be assertive and somehow disdainful.

William finds me in the kitchen, crying.

'Stop tormenting yourself,' he shouts, tearing the new letter out of my hands. He crumples it up and throws it in the bin. 'There,' he says, his neck taut with anger. 'That's what you do with them.'

Later, while William is out, I fish the letter from the rubbish and flatten it out. It's covered in multi-coloured stains and blobs. I think, How apt, considering the content.

> *Do you feel dirty,*
> *When you have a murderer's hands on your body?*
> *Those fingers smearing her blood across your skin.*

I reread the words. No 'murdering whore' this time, but the message seems to have stepped up a gear in viciousness. With a flash of intuition, I realize that she's seen me in the shop.

39

She's there.

I recognize her neat grey-blonde hair on the Express checkout the moment I go in.

I charge into an aisle, out of sight. I prop myself up against a freezer unit and push my hands down to my wrists amongst the crackling bags of frozen peas and sweetcorn in an attempt to cool down and compose myself. It's important to look completely unfazed and calm when I appear in front of her.

I hurry round the shop selecting ten things at random, the maximum number of items I can take through the till so that I can have as long as possible with her.

There are four customers before me. I crane my neck to watch her. I notice that she deals with each one extremely efficiently, exchanging only the minimal conversation required; no jokes and cheeriness and passing the time of day.

It's nearly my turn. The man in front of me places the Next Customer divider down on the conveyor belt and I slowly unpack my shopping. Now I'm this close, I hardly dare to look at her. The ring on her wedding finger surprises me until I see it for what it is: a disguise, a wish to appear as a respectable married woman. She's also wearing a gold chain just visible at the collar of her uniform and tiny gold cross earrings.

'Afternoon, dear,' she says, her gaze gliding over me as she reaches for the first of my purchases.

'Good afternoon,' I say loudly, to attract her attention.

'Need any help packing?' she asks, without lifting her eyes, beeping my items through at high speed. She doesn't wait for a reply; she pulls a carrier bag out from under the counter and starts plonking everything in.

'It's OK.' I grapple the bag from her. She spins her chair back to the till and informs me of the total price. It doesn't register immediately – I have to look at the amount on the display in front of me.

I can sense the murmurings of irritation in the queue as I hunt through my handbag for my purse. I'm flustered, over-heating. The woman sits calmly upright – the serene model of Customer Care politeness.

I pull out a ten-pound note, then change my mind – to louder grumbling from the queue. My card has my name on it. I hand it over and wait for the penny to drop.

The woman has spoken. She repeats her question. 'Do you want cash back?' She's finally met my eyes, not with any recognition but patronizingly, as if she considers me to be a little strange. I shake my head dumbly.

'Enter your pin number, please.'

My fingers feel numb. I mis-key, have to cancel and start again.

'Your receipt and card.' The transaction is complete.

And then, just as she's leaning forward to begin with the next customer, I speak.

I know it isn't her but I say the sentence that I've been practising anyway. I can't imagine walking away from the shop without doing so. I just can't.

'I know it's you sending the letters.'

'Pardon?'

I repeat it. She looks at me, glances at the next customer, then back at me. I can tell that she thinks I've got a screw loose.

'The letters,' I say.

'I'm sorry, dear,' she says. 'I really don't know what you mean.' And for the first time, her trained politeness cracks. She shrugs, pulls a face at the man behind, as if to say: 'Oh God, I've got a right one here.'

I emerge into the street and all I can see are eyes watching me; I'm a freakshow.

Amusement, pity, mockery.

Choked with humiliation I blunder through them, and then I begin to run.

40

The letters keep coming. Some are short and cryptic:

> *I'm waiting,*
> *Waiting for a chance.*
> *Are you ready for me?*
> *I'm coming.*

Others are longer and more detailed; it's these I dread most.

> *What would a child of yours be like?*
> *What would two murderers create?*
> *Can you picture him? I can.*
> *Big baby eyes which have no soul.*
> *A monster.*

My trail of the letter-writer is stone cold.

I believe that this person must be watching me. How else could they tap into my fears so easily? How else could they hit the nerves they do? Whenever I go out, I'm on high alert. I scan every face, challenging them to step forward and reveal themselves, even though in the pit of my stomach I'm scared to death.

One afternoon, when I'm walking back to the house from a lunchtime meeting with a client, there's a woman standing outside a neighbour's house. I don't recognize her and something about her demeanour strikes me as odd. When I get closer, our eyes meet. I stop suddenly on the pavement, unable to move forward and unable to look away. The woman turns abruptly, then, fumbling with her keys, she rushes inside.

As I continue on my way, in as dignified a manner as I can muster, I sense her watching my progress from behind her blinds, waiting until I'm safely gone.

I'm ashamed to think that I have just caused someone else to feel afraid.

William comes up behind me. 'Boo,' he says softly.

I shriek and he leaps back.

'You scared the hell out of me,' he says. His arms come around my chest. 'I can feel your heart beating,' he whispers.

We watch TV – a documentary on lions. I lie with my head on his lap and he strokes my hair. The next thing I know, William is shaking me awake and leading me upstairs.

I lie fully clothed on the bed and William kneels beside me; he begins to undress me and I feel my body soften under his caresses.

Those fingers smearing her blood across your skin.

I tense. William murmurs, 'Relax.'

He tracks kisses across my neck, his hands play in my hair. His face is the usual mixture of seriousness and desire, which makes my heart fill up. I want to believe in this moment so I close my eyes and try to hold onto that image as his mouth and hands travel down my body.

Those fingers . . .

I resist the urge to push William away; I won't let her spoil this. Instead I turn over, bury my face in the pillow, grit my teeth and wait for him to finish.

A woman barrels into me in the street. I am mesmerized by a mess of yellow-white hair; some of it sits in a knot tied on top of her head with a wide, orange elastic band, the rest hangs in greasy strands down past her shoulders. The knot wobbles as she waggles her finger at me.

'You,' she accuses.

The hairs on the back of my neck spring up. I stand still. It's her. Here she is. It's time.

Her face is mottled; her eyes are tiny, lost under sprouting grey eyebrows. 'Watch where you're going, bitch.' She spits her anger at me.

I mumble, 'I'm sorry.'

People are slowing down to watch.

'It's a bit late for sorry, Miss La-di-da,' she shouts. Her long coat bulges from the layers underneath. Bright green Argyll socks show above a pair of scuffed men's shoes with newspaper stuffing at the heel.

Someone laughs and she spins round. The finger, like a divining stick, waggling away, locates the culprit in the crowd – a bloke about my age.

'You,' she hisses and charges at him, her plastic carrier bag swinging wildly.

His head flicks back, his eyes bulge like a spooked horse and he legs it down the road, with the woman giving chase. I am too tired to find it funny. I continue on my way; I would have taken a taxi if the nearest rank hadn't meant retracing my steps.

William catches me reading the letters which I've been keeping hidden in a folder in my office. He rushes over, snatches the folder out of my hands, twists it, bends it and dumps the lot in my wastepaper bin.

'See?' he shouts. 'See how easy it is?' He stands in front of the desk, his voice lowered and softer. 'Why do you do it, Laura? It's ridiculous. You're just upsetting yourself.'

I don't say anything.

'Can't you see that's what she wants?' He raises his hands in exasperation. 'Can't you see you're letting her win?'

I jump at his words. 'So you do believe in her.'

William turns abruptly, slamming the door behind him. When I hear him in the kitchen, I escape with the file upstairs. Rose's room is the only place I can be sure William will not find it. I flatten out the worst creases and slip the folder under the mattress.

When I hear the front door banging closed, I go over to the window. William stops to button his coat, pull his collar up against the wind. I bob out of view, certain that he's about to look up at Rose's window but when I peer round, he's already halfway down the street. He has his camera bag with him, so he could be gone for a while.

The Crescent is empty.

My eyes are drawn to the panorama of windows in front of me. There are dozens of different ones, all sizes and types – huge sheet windows, little portholes, dormers and sash. Some are curtained, or have blinds, others are bare.

As soon as I realize I can be seen, I step back.

Somewhere in David's airy, spacious house the phone is ringing. I imagine a muted sound purring out across the tranquil cream setting. I let it go on for a long time.

I think, Forget it, there's no one home – but I keep holding on. Perhaps they're in the kitchen; perhaps they're in the garden. 'Is that the phone, dear?' Tugging off outdoor shoes, stepping lightly in soft socks across beige tiles.

But finally the answerphone takes the call. '*David and Trudy aren't here to . . .*'

I disconnect. David's voice is higher-pitched than I remember.

Debbie's mobile rings once, twice, and abruptly stops. I try again. It switches immediately into Voicemail. No chance to say *sorry*. No chance to say *remember*.

I'm still mad at you – that's what her silence means.

I don't know why, but I seem to be shaking so I sit down on my bed.

'God, Laura,' Nat says. 'You look terrible. Are you ill?'

I try to say no, but I can't form the words. Something's not right. I lean against the counter. I'm having trouble breathing.

'Go and sit down,' she orders. 'I'll bring a drink over.'

We stir our cappuccinos. Nat has brought a cocoa shaker to the table and we sprinkle, drink some of the froth, sprinkle more powder on top. We do this in silence. Perhaps looking at us, you'd think it was companionable but it's not – it's awkward. Nat's disappointment in me is like a grumpy third party sitting at the table. I'm already regretting coming here but I didn't know where else to go.

I feel screwed up tight inside.

'Laura,' Nat says finally. 'What's wrong?'

'I'm getting hatemail,' I blurt out.

'What?'

'These – horrible – letters about me and William.'

'What do you mean horrible? What do they say?'

'Sinister things, nasty things.' I shiver. 'Some of them start with "murdering whore".'

'Murdering whore!' Nat's face opens up with amusement but she quickly becomes serious. She touches my hand in apology. 'I'm sorry, it just sounded so melodramatic, like something out of the Dark Ages.'

I nod. 'I know. It's stupid, isn't it? It's stupid, stupid to let it bother me.' I start to laugh but it turns to sobbing. I gulp and hiccup as I try to make myself stop. 'I'm sorry, Nat. I'm an embarrassment.'

She brushes my damp hair gently from my face. 'I didn't realize you were so upset.'

'They make me feel dirty and bad . . . They say if I have a baby it will be a monster. They say William has . . . blood-smeared fingers . . . and that they're coming to get me.'

'God. That's awful.' She is shocked.

'They say they're watching me and they're waiting. I don't know what they're waiting to do, Nat, but I'm frightened to go out, and I hate staying in.'

Nat looks alarmed. 'Have you told the police?'

'Wills says they can't do anything.' I look at Nat. 'He received a couple of letters before, when Rose died . . . when the police took him in for questioning.'

'Well, there you are, then.' Nat sits back. 'Nothing happened to him, did it? I guess they'll just stop sending them in the end and in the meantime, don't read them. Throw the wretched things straight in the bin.'

'That's what he says I should do, but I can't.' I lean forward. 'You see, I think there's a hidden clue in each of the letters, and each clue gives a different part to a message. So I can't afford to miss one. I have to read them all to work out the message so that I can be ready.'

Nat fiddles with her cup. 'Do you think you should go and see a doctor?' she asks suddenly.

'No,' I say, surprised. 'Why, do you?'

'I think it's something you should consider. I mean, you look awful – you're obviously completely stressed out.'

We sit in silence for a moment.

'You never seem happy,' she says gently. 'These days.'

I shrug.

'You've been like this ever since you started with William.'

'What do you mean?'

'Nothing. Forget it.'

'Come on, Nat, what are you saying?'

'All right. What I meant was, being with William doesn't seem to be very good for you. Nothing about it seems right.'

I don't even bother to respond. I pick up my coat and bag and I leave. I don't know whether Nat calls out to me. I just walk out of the door and I don't look back.

*   *   *

William's gone shopping. He tried to persuade me to accompany him, but I lied that I needed to finish some work; I simply couldn't face going out.

As soon as he left I locked all the doors. I do this automatically now whenever I'm alone in the house. It gives me peace of mind.

'I want to bring you back something nice,' William had said. 'What do you fancy?'

I could tell he wasn't going to be happy until I'd named a treat.

'Ice cream. One of those posh ones.'

'Flavour?'

'Surprise me.'

He'd looked pleased with his mission and now I'll have to pretend to be delighted with whatever he chooses, even though the mere thought of ice cream makes me feel sick. I haven't been running for ages and it's really starting to catch up with me. I constantly feel bloated, and just now when I jogged up the stairs, heavy flesh juddered on my bum and thighs.

I look down at my stomach and pinch it viciously.

I miss running badly. I'm cooped up, so cooped up.

From Rose's window I picture myself, running through the streets, criss-crossing the town; my hair, a blonde flag of freedom streaming in the wind behind me. I can almost smell the air: salty at the seafront, pub and grub odours further inland, the chemical perfume of washing powder as I run past the laundry block of the student accommodation. I hear the thud of my trainers, the swoosh of slowing cars, the manic chirping of birds diving into their chosen roost before they settle for the night.

There's no wind today; it would have meant I could have run further, stayed out for longer.

I wait for Wills in the kitchen. I don't know how time passes.

'It's muggy out,' William informs me and proceeds to clatter around, opening doors and windows, exclaiming: 'Haven't you noticed how stuffy it is in here?'

'Good job I've got this to cool me down,' I joke. The largest tub of chocolate cookie crumble ice cream is on the kitchen table in front of me. William's remembered correctly that this is my favourite, but I look at the daunting richness of it with apprehension.

He's bought himself his favourite cheesecake from the fancy bakery and so we sit opposite each other in what William believes to be companionable indulgence. Every spoonful sticks in my throat, but I keep on going and going and going.

William chats about the Brighton diving project which is nearing conclusion. He's currently preparing for a meeting where they'll make the final selection of photographs. I half-listen; my mind keeps traipsing away. The waistband of my jeans is cutting into my flesh. I surreptitiously undo a button and my stomach flops free.

'You're enjoying that,' William states, meaning the ice cream.

'Mmm, delicious,' I agree, and I keep digging away with the spoon until there's only a small hump left in the bottom of the tub.

I make an excuse that the house is warm in order to change into a loose summer dress. There are red lines all across my stomach and short zigzag marks on the outside of my thighs which on closer examination in the mirror turn out to be the imprint of the seams.

Downstairs, as I stand looking out of the window, I catch William studying me. I realize the light is illuminating my body through the thin cotton. I quickly move to sit primly on the other end of the settee. Right now, I couldn't feel any less sexy and I really don't want to encourage any lustful thoughts in Wills. I glance over at him. A shiver goes through me as I read not desire but tenderness in his eyes and realize that William suspects I'm pregnant.

A monster.

Blood rises to my face. 'I've put on weight.' I fold my arms across my stomach. 'No more treats like that for me for a while,' I add in as light a tone as I can muster.

'You look lovely,' he tells me. 'In fact, I prefer you with a bit of flesh. You were too thin before.'

'I hate being this size,' I say, and I can tell William's a little alarmed by the vehemence in my voice.

'Why haven't you been running?' he asks after a moment.

I'm surprised. I hadn't realized he'd noticed. 'I haven't felt up to it recently.'

'Why not, Laura? Do you feel ill?'

'Just tired.'

He cups his hand to the side of my face; his palm is warm against my cool cheek. I love it when he does that. I lean against it and close my eyes.

I think, Don't move. Please don't move. I'd be happy if everything stopped at this moment.

41

'How are you doing?' Ben asks.

'OK.'

'You look tired.'

'Yeah,' I say. 'I am a bit.' I glance at my watch; William's only been gone five minutes although it seems much longer. I wish I could have forced myself to go to the off-licence instead of him. I know they were both expecting me to offer, but I just sat there like a lemon. William had given me a long, quizzical look before getting up.

What that means is, I'm left talking to Ben who slouches on the sofa with one leg crossed, idly tapping the beer bottle on the sole of his trainer.

'Dad said some psycho's been sending you letters,' Ben says.

'Oh, I didn't know he'd told you.' Blood rushes to my face.

'He's worried about you.'

I shrug and try a smile. 'There's no need. Although, actually, the letters are pretty upsetting.'

'I heard.'

I wonder just how much William's told Ben. I wonder what else they might have discussed.

'As long as you don't let the crazies get to you, Laura.'

'I'll try not to.'

Ben suddenly sits forward, elbows on his knees. 'I meant it, you know, the other week, when I said I was pleased about you and Dad.'

'Thanks, Ben,' I say, carefully but sincerely. 'That means a lot.'

'It's about time he had some happiness. After all, he gave up so much for Mum.'

'I'm not sure he'd see it that way.'

'I wasn't talking about Mum's illness,' he replies, and then stops.

I look at him blankly.

'Oh shit,' he says, groaning. 'God, I thought you knew and now I've put my foot in it.'

Jittery nerves immediately start up in my stomach. I think, No more surprises; I can't handle any more surprises. 'Well, there's no need to say anything else,' I tell him hurriedly. 'Just forget it.'

Ben gives this some thought. He tap-tap-taps the bottle on the bottom of his trainer. 'I think you should know,' he says eventually. 'It might help you understand this dysfunctional family a little better.'

'Perhaps you ought to talk it over with your . . . with William first,' I say, and start to get up.

'Years ago,' Ben announces, 'Dad had an affair.'

I slide back on the seat. Ben continues to tap-tap-tap the bottle as he speaks.

'It wasn't a fling or anything; it was serious. I was only about twelve but we – me and Alex – found out about it. We were back in Barcelona for the Easter break and I saw Dad with her in the street, and somehow it was obvious that they were together. They looked very happy and I remember thinking it seemed right. We met her, too, when she came to a party at the apartment and I talked to her; she was a nice woman, very gentle.' He pauses and glances at me. 'I suppose it seems a bit odd me talking about this?'

'A little,' I admit. My throat croaks and my lips feel dry; I lick them.

'Perhaps that's what comes of spending most of your child-hood in boarding school. You end up seeing your parents more objectively; actually as *people*. For good or bad.' He gives a little smile. 'Anyway, the thing was, Mum and Dad hadn't been happy for a while. There was always a big fuss and excitement and fun when we first arrived in the holidays, and they were fine in a family group or surrounded by friends, but you would never find them alone together. They just weren't interested in each other's company.'

I'm confused: Rose and William loved each other, I know they did – I witnessed it daily – but now Ben seems to be saying something different. I wish I had left the room now; I don't want to hear any more. I'd like to stick my fingers in my ears, sing la-la-la loudly until Ben stops talking.

'Anyway, one summer holiday it was obvious Mum had found out about the affair, and she seemed to be punishing him. It was awful. She was pretty mean to him. She was hurting, I suppose, but we didn't see it like that at the time. We'd always been Daddy's boys and we just saw how miserable he was.

There was a particularly shitty period like you get in films where everything is done via the children: *Would you ask your father to pass the salt? Would you ask your father to fix the tap?* He shakes his head. 'A nightmare.' He pauses briefly. 'She kept it up for weeks. We still went on family picnics and to the beach and did all the things that "nice families" do, but for the entire holiday, she didn't say a single word directly to Dad. I'd escape out on my bike for hours and when I had to be at home, I stayed in my room, stuck my Walkman on and blocked it all out. But Alex couldn't detach himself. At first he tried to trick Mum into saying something to Dad, then he stopped talking to both of them in retaliation; for a while he wouldn't even speak to me. He completely lost the plot – he was getting bullied back at school in England – he was totally losing it with everything.'

'How did it end?' My voice comes out in a whisper.

'I don't know; it just did. When we were due to go over to stay with them for the next holidays, Alex couldn't hack it. He got so wound up and ill that the school doctor declared him too unwell to travel. Mum and Dad changed their arrangements and came to us – to here, in fact – for Christmas and when we arrived, they were like different people. They seemed in love, madly in love, more demonstrative than I'd ever seen them. They held hands, they cuddled up together on the settee – it got to be so embarrassing it was almost as traumatic as them falling out.' Ben grins. 'Alex was furious. He called Rose psychotic and Dad a pushover.'

Ben places his bottle on the coffee-table. He picks at the label. 'I was relieved, of course. I mean, thank Christ it was over! But after a while I began to feel there was something different about Dad, and that behind all the lovey-dovey giggling and clinking of wine glasses, he was actually sad.'

We hear the key in the front door and look guiltily in that direction as if we've been caught being naughty.

'I know that he loved her,' Ben rushes to say, frowning, looking anxiously at me. 'Mum, I mean – in a whole lot of ways. But he loves you, differently. That's all I was trying to say. That sadness, that shadow, has gone.'

Do you think you're special?
Do you think he won't do the same to you as he did to her?
What's to stop him?
One way or another.

*   *   *

It seems only fair to William to tell him what I know.

'My God, my God,' he says, and covers his face with his hands. He remains like that for several minutes. Minutes where I kick myself that I've made completely the wrong judgement.

'I need a drink.' He fetches an open bottle of wine and pours us both a large glass. 'I've always kidded myself that the boys were too young and wrapped up in their own lives to notice that there was something going on between me and Rosie.'

'I'm sorry, Wills. I wish Ben had never told me.'

'No, I'm glad. It's better this way.' He takes a long drink of wine. 'Right. Let's get this out in the open.' He breathes deeply to compose himself and I find myself taking a deep breath, too, as if I'm about to be submerged in water.

'I was on the verge of leaving Rosie.' He stops and looks down at his hands. 'I don't know how to talk about this,' he says, but almost immediately begins to speak again. 'Rosie was unhappy with a lot of things – though mostly me – and our marriage had been struggling for some time when I met Evelyn. We hit it off immediately; she was a sweet, kind woman and didn't seem to hate me!' He lets loose a short, mirthless laugh. 'Things went from there and were great until one of our friends told Rosie and she hit the roof. She did all sorts of crazy things for a while and just when I thought she'd calmed down and we could talk, she started her silent treatment. I tried to get her to discuss things but in the end I gave up. I couldn't get through.' He glances at me. 'This had already been going on for a few weeks when the boys came for the holidays, and, as you know, it continued all the way through. When they left, it was so quiet and awful, I couldn't stand the thought of living like that any longer and I told Rosie that it would be better for both of us if I left.' He smiles weakly. 'I'm sorry; this doesn't put me in a great light.'

'It's your past, Wills,' I say quietly. 'Everyone's got one.'

'Anyway, Rosie was always full of surprises. She disappeared for a few days and when she came back, she said she wanted us to try again. I felt I owed her that and so I agreed. Once things had settled down a bit, we began to rediscover each other all over again, and for the first time in years we actually appreciated and liked what we found. In the end I had to tell Evelyn that I was staying with my family; with Rosie.'

He leans his head against the back of the settee.

'I did love Rosie,' he says, and looks me straight in the eye. 'Is it all right to say that?'

'Of course it's all right. I know you did.'

We sit in silence for a while. I think I can hear children

shouting. It's about the usual time they play outside before they're called in for the night.

'I've been wondering whether we should think about moving,' William says suddenly. 'This house holds a few too many ghosts, too many memories. Don't you think it's time we made some new ones of our own?'

'Where would we go?'

He opens his hands wide. 'The world's our oyster. We always used to talk about travelling, didn't we?'

'Leave everything? Our families and friends?'

'You visit them, they visit you.'

I stumble over my reply. 'I really don't know. I'll have to think about it,' I say, although I don't know what there is to think about. Who would there be to stay for, after all?

42

'Are you sure you're going to be all right?' William asks for about the zillionth time. 'I can always delay . . .'

I press my finger to his mouth to stop him talking. 'I'll be fine,' I reassure him. 'Don't be silly.' I know how important this assignment in Cornwall is to William and I'm not about to blow it for him by behaving like a baby who can't be left alone for five days.

The car is packed. It's taken over an hour to do it. There's an amazing amount of equipment. A lot of it is William's own, which has all been checked and serviced. Some is specialist stuff which he's hired to replace that which he's left behind in Barcelona. Three wetsuits hang on the suit rail; the car already reeks of warm rubber.

William goes for a last-minute check round the house while I stand in the open front doorway waiting to wave him off. The Crescent's quiet; all the kids are in school. It's a lovely day – dry and cool. The sort of day that tempts you outside, that reminds you of afternoons spent walking along the beach, or through woods collecting chestnuts for roasting.

As soon as I close the door behind William I feel depressed by the dinginess of the house. I sit in the office and make a To Do list but the whole time my mind is skirting around the most important issue, the thing I've been planning to do ever since William told me he was going away. With no prospect of being caught, I'll have plenty of time to study the letters and work out their meaning once and for all.

I pull the folder out from under Rose's mattress. When I open it, dislodged dust makes me sneeze and the sickly perfume from the letters coats the roof of my mouth. I open the windows and sip at the fresh air. The sky is completely clear; there's not a single cloud.

I hear Rose chastising me: '*Why do you want to be stuck indoors on a day like this, girl? Get out there.*'

As her words hit home, a flush creeps up my body, like a stain. I feel ashamed that I have allowed my life to be reduced to this tiny, bite-sized version. I've been pretending to myself that I can carry out my business in this half-hearted manner, but I don't have to look at my diminishing number of clients to know that it isn't working. I have kidded myself that it's enough for William and me to stay at home most evenings and at the weekends, and I have lied to myself that running had become an obsession and I needed to cool off for a while. It's the one thing that I'm sure I love, that I know is one of the best parts of me.

Like a kid woken early in the morning to go on a surprise trip, I feel sluggish but exhilarated. I dust off my bum-bag, dig out my trackpants and T-shirt.

On my way out, I pause momentarily with my hand on the

door handle. The fear hasn't gone; I can't simply scoop it away like a pile of rubbish into a bin, but within it is a seam of pleasure and excitement that I tap into; a root sucking up sustenance. I think of Rose's encouragement as I pull open the door.

Outside, the air catches in my chest. It's colder than I had imagined. A gusty wind is rolling in from the sea, charging through the streets and bouncing into everything in its path. As I walk to the end of the square, I feel an overwhelming instinct to look behind me, and when my eyes are drawn to the top of the house, it's as if I'd known: a shadow flits across Rose's window.

I reason it out – a cloud passing in front of the sun, something moving in the building opposite, perhaps – but I wave anyway. I wave to Rose who's given me the strength to be out here, who's been rude enough to set me back on track. *'Stop moping, Laura.'*

I run down to the promenade. It's quiet, but the few people around seem unusually cheerful and friendly. I'm surprised how many of them acknowledge me, how many say a spirited hello as the wind buffets them.

On the way back, I take a detour to Nikki's juice bar. I sit on a bar stool and sip a carrot, celery and soy-sauce cleanser.

'Haven't seen you around so much these days,' Nikki says in her slow, soft voice. Behind her tough-looking cropped hair and piercings her face is remarkably childlike with absolutely flawless skin. Along with her dawdling speech, she has a serene way of moving which might lead you to suspect she's a dopey, drippy cow, but in fact she's one of my most successful clients. Not only does she make a reasonable living out of this tiny five by ten feet space but she also owns a hat boutique, has shares in an antique jewellery shop in the Lanes, and her seaview apartment is fully paid up. She doesn't need to work here – she's told me before; she does it because she likes to meet people and because she finds the work therapeutic.

'I've not been feeling so good,' I tell her.

'Symptoms?'

'Well, stress, really,' I mumble vaguely. 'Nervy, insomnia, demotivated – that kind of thing.'

Nikki wipes her hands on the cloth tucked into her waistband, cocks her head to one side as she assesses me. 'I'll make you something to take away,' she says.

She snips expertly at a tray of wheat grass with a glinting pair of elongated, slim scissors and it seems like magic when the whole mini-lawn ends up level. The aromas of ginger and sesame waft over me. In the background, jingly relaxation music is playing.

Nikki places a plastic container on the counter in front of me. 'You need to keep it in the fridge and have it over the next three days,' she tells me.

I prise the lid up a little. The mixture looks sludgy and smells potent – the kind of drink you need to hold your nose to swallow.

'For positive energy,' she tells me. 'On the house.'

On the way home, I buy fresh bread and a bunch of dwarf sunflowers. I pop my head round the door of Angus's shop and wave to him. He's busy with a customer.

'Come and see me soon,' he calls over their head.

As I walk, I picture myself describing my day over the phone to William, hearing his relief, making him laugh. It seems ages since we really laughed together.

When I get inside and the empty house greets me, I bustle away my falling spirits. I put on the radio, fill the coffee-maker, arrange the flowers in a vase. I sniff Nikki's concoction and put it in the fridge, deciding to leave the first batch until tomorrow.

When the evening draws on, I close the curtains, switch on the TV and lie on the sofa waiting for William to call.

He rings late. 'Sorry, darling, I couldn't get away any sooner,' he says. 'Is everything OK there?'

I tell him about my afternoon and it's how I imagined; the pleasure in his voice is evident and he's full of news, too.

'There's going to be the chance for some amazing pictures,' he tells me. 'It's beautiful here. I'm going to bring you with me next time,' he promises, and my heart turns over.

Before going to bed, I do a final check of the doors and windows. A little unnerved, I now regret watching all those scary movies as I make my way round the big, creaky house. I tell myself it's understandable as I haven't been alone here at night before. I just need to get used to the noises it makes.

I was unsure if I'd remembered to close the windows in Rose's room this afternoon, but I evidently had as the air is thick with the scent emanating from the letters. I check the lock is secured and then bend down to the bed. I slide my hand under the mattress for the folder but my fingers find nothing; it's gone.

Panic blooms in my head until I recall taking it downstairs with me this afternoon. I almost laugh at my stupidity and plump down on the bed to recover myself. The smell of perfume rises again; the hairs on the back of my neck prickle as the scent intensifies.

I recognize it now. I don't know how I missed it before – it's Rose's perfume. The scent on the letters is the same as the perfume she wore every day until she died.

I'm choking on cloying lungfuls of the stuff. I'm suffocating. I manage to push myself up and flee the room.

I fly down the stairs and into my bedroom, locking the door behind me.

43

The next morning, the twelfth letter arrives. I stare at it. The idea of opening it is horrifying but inevitable.

I walk slowly to the kitchen. The envelope is saturated with scent; I feel the paper sticking to my fingers.

I sink onto a chair and slice open the flap with a kitchen knife.

> *You're the cuckoo in the nest.*
> *Getting fat in someone else's house.*
> *Find your own house, your own life.*
> *This one doesn't belong to you.*

It's all clear to me now. I've been an idiot to have missed it. Stupid, stupid, stupid. It's the same jabbing voice, the same trenchant words which can U-turn on you in the blink of an eye.

I fetch the other letters and read them in order and it's as plain as can be. I remember the photographs. They're where I'd hidden them on the bookcase in the living room. I hear myself gasp as I remove them from the packet; my hands are shaking as I sort through the ones of William and me.

Eleven photos.

So obvious now, the message that she intended to leave us: *I'm keeping an eye on you.*

Her spirit is everywhere. Every bit of this house has her mark on it; every item has been touched or looked upon by her.

I retreat to my bedroom and pull the duvet over my head.

At six o'clock I force myself downstairs. Last night William said he'd probably call some time between now and eight. Last night seems a world away.

I venture into the kitchen for some supplies. I try to drink some of Nikki's juice mix but I gag on the thick liquid so I take two bottles of water and a packet of plain biscuits for later. I stretch the phone cord into the hall and sit on the bottom step to wait. It seems the most neutral territory – a passing-through place which nobody can really claim.

There's a draught from the front door. I hug my frozen knees and stare at the phone, desperate for William to call so I can go back to my room. Minutes slouch by.

When the phone rings the noise is immense; my heart feels as if it's been jump-started.

'How are you, Laura?'

Tears hover. William rushes on, full of his day – he talks about sea squirts and a conger eel which was almost two metres long.

'It scared the hell out of me,' he says, laughing.

He takes me at my word that everything is fine.

* * *

There are now twelve letters. The thirteenth is going to come on Friday. I realized this when William was talking about Saturday, the fourteenth – the day he'll get back.

Friday the thirteenth, the thirteenth letter.

And it will be the one that all the others have been building up to.

I know it, the house knows it. The air seems taut as if the walls are holding their breath.

The next two days crawl by.

I only emerge from my room to wait for William's evening call or to visit the bathroom. I drink water in the day but never in the evenings, to keep the number of trips to pee to the minimum. I can't eat. I have trouble even swallowing a bite of biscuit – it clumps in my mouth and I end up spitting it out into a tissue.

Every now and then it occurs to me to abandon what I'm doing; to simply get up and walk out and drive over to Mum and David's, or to ring someone up and tell them what's happening, and see how ridiculous it sounds. Somewhere, in the recesses of my mind, I know that this is not normal behaviour, that the situation I'm in isn't real.

Yes, I know that, but at the same time I have this pressing need, an almost physical compulsion, to bring this whole thing to a conclusion. I have to see it out.

I owe it to Rose.

On Friday morning, at the clunk of the letterbox, my stomach heaves and I taste bile in my mouth. I can see as I go down the stairs that there's only a single white envelope on the floor but I still don't believe it until I pick the letter up and turn it over. It's a bill. Addressed to William.

I rush to unlock the door, bang my way outside. The postman is next door getting a signature for a package. He looks over at me and says, 'Morning.'

'Have you . . .' My voice is hoarse, unused. I clear my throat. 'Haven't you got anything else for me?'

'You expecting something, love?' he says cheerfully, checking through the bundle in his hand while I wait. 'Sorry, love. Nothing here. That's your lot.'

44

Sleep has sucked me down so deep that I don't hear William arrive home. I'm just suddenly aware of a presence close to me, and the stink of perfume. I lurch awake, give a yelp of fright.

William is sitting on the bed next to me; a bouquet of lilies lies between us.

'Sorry, darling. I didn't mean to startle you.' The wrapping paper crackles underneath him as he leans forward and kisses me on the lips.

I recoil from his touch, swing myself up off the bed, so quickly, the blood doesn't have time to reach my head. The lilies are stinking.

William is talking and the words are hitting my brain and bouncing straight off. There's a spiral and I'm spinning in it, spinning faster, faster, faster. There's a roaring in my ears. I feel William's hands on my arms as he tries to pull me towards him. When I resist, he tugs harder. I stagger backwards and, as I feel my legs give way, I shut my eyes.

*   *   *

I'm back on the bed. I'm snivelling into sodden tissues, snivelling and spluttering and trying to make sense except I don't make sense. Not even to myself. Each sob drags me further away. I am looking at William's face through a hazy blackness. I think, How can you see colours with your ears – but at the same time I know this is nonsensical.

I surface. All the shapes of the room zoom into focus. The pillow is soft under my head, William's cool hand is pressed on my forehead. The expression on his face is devastating.

'It'll be all right,' he tells me.

'I've betrayed her,' I tell William urgently. 'That's why she's angry.'

'Who's angry?'

I'm annoyed at his stupidity. How can he not know? 'Rose, of course.'

He flinches. 'Rose is dead, Laura,' he says quietly.

'I've stepped into her shoes,' I tell him. 'I'm the cuckoo in her nest, with her husband.' I sit up so that I can make the point more effectively. I search his eyes. 'Can't you feel it? The whole house is pulsing with her anger.'

William shakes his head slowly.

'Then what about these?' I scrabble out the pile of photographs from under my pillow. 'This one and this and this and this.' I slap, slap, slap them down on the bed in between us like a high-speed game of Snap.

'Stop it,' William says, and he yanks my hands away and presses them down into the mattress. 'Laura, listen to me. You're upset. You've got it all wrong. For God's sake, Rose is dead. *She is dead.*'

I suddenly feel woozy with tiredness; my whole body is so tender that when I sag against William, my flesh feels bruised. I hang my head.

'I shouldn't have left you.' He tilts my face towards him, lifts my chin. 'Look at me, look at me. It's all right. You shouldn't worry. Rose wanted us to be together.' I feel his breath on my lips, then on my ear as he places a kiss there. 'She knew long before anyone did that it was going to be us together,' he says. 'It was what she wanted. She thought you would be good for me and she loved you, Laura, she really did. And she knew that I'd look after you, as I promise I will. So it's fine. You've got it wrong – she wouldn't be angry, it's what she wanted.'

William's words meander through my brain; his caring, loving words, wander, wander, wander.

Then they strike home.

'What did you just say?' I knock William's hands away. 'You discussed this with your wife? She . . .' I search for the word '. . . selected me?' My voice rises. 'You're saying she groomed me as her replacement?'

'No, that's not how it was.' William's response is clipped, sharp. 'For God's sake, Laura, isn't there any way of talking properly with you?'

I shuffle up the bed away from him. 'No,' I say. 'This is too weird.'

William doesn't move.

'Could you go, please?' I ask him. I grab a pillow and hug it to me. 'Could you please leave me alone?'

45

There's a bee buzzing. How did it get in?

I open the windows and try to waft it to its freedom. It's stubborn, or stupid, blundering past the exit point each time. I'm about to give up when it crawls across the frame of its own accord and out to the air – a stumbling start before it curves away as it gains velocity.

I try and hold it in my sights but its journey is too erratic so I give up.

I have come to my senses. I no longer feel there's a spirit of Rose, trying to tear me away from her husband; and I do understand that there is some crazy person out there who writes crazy letters which have nothing to do with my life.

There is, however, a heavy presence of memories in Rose's room and that is why I'm in here. I've come to try and think through some of the past conversations I've had with her, so as to understand.

Downstairs it's hard to keep a train of thought going, what with William so close, and him trying so hard to keep things real – offering cups of tea, showing me some of his shots from Cornwall, suggesting an evening stroll.

I leave the windows open and lie in a shaft of sunlight on the floor. I can see the sky – TV aerials, satellite dishes and a plane. Sounds filter up – car doors slamming, a car alarm, the plane's engine. The dustcart is rumbling its way round the Crescent, wheelie bins clattering in its wake. A beeping starts up as the lorry reverses backwards out of the tight road.

Downstairs, a door slams shut and the blind in Rose's ensuite bathroom clatters from a sudden pull of through-draught.

'Go out somewhere with William, please, Laura. He's bored and I'm tired and need to sleep. You look as if you could do with a walk – you're rather pale. Fresh air will do you both good.'

And so I went downstairs and told William about Rose's suggestion.

'You don't have to,' he'd said immediately, but I'd pressed him to go. Rose had made me feel sorry for him, and I wanted to please Rose.

It was a summer's day but muggy and overcast, not sunny. We drove to the Downs and it drizzled as we walked across them. We exchanged some small talk but for the most part remained silent. I remember that William's self-containment had made me uncomfortable, and I'd spent most of the stroll filled with a childish and ultimately impotent desire to utter some profundity which would impress him.

When we got back we went upstairs together. Rose was lying in bed.

'Look at you both!' she exclaimed. 'Come close. Let me breathe in that wonderful outdoors smell.'

William sat on her bed, and I pulled up the chair from the desk and sat on her other side.

William began to talk and as he did, he transformed our walk.

Rose closed her eyes; her whole body seemed to sink into the bed as she immersed herself in all the beautiful details he'd noticed: the pattering of the raindrops on the hedge leaves; the twittering of the skylark which you couldn't see because it was so high up in the clouds; the hips on the wild rose which were beginning to redden; the stench of the fox musk.

I believe that was the first time I saw what she meant about his passion for life; and the fact that it was obscured by his quiet manner made it all the more forceful when expressed.

When William had finished speaking, I felt that I was intruding on an intimate moment, but to move would have spoiled it, too. William waited for Rose to open her eyes and they held each other's gaze for what seemed like a long time.

Rose's face is as clear to me today as it was then, when she finally turned her attention to me, but what I'm no longer certain about is how to read the expression I saw there. What I took to be love and pride in William might simply have been her checking out my reaction. 'So, what do you make of him now, love?'

I remember back to a time in the first few months that I knew the Claymores. I'd been given a free shiatsu massage treatment for me and a friend as payment in kind from a client.

When I offered Rose the chance to accompany me, she considered it for a moment and then said, 'I don't think so, thank you.'

'Why not? You feel wonderful afterwards.'

'My body's not so pretty these days, and I wouldn't want to undress in front of anyone.' She paused. 'Why don't you take William? He's a bit stressed at the moment.'

Before I could say no, she'd called him in. He flashed me an apologetic look, but Rose's intentions steamrollered us both and off we trotted.

'You're glowing,' William had said when we came out of the salon.

'You, too.'

We'd gone to Alessandro's and I noticed how relaxed William seemed – and how handsome he was, too.

'She forced us to go out together,' I tell William. 'She even contrived to get us sitting down here talking. All the time she was plotting.'

William's a tight-lipped statue; his back is rigid, his hands lie motionless in his lap.

In contrast, I rock forward on the chair, shuffle around, look down, fiddle with anything that comes to hand. The cup of coffee is cold; I haven't drunk any of it. Neither of us have touched the biscuits that William's put out. They're chocolate chip cookies, my favourite, and William's bought them to please me, but I feel numb to his little kindness.

'Doesn't it bother you at all?' I ask him. 'For God's sake – she was a match-maker for you, her own husband. Didn't you think that was a little bit crazy at the time?'

William looks hurt. 'You're distorting how it was,' he tells me. 'Don't make it into a sinister game that Rosie was playing, Laura.'

'I'm sorry, but that's how it feels.'

William sighs. 'She told me she didn't expect – or want – me to spend the rest of my life alone but we didn't discuss suitable wives and she certainly didn't dictate or even openly suggest that it had to be you.' He pauses to gather his thoughts. 'She made it clear that she liked you and hinted that she thought we'd be good together, but she did *not* make it happen.'

I jump in. 'How can you be sure? I mean, could you, hand on heart, say that Rose hasn't influenced your choice in any way?'

He hesitates and it's one of those massive pauses. The room swells with eeriness, as if something cataclysmic is about to happen.

'This is ridiculous,' he shouts. 'You're creating this atmosphere. You're creating this out of nothing.'

He comes round to my side of the table, leans over me and his eyes fasten onto mine. 'I love you,' he says.

But it's as if I've been covered with this invisible, impenetrable film; his words slide off me and I look away.

We've retreated into separate rooms. William is back in his marital bedroom.

I lie on my bed. There are still some of his belongings around – a book about the Andes he was reading at night, a gungy bottle of sun cream.

We avoid each other day after day. Sometimes the house seems so large that I have no idea where he is, or whether he's out. Sometimes it feels tiny and we're forever bumping into each other – in the hall, in the kitchen, on the landings. I keep away from communal areas as much as I can, going out to eat although I rarely feel hungry.

I've lost pounds, but my body doesn't look good. I'm like a balloon that someone's pricked. I've got wrinkled pleats of skin everywhere and my face feels desiccated no matter how much moisturiser I rub in. I feel cold all the time too; my hands and feet are permanently chilled.

I don't hate William. I miss him.

Sometimes there's nothing more I want than to cuddle up beside him and listen to his stories about the sea or faraway countries. At night, I wish he'd just come in and get into bed and let our bodies speak up for our feelings. But even though I wish it, every night I lock my door and the one night when he does come and try the handle, then gently tap on the door, I lie huddled up, holding my breath, until I'm sure he's gone away.

Because whenever I see him, Rose isn't far behind; taking sneaky looks, talking William up, talking Adam down. Everything I thought and felt has to be dragged from the past to the present and looked at with new eyes.

I doubt my love, I doubt my decisions, and I doubt myself.

I ring Mum. I get her answering machine.

I ring Debs. I get her silence.

I ring Nat. I'm incoherent – blubbing down the phone.

'I'll come,' she says. 'I'm on my way.'

William lets her in. I hear her voice. I wait anxiously, straining to listen; frightened of what each might say.

Then Nat pops her head round the door. 'Uh-oh,' she says. 'Look at the state of you.'

I immediately burst into tears. She sits beside me, holds me tight, strokes my hair. When my crying has subsided, she suggests we go downstairs.

I shake my head. 'William's there.'

'No, he's not. He's gone out. He said we've got the run of the house. He'll be gone for a few hours. Why don't you go tidy yourself up a bit and I'll get us both a drink.'

Nat's searching the cupboards when I enter the kitchen. 'Where do you keep your booze?' she asks.

I go to the living room and return holding aloft a bottle of whisky .

'Well done,' she tells me. 'Right – sit down.' She mixes us both a hot toddy with honey. It smells delicious.

My eyes are puffy and sore and I can't stop sniffing, but I've tied back my hair and washed my face and hands, and I not only feel less grubby but more composed.

'So, what's going on?'

I tell her the whole thing. Nat remains silent after I've finished.

'Don't you think it's wrong, too, Nat – or am I being over-sensitive?'

'I don't know.' She puffs out her cheeks, shakes her head as if to say: 'This is a tricky one.'

I rub my eyes, and the tender skin protests. 'Everything's been turned inside out.'

'He seemed very upset, and worried about you,' Nat says slowly. 'So he obviously genuinely cares a lot about you. More than I ever gave him credit for,' she adds, looking shamefaced.

I think about this.

'Do you love him?' Nat asks suddenly. 'He's in the same position as you, after all. Does he believe your love is real? Or does he suspect that Rose worked her magic on you, too?'

I clench my fists. 'I'm so mad at Rose,' I tell Nat. 'I feel used and conned and as if I've been brainwashed. There was stuff she said – like she used to imply I could do better than Adam – but of course now I think that was only because she'd earmarked me for William.' My voice wobbles and I fight to keep calm. 'All the talks we had seem worthless, everything I confided in her seems as if it was simply material – ammunition – for her to use, to create what she wanted.'

Nat pushes back her chair, and reaches behind her for the whisky bottle. 'Do you know what? I think you should forget Rose; the important point is whether you and William want to be together.' She glugs a large measure into each glass.

'But you're against the idea, aren't you?'

'I want to help you,' Nat says quietly but forcefully. 'It's not up to me how you live your life. I've thought about that a lot these last few weeks.'

'Nobody believed in us from the beginning,' I say. 'And I just wonder whether you all were right.'

I'm in my room, attempting to immerse myself in a book, when William knocks. He pushes the door open.

'Can we talk?'

I'm lying on my side and when William sits down against my stomach, the warmth of him is unexpected but nice. He pushes his hair clear as it falls across his face.

'Have I lost you, Laura?' He frowns as he studies my face.

'Oh Wills,' I say. I want to reply, 'No,' but instead what comes out is, 'I don't know.'

'I love you,' he says. 'I really do. You're wonderful – funny, loving, sweet company. I've discovered that for myself,' he smiles wryly. 'And I want you to believe that I never seriously considered us having a relationship until you moved in and we started spending time together.'

It hits me that William's about to say, 'But . . .' I struggle upright, sit cross-legged and wait.

'But I think we may have too much going against us.' He pauses. 'To carry on. To make it.'

William has given up; he's given up on us.

I press my face into his neck and he holds me tight as if he's never going to let me go and he rocks me while I cry.

I cry for Wills, who has to suffer another loss so soon after Rose. I cry for myself. I cry for our love smothered in its plump infancy. And I cry because it's the end. And it's sad. An ending is always sad.

46

Hours, days, three weeks pass in muffled blandness in a house where the phone buzzes gently with friendly chatter, post comes in soothing, ordinary envelopes and the hardest decision I have to make is which programme to watch on TV. Mum drifts by the sofa, stops and chats if I want to, leaves me alone if I don't. David, a soft-footed giver while I'm asleep, leaves gifts of magazines and chocolates.

This afternoon, I wake to find the day's offering lying on the coffee-table beside me. A model, with perfectly made-up expressionless eyes, watches as I stretch and yawn and automatically reach for the remote control. I adjust the cushions behind me and lean back against the padded softness. The house is absolutely silent. Mum and David are out at the golf club; it'll be evening before they return.

Over on the table, a perfect mouth with perfect teeth mocks me.

I decide I have to get out.

*   *   *

I drive across town seeking out familiar streets. On the cusp of winter, the town looks shabby; a layer of grime covers the buildings and roads. Spartan trees poke knobbly branches towards the dirty clouds.

In the street where I park, rubbish has blown out of a skip and lies in huddled groups where the wind has abandoned it. The air feels damp and thin. I take my time warming up. I roll my shoulders, reach down to my toes; the tips of my trainers are already staining grey.

Running is more difficult than I remember. My chest is tight, my breathing laboured; thick saliva gathers in my throat. I ease off my pace.

Ahead, a short pink and yellow figure waits in the middle of the pavement: a pastel beacon amongst all the dreariness. The little girl watches me approaching, hands on hips, her bare pre-pubescent midriff bulging out between hip-slung trackpants and short jacket.

'You're fat,' she sneers from two metres away. 'You're a fat cow.'

I choke on the laughter which bubbles up; I slow down and stop.

Her chubby face grows furious, her eyes narrow. A two-tone candy-coloured tyrant, she glowers at me, which makes me laugh even more.

I set off again, a grin stuck on my face. I look back over my shoulder.

'Fuck off!' she shouts, and jabs her fingers up in a 'v'.

By the time I reach Mum's old house, my throat is scraped raw and my ribs feel as if they'll snap under the pressure of my expanding lungs. I stop and hang my head until my heart calms down.

The front garden has been culled. All the shrubs and roses have been dug up and replaced with gravel; the hedge on the left-hand side is the only living thing which remains. The façade has changed too. The windows are shrouded by stark, white blinds; a new glossy red door gleams its warning against getting too close.

I run on. Evening descends and the light darkens into the sallow violet of winter dusk. I've strayed from my original route, heading further than I am capable of running at the moment. I will have to catch a bus back to my car.

I think, This is a bad idea. But it doesn't stop me.

It's dark by the time I get to Adam's flat.

He isn't home; his van's not outside and there are no lights on. I hesitate on the street for a moment and then duck furtively down the path before someone spots me. I stand outside the porch looking at the fuzzy outline of Ad's old Aran jumper, his walking jacket and the hook of an umbrella handle leaning up against the glass.

I imagine ringing the bell. I imagine Adam answering the door, taking one look at me, giving me a hug and a quick kiss and then hustling me inside.

'Hey, babe. How are you? Go and take a seat.'

I'd sit in the lounge; around me would be a few new things – perhaps a new side-table handy for Adam to put his beer on, and a photograph of the stately home garden on the chimney breast, but everything else would be familiar – the sunset picture we bought in Devon, the red and green rugs we chose from Ikea.

'I've just got back from work,' Adam would say, padding towards me in his chunky woolly socks, holding out a beer. 'I'm afraid there's nothing to eat in the house.'

We'd phone up for a take-away.

'What do you fancy, babe?'

'The usual.'

And while he went out to phone the order through, I'd settle back on the settee and start to notice more: I'd see that the holiday photographs of us are still up on the far wall, my books are still on the shelves, and pushed to the side of the two-seater settee are my old fluffy slippers, left there as if I'd been away but would be coming back and needing them.

A car pulls up. I spin round, my heart pumping. Now I'll have to face him.

But it isn't Adam. It's the couple from the first-floor flat next door who we sometimes say hello to in the pub. I bend as if I'm busy tying my shoe-lace, and as soon as they're inside, I walk-run down the path and then sprint away, sprint as fast as my aching legs will allow, telling myself 'That was close, that was lucky.'

A few days later, when I am about to cross Church Road, I see Adam in his van. Debs is with him. I hear the beeping of the pedestrian lights and feel the rush of people pushing past while I stand still. The shock drills deep into my veins and drains my heart. After all she said.

They are laughing. Debbie's hair, a silky block, screens her face as she leans towards him. Adam's face is creased, his mouth broad in laughter; he shakes his head as if it's all too much, all just too funny.

Cars start moving. I step back from the kerb, but not quickly enough. Debs turns forward and sees me. Mid-laugh, her mouth falls open. The van glides by.

Stupid, stupid, stupid.

Stupid to imagine Adam would mothball himself for months just on the off-chance that I'd come back. Stupid to think he'd even want me back when I'd treated him so badly; that he'd say, 'Let's wipe the slate clean, babe,' as if he was some kind of emotional simpleton.

Stupid to trust Debs.

47

'Hi, Loz,' Debs says. 'You going to invite me in?'

I don't say yes but she steps inside anyway, bringing a swirl of cold air with her.

We stand opposite each other in the hall. I'm trembling. I stare mutely at Debs who jiggles up and down as if she needs the loo. She looks at me, nibbles at her bottom lip, jiggles a bit more.

'God, Loz,' she bursts out, 'I knew you'd think the worst. When I saw the look on your face, I knew exactly what you were thinking, you silly cow. I asked Adam to stop, but someone nearly drove into the back of him, so he had to keep going and by the time he pulled over, you'd gone.' She puts her hand on my arm, squeezes it gently. 'It was a coincidence. One of those mad coincidences. I'd taken my car in for an MOT and Adam was at the garage getting his tyres changed so he gave me a lift into town.' She opens her eyes wide. 'You know how Adam rates me,' she says. 'I'm surprised he even offered, but I guess he's too much of a gentleman to ignore me.' She grins. 'Plus I did kind of hint rather heavily.'

She takes off her coat and gives me a little push. 'Come on then, you big dope, show me round your mum's new pad. Ooh – nice,' she says appreciatively as we enter the living room. 'Very nice. She's done all right for herself, your mum. Good for her.'

We sit in the armchairs that look out over the garden. The lawn has been freshly cut and it looks as soft as a carpet. David's pride and joy.

Debs is watching me. 'You OK?'

I nod. I just need a minute to catch up, to take everything in.

She frowns. 'You do believe me, don't you? About Adam, I mean.'

I nod again, not trusting myself to speak yet.

'Well, you're Little Miss Chatty,' she says after a moment.

'I said all those horrible things . . .' My voice cracks.

'I said plenty back,' Debs says – a rapid-fire reply. 'So let's call it quits.' She pulls her hair forward over one shoulder, purses her lips. 'The thing is, I've missed your naïve ways, your soppy take on life. I've had to manage all that prim, sensible stuff by myself and it's not been easy.'

I can't help smiling. 'So?' I ask. 'How've you done?'

'I know Andrew's a shit, Loz, so I'm trying to steer clear of him.' She shrugs. 'Ironic, isn't it? After me banging on all the time about not being tied down and all that, I meet the one person I'd really like to be attached to with a ball and chain.'

'You said "trying"?'

'Some times harder than other times. I still fancy him like mad.' She giggles. 'And if he catches me in a weak moment, then I choose to forget everything I've just said – just for a while, though,' she adds. 'And the weak moments are getting less.'

I've hired a van to collect my things from William's. When I phoned to arrange a date, he had asked me if I wanted his help or his absence.

'I'd like to see you,' I told him because I felt I owed him that at least, but now I'm nervous, unsure of what to expect.

I hit heavy traffic coming into the town centre. The traffic-lights go green and nothing moves; red, then green again. The van radio bursts into life. Too late to take a detour, it informs me that there's been an accident just ahead. Long delays are expected.

I phone William to explain.

'No problem,' he says, and his voice sounds relaxed, even happy. 'I'll be here. I haven't got any plans for this afternoon.'

I put my mobile on the passenger seat, then pick it up again. Yesterday Adam called me. I flick to my Received Calls memory just to see his name recorded there.

I skip over the faltering start to the conversation, my pathetic attempt at a joke. I even skip over Adam's rushed and apolo-getic explanation of how the stately home garden is going. I do linger momentarily over his: 'Enough of me, what about you, babe?'

Babe, babe, babe.

I skim over the rest of the thirty-two-minute conversation although it's stored in my head, every scrap and crumb of it for future reference, until I reach Adam's last words, spoken so softly that I had begun to lower my phone from my ear, and only just caught what he said.

Now they're on a loop in my brain.

'I miss you, babe.'

William kisses me on the cheek and compliments me. 'You're looking good, Laura.'

In a rush to return the compliment, I stumble over my words. William looks awful. He's wearing a linen shirt and jeans which both hang off him, and it's terrible to see how haggard his face is.

We go into my office.

'I hope you don't mind?' he says, indicating the boxes that he's packed up for me. 'I thought it would speed up the process.'

I shake my head.

'I threw some stuff away,' he tells me. 'That I knew you wouldn't want.'

He means the letters. I'm touched he thought to do that and I'm so glad they've gone, that I won't have to see them again. I don't ask him if more have come because I don't want to know.

'Thanks, Wills.'

'How have you been coping without all your files and stuff?' he asks.

I tell him how I've had some time off work, but that recently I've had several meetings with a bloke who in theory is my competition but who in reality is almost certainly going to become my future business partner.

'I like the sociable side of the work, and he's a genius at the practicalities,' I explain.

'Sounds promising,' William says, his voice warm with approval. He leans against the desk, showing no signs of being in a rush to leave me alone. I begin emptying the desk drawers.

William tells me that the assignment he did in Cornwall has been nominated for an award and that another project has come through because of it.

'The Greek Islands,' he tells me, and his face lights up. 'It's going to be fantastic, but they need a high level of fitness; there's a lot of sailing and kayaking involved, as well as diving.'

I glance at him.

'I've put myself on this crazy training schedule,' he says, pulling at his loose shirt. 'Look – it's nearly killing me.'

'You mean . . .'

William catches my expression. 'Oh, Laura. You thought I was pining away?' He smiles gently. 'Really, I'm fine. There's no need to worry.'

We stand at the back of the van once the final box has been put inside.

'I hope you'll be happy.' He touches my face, withdraws his hand quickly. 'No,' he continues. 'I *know* you'll be happy. No tears,' he tells me, and places a kiss on my forehead. 'No regrets.'

He steps back.

'What were we doing?' I ask William as I'm getting in, because it seems important to know and I think he might have the answer.

He hesitates before replying and he suddenly seems miles away.

'We just got caught up in something,' he says quietly. 'Perhaps that's what it was.'

*　　*　　*

After William has closed the front door behind him, I start the ignition and as the van begins to roll forward, I take a last look at the house, my gaze travelling upwards to Rose's room.

A flare across the shadowed window leaves a momentary star-burst on my retina. I shield my eyes to see. I think, What am I looking for? A sparkle of sunlight on the window, the glint from a champagne glass held up in a toast, the flash of a camera? I strain my eyes to catch it again but there's nothing. Of course.

I nudge the van out onto the busy coast road. The sun emerges from behind a cloud and momentarily blinds me before another drifts across to spoil its fun.

I feel strange but I don't know in what way. I feel that I should be able to identify this peculiar mood but the more I try to pin it down, the more it eludes me. I watch the strobing brake-lights of the car in front in the stop-start traffic. I look at the sea glittering on my left. I watch a man coming towards me, struggling against the tide of pedestrians streaming in the opposite direction; he bumps and apologizes, twists and side-steps, bumps and apologizes again.

Then, like a shy creature emerging from its hideaway now that the coast is clear, something stirs inside me. A sensation is swimming up, slowly at first, than faster, faster as it gets closer to the surface until it bursts through, glossy in its clarity: a memory.

Debs and I were sitting on my bed. All those things we'd said we were going to do before we left school – snog Mr Fletcher, rip up our books and scatter them like confetti throughout the corridors, shout out obscenities in the last assembly – we hadn't done. We'd just walked out at the end of the day with everybody else, and that was that. And now it was too late; we were never going back.

Debs and I looked at each other for a long time without speaking. Then she stood up, took off her blazer, took off her skirt, started unbuttoning her blouse.

'Come on,' she said in a theatrical voice. 'Divest yourself.'

We stripped down to our underwear and Debs fetched my wastepaper bin and placed it in the middle of the floor.

She folded her blazer and put it in the bin, and held her cigarette lighter to the material. She was bent over, with her skinny bum in her frilly pink knickers poking up in the air, but I tried not to giggle because Debs seemed so serious.

It had been raining that day and the damp wool smouldered, but wouldn't catch. But Debs wouldn't give up. She kept trying and trying until a tiny flame flickered into life.

'Gotcha.'

She jumped onto the bed and pulled me up with her and we held hands and bounced on the mattress in our bras and knickers, shrieking and yelling while a wisp of pale smoke curdled the air.

The memory drifts away, leaving the present burned clear. I don't ever have to go back to their house. It's over.

This thought feels so big and bright, that when I glance up, I almost expect to find the dazzle of sun in my eyes again.